PRINCE OF HAWTHORNE PREP

JENNIFER SUCEVIC

ALSO BY JENNIFER SUCEVIC

Campus Flirt (Novella)

Campus God

Campus Heartthrob

Campus Hottie

Campus Legend

Campus Player

Claiming What's Mine

Confessions of a Heartbreaker

Crazy for You (80s short story)

Don't Leave

Friend Zoned

Hate to Love You

Heartless

If You Were Mine

Just Friends

King of Campus

King of Hawthorne Prep

Love to Hate You

One Night Stand

Protecting What's Mine

Queen of Hawthorne Prep

Shameless

Stay

The Boy Next Door

The Breakup Plan

The Girl Next Door

DELILAH

"Better hurry up," Mom calls from the kitchen. "Jasper will be here any second, and you don't want to keep him waiting."

No, we definitely wouldn't want to do that.

The thought of seeing my boyfriend makes my belly pinch. Deep down, I know it shouldn't be like that. But there's no getting around it, that's exactly the way he makes me feel. Nervous and on edge.

With those thoughts clouding my brain, I smooth a hand down my navy blazer before running a brush through my long, blonde hair. Just as I pick my backpack up from the floor near the narrow desk shoved against the wall, there's a blast of a horn from outside. The knowledge that Jasper is waiting in the driveway has me quickening my step.

As I head out of the tiny bedroom, Mom waits in the living room with a stainless steel to-go container filled with my favorite coffee blend. I flash a grateful smile before nipping it from her outstretched hand.

"Thanks. I really needed this."

"I know. You were up late studying. Again." She arches her brow in a look meant to convey concern.

With a shrug, I bring the cup to my lips and take a sip. For me, there's only one way out of this town and that's with hard work and high grades which will hopefully end up with me being awarded a full academic ride to one of the state schools.

As I bring the steaming brew to my lips, a longer blare of the horn fills the air.

Instead of getting annoyed, Mom shoos me toward the door. "Hurry now and I'll see you at school."

I draw in a shaky breath and jerk my head into a nod before crossing the cramped space. With each footfall, I feel like I'm walking to my death.

Am I being a tad melodramatic?

Maybe.

The horn sounds for a third time.

Then again, maybe not.

With a final wave, I wrap my fingers around the handle and yank open the door before stepping onto the front stoop. My eyes reluctantly lift and settle on Jasper, who lounges behind the wheel of his sleek silver Porsche 911.

As soon as our gazes lock, he throws his hands up in an impatient let's-go gesture.

That's all it takes for the vague feeling of unease to congeal into a painful knot at the bottom of my belly. With any luck, I'll only have to listen to him bitch about me taking too long and keeping him waiting. The last thing I want to do is fight him off this early in the morning.

It's becoming an everyday occurrence.

There have been a handful of times when I've casually mentioned that it would be easier for me to catch a ride to school with my mother, since she works in the office at Hawthorne Prep, but he always quashes the idea, insisting he drive me instead.

It takes some mental prodding for me to force my feet into movement. I remind myself to paste a smile on my face as I walk around the hood of the sporty little vehicle and slide onto the plush leather seat beside him.

Before I can even get out a greeting, his hand snakes around the nape of my neck before dragging me closer until his lips can crash onto mine. I'm not given a choice to open. His tongue pries the seam of my lips apart before delving inside and wreaking havoc.

I would consider this kiss a fair representation of my boyfriend.

Punishing.

Slightly mean.

Angry.

At this point, my acquiescence is expected.

I'm ashamed to admit that in the six months we've been together, it's become easier to give him what he wants and hope the price extracted isn't too steep. So far, it hasn't been, but I know that will change. Time is quickly dwindling. I can hear the faint ticks of the clock in my head.

When the front door of the house slams, I press my palms against his perfectly pressed white shirt and gently push him away.

"Mom is coming," I say breathlessly, never more grateful for an interruption than I am now.

He grumbles under his breath as his gunmetal gray eyes stay pinned to my swollen mouth. "That woman has shit timing."

Agree to disagree.

But I'll keep that to myself.

When Mom's footsteps slow near the driver's side door, Jasper's expression magically transforms as he presses the button to unroll the glass that separates them.

"Hey, Ms. Robinson. You're looking lovely this morning." He doesn't spare me a glance as he reaches out and squeezes my bare thigh with rough fingers. "I've told Delilah that she must get her stunning looks from you."

It's a challenge to sit beside him with a straight face. If she only knew what he was truly like and all the crap he talks when we're alone, maybe she'd rethink her stance and stop nominating him for best boyfriend of the year.

Mom's bullshit meter must still be on the fritz, because she beams at him like he hung both the moon and stars. I wish she'd open her eyes and see that he's nothing more than a mean-spirited kiss-ass instead of constantly pushing me into his arms. According to her, we're a match made in heaven.

That's a frightening thought.

If Mom had her way, I'd attend whatever four-year institution Jasper gets accepted at, we'd get engaged midway through college and married directly after graduation. Then, I'd live out the remainder of my days in a sprawling mansion in Hawthorne without a care in the world. A Cinderella dream she wishes could have played out for herself.

Even when I provide examples of Jasper's cruel behavior, she'll chide me, saying no one is perfect and we all have our faults. I can't argue with that. The problem is that mean and spiteful just so happens to be Jasper's default setting, and nothing will change that.

The other issue—and this one is ridiculous—is that I'm loath to burst her little bubble of happiness. The woman has sacrificed so much for me to attend Hawthorne Prep and rub elbows with the right kind of people. And by right kind of people, I'm talking about the ones with money and clout who lord it over this small community.

Unfortunately, I'm no longer able to continue the charade.

This relationship has reached its expiration date. Whether Mom can wrap her head around it or not, Jasper and I were not meant for the long haul. There isn't a happily ever after written in our future. As we speak, I'm quietly working on an exit strategy.

I just have to…time it right.

Otherwise, there'll be hell to pay.

Even the thought of his wrath is enough to make my heart spasm.

Mom's hand flutters to his forearm before giving it a squeeze. "I've told you a hundred times that when we're not at school, you can call me Carrie."

Jasper flashes a grin. "All right, Carrie."

If it's possible, her smile grows wider. "You two are so adorable together," she says with a heartfelt sigh.

I'm half afraid she's going to whip out her phone to capture this moment for posterity.

After a few seconds tick by, she blinks and glances at her silver wristwatch. "You two should probably get moving so you're not late."

Jasper nods. "Funny, I just said the same thing to your daughter."

His fingers tighten around me, digging into my flesh.

What a liar. He does it so smoothly, it's almost frightening. Or maybe I'm terrified because I know precisely what he's capable of. And that's anything without so much as a hint of remorse.

Mom waves before heading to the garage and the rusted-out Honda Civic parked inside the tight space. As soon as her back is turned, he stabs the button to roll up the window. Once it reaches the top, his eyes flicker in my direction. "It's un-fucking-believable that you'd rather show up to school in that rusted-out piece of shit than this sweet ride." He presses his lips into a thin line and shakes his head. "How embarrassing."

At the beginning of our relationship, that nasty comment would have wounded me. Half a year later, it's water off a duck's back. Instead, I shift in the seat and stare longingly out the window.

We both hear the engine sputter to life.

"Is your mom ever gonna get a new car?" He squints toward the garage as disgust morphs over his features. It's almost like there's a stench in the air offending his nostrils. "What's it from? The early eighties?"

My gaze is reluctantly drawn to the old Civic. It's one of two things that we still have of my father's. It's stupid that I'm so sentimentally attached to it.

It's just a car.

After Dad died of colon cancer when I was seven years old, Mom was so broken hearted that she packed his things and donated them to charity. All the photographs were boxed up and placed in the attic, never to be seen again. It's as if she thought it was possible to lessen the pain of his loss if she erased him completely from our lives.

The other thing I hung onto is his camera. It's an old Nikon that still takes great pictures. I usually have it packed away in my school bag, because I never know when inspiration will strike.

Jasper understands why both the car and camera are important, but he doesn't give a damn. He's more interested in outward appearances and enjoys having the shiniest toys and the best of everything. It's only recently that I've wondered why we're together when I don't fit with the image he projects to the outside world.

Sometimes, I suspect I'm one of those shiny toys.

Instead of mentioning the sentimentality of it, I mumble, "It's not that old."

He snorts. "Maybe, if it were the early nineties."

It's a relief when he drops the conversation and shifts the car into reverse before stomping on the accelerator. My heart gets lodged somewhere in the vicinity of my throat as I quickly snap the belt into place.

It's a wonder he hasn't killed himself or me yet with his reckless driving. It feels like I'm taking my life into my hands every time I reluctantly slide onto the leather seat next to him. Once we're in the middle of the street, I barely have time to huff out a breath before the Porsche shoots forward, zipping down the road and out of the small subdivision at the southern end of Hawthorne.

It's almost ironic that after crossing over the train tracks that divide the town in half, the houses become bigger, and our surroundings appear less dilapidated. The lawns grow in size and the architecture is more impressive.

I suspect the Hawthorne family intentionally designed it that way. Money and status have always been important here.

Without them, you're nothing and no one.

Once we make it through the small center of town, passing by Rothchilds, a regional chain store owned by the Rothchild family, and the local Second Chance Theater, we leave the community behind in the rearview mirror as we head north onto a long stretch of country road surrounded by farmland before turning onto the winding drive that leads to Hawthorne Prep. As much as I despise this place and everything it stands for, it's a relief when the gated campus comes into view. I search my mind for an excuse to escape Jasper's suffocating presence.

"This weekend is gonna be epic," he says, breaking into the whirl of my thoughts. When I remain silent, he spears a merciless look in my direction. "My plan is to score on the field, and then with you afterward."

When my eyes widen, a slow grin moves across his face.

"I've given you more than enough time, and I'm done waiting."

Just like that, my mouth turns cottony as my heartbeat hitches before pounding a painful staccato against my ribcage.

The silence that follows that announcement is brutal.

He hikes a brow. "What's wrong? Nothing to say?"

My teeth scrape against my lower lip as I give my head a slight shake. The steely determination in his eyes tells me that any argument would be pointless. It seems almost unfathomable that I spent years craving his attention and now, I'd prefer he forget about my existence. Figuring a way out of this relationship feels even more imperative.

Otherwise...

A cold shiver slithers down my spine.

I can't bring myself to consider the alternative.

DELILAH

It's a relief when Jasper shifts the Porsche into park, and I can escape the claustrophobic confines of the sumptuous interior. My trembling fingers fumble for the handle before shoving it open as I grab my bag off the floor and slip soundlessly from the vehicle. Once outside in the crisp fall air, I suck in a shuddering breath, hoping it will steady the turmoil that roils inside.

It doesn't.

I don't make it more than two hurried steps when Jasper throws an arm around my shoulders and tugs me close before nipping my ear with sharp teeth.

"I seriously can't wait to pop your cherry," he growls loudly enough for the people closest to us to overhear.

"Jasper," I gasp, mortified that he would blurt out something so intimate in the school parking lot.

"What?" he says with a smirk, getting off on my embarrassment. That's exactly the kind of guy he is.

"Lower your voice," I mutter, peeking around to see if anyone is paying attention to our conversation.

"What's the matter, baby? You don't want everyone to know you're still a virgin?"

"Why would I? It's not anyone else's business." There's so much heat filling my face that spontaneous combustion seems imminent. Maybe that would be a blessing.

"You're so fucking cute," he says with a laugh, pressing me closer.

"Yo, Morgan!" someone shouts.

Jasper straightens, glancing around. As soon as he spots his friends, he pivots, steering us toward the rowdy group of football players. The muscles in my belly contract until it becomes painful.

I'll die of mortification if he brings this up in front of them.

After a few reluctant steps, my feet grind to a halt as I duck out of his arms. "I, um, need to talk with Ms. Pettijohn before first hour."

"Blow her off," he says easily. "I don't understand why you agreed to TA for that old bitch."

I frown. "I like her."

He snorts and shifts his weight. "You must be the only one."

He's probably right about that. There aren't many students at Hawthorne Prep who like the older woman. What Jasper doesn't realize is that it's not easy to be around all these kids who are drowning in money when you barely have two nickels to rub together.

But the teachers do.

Even though there should be a natural respect for not only someone older but also in charge, there isn't. A lot of the students walk around here like they're better than everyone else, including the staff. So, I can understand why Ms. Pettijohn takes a hard line with most of them.

I scramble back another hasty step, only wanting to distance myself from him. "I'll see you later, okay?"

Instead of answering, he swallows up the space between us before locking his fingers around my wrist and jerking me forward. His lips crash onto mine and his tongue invades my mouth with harsh strokes. One hand snakes inside my blazer to grope my breast. A few of his friends hoot and holler as I press my palms against his chest and shove him away.

"I need to go," I say breathlessly.

"Whatever," he grumbles as his tongue darts out to lick his lips.

That's all the signal I need to spin around and flee before he changes his mind. Thankfully, we don't have any classes together. Lunch is the only time during the day when I'm forced to interact with him. I shove that thought from my head as I hurry along the sidewalk that leads to the school entrance.

"Damn, your man is fine." Sloane and her wannabe clones sidle up beside me.

"Yeah, he is," Aubrey, her trusty sidekick echoes, craning her neck to get a better view.

A shudder of distaste slides through me. If they want Jasper, they're more than welcome to have him.

"You're so lucky," Annabelle sighs, sounding like a lovesick puppy.

At the moment, I'm wishing that weren't the case.

Over the last three years, I've become friends with these girls.

Well…maybe *friends* is a bit of an overstatement. We're more like frenemies. What I've learned is that it's easier to be in their good graces than on their bad side. I've witnessed them fall upon their prey and rip them apart like a pack of bloodthirsty jackals.

It's a frightening sight to behold.

Especially Sloane. She's the leader of this little girl gang and has been queen bee since I stepped foot on campus freshman year. Her blue eyes glitter with self-importance and malice.

I give her a bit of side eye. I'm always conscious of what I say or do when in her presence. You never know what seemingly innocuous statement will be used against you at a future date.

"Speaking of fine," Sloane says, attention fastening on to someone walking toward us.

When the delicate hairs on my arms rise, I know exactly who she's commenting on. Even though I should keep my head down and pretend I don't see him, my gaze unconsciously lifts, colliding with his. A zip of energy sizzles through my veins, electrifying my insides. It's as if a switch has been flipped and my body is being woken from a long, dormant slumber.

Austin Hawthorne.

I don't understand what it is about the inky-haired, green-eyed boy that sets my nerves on edge and makes my heart skip a painful beat every time I catch sight of him. This attraction isn't like anything I've experienced before. I can only liken it to a magnet, drawing me closer against my will. Everything about him screams danger. I've witnessed his short fuse for myself. I've seen him throw punches without the least bit of remorse.

Unlike my boyfriend, he only does it when provoked.

Jasper goes out of his way to needle him. That has everything to do with them both being quarterbacks and Austin showing up out of nowhere at the beginning of the school year.

Ever since I showed him around HP, I've done my best to avoid the muscular football player. What I've found is that it's impossible to evade the intensity of his gaze. Whenever we're in the same vicinity, his attention stays pinned to me. My back could be turned, and I'd still feel his penetrating stare licking over me.

I've come to both love and hate it.

"Too bad he's a Hawthorne," Aubrey sighs, voicing what all the other girls are thinking.

They might want to throw themselves at him, but they wouldn't dare.

In this town, the name Hawthorne is a dirty word. Everyone would still be snubbing the twins if not for Kingsley Rothchild dating Austin's twin sister, Summer. Now, the loathing is more of a lowkey simmer. The Hawthorne name might be stamped across the front of the building, but Kingsley runs this place. And no one, not even Jasper, is willing to incur his wrath.

Even though I'm helplessly ensnared by Austin's gaze, I'm aware of Summer and Kingsley at his side.

There was a time when Kingsley was the ringleader in making their lives hell.

Especially Summer's.

I have no idea what happened to change that, but for the moment, there's peace in the kingdom.

Let's hope it continues.

As they move toward us, I'm powerless to break the trance that has fallen over me. My heartbeat increases, pounding more harshly against my ribcage with every footstep. Even though I should yank my gaze away, I'm unable to do it.

I'm trapped within his penetrating depths.

If I'm not careful, I'll drown in them.

As soon as we pass and our gazes are no longer able to cling, my muscles loosen and everything inside me wilts with relief.

Sometimes, it feels like I'm caught between these two boys. There's one I want desperately to get away from and the other whom I find myself irresistibly attracted to.

All I know is that whatever happens, it won't end well.

With my tray in hand, I join the line of students waiting to checkout. The dining hall at Hawthorne Prep in no way resembles a school cafeteria. The meals are served on fine-boned Lenox china and there's a chef who prepares all the menus. The food is more on par with a high-end restaurant than a high school cafeteria.

Not that you can't enjoy a burger and fries here, but you can also find crowned roast of pork with mushroom dressing or duck breasts with apricot chutney, if that's your preference. It's outrageously expensive, and my scholarship doesn't cover the cost. Most of the time, I pack my own meal. PB & J, a small baggie of pretzels, an apple, and maybe an organic fruit snack.

If I'm running late, I'll splurge and buy lunch.

Like today.

The place is gorgeous with weathered beams that cross the double story vaulted ceiling and arched stained-glass windows that allow shards of bright sunlight to flood into the space, giving it a warm feel. Gold-leaf framed photographs of the founders and first graduating classes dot the walls at strategic intervals. My eyes settle on the heavy wooden chandeliers that hold thick white tapered candles. The architecture and attention to detail is stunning.

From all outward appearances, this place resembles a sanctuary.

It's the furthest thing from it.

There is no peace to be found.

Perhaps if I was here alone, it would be possible to enjoy the ambiance. But in this environment, one needs to be constantly on guard and watching your back.

Otherwise, you'll find yourself stabbed in it.

A bark of laughter shatters my thoughts and I'm jarred back to the present. As soon as my gaze collides with Jasper, he waves impatiently. He and his friends are seated at the table centered directly in the middle of the cafeteria. Only the most popular people are allowed to sit there. At Hawthorne Prep, there's a strict social hierarchy that is adhered to. Being invited to lunch at the epicenter of it is much akin to receiving a golden invitation that solidifies your popularity at the prep school. The inner ring of tables surrounding the coveted one is known as the second tier. The rings continue to fan outward until they reach the edges of the cafeteria.

The furthest one from the center is known as no man's land.

The goal of everyone who sits at the outer tiers is to gradually work their way inward. Even moving a couple rings is an accomplishment to be celebrated and unlocks coveted social invitations.

I'm something of an anomaly. Given that I'm a scholarship kid, I shouldn't be allowed anywhere near the center.

Trust me, I've heard all the grumblings.

Especially from other girls.

Ever since I started dating Jasper, my social standing has skyrocketed.

At first, I was thrilled by the attention. When you're used to being invisible, having popularity thrust upon you can go straight to your head. Suddenly, there were football games, parties, and hanging out with the elite of Hawthorne Prep. I'd stupidly thought they would become friendlier now that I was one of them.

But that's the problem—I'm still not one of them.

I'm Jasper's girlfriend from the wrong side of town whose mother works as a secretary in the school office. It didn't take long for the rose-colored glasses to fall away.

The other exception to the rigid social structure at HP is Duke Carmichael. Like me, he's a townie here on scholarship. He's also one of Kingsley's friends, which means he's been grudgingly accepted by his peers.

Ironically, the blond, muscular boy doesn't give a crap about popularity. He has the tendency to hang back from social situations with watchful, whiskey-colored eyes. Nothing gets past him.

Unlike Kingsley, he doesn't play football. He's a lacrosse guy. Duke stands well over six feet tall with broad shoulders and brawny arms. His hair is slightly longish and always disheveled in a way that looks intentional. Especially when he plows a big hand through it.

Except that's not the case. I've known him since elementary school, and he's never given a damn about those kinds of superficial things.

Even though I've never been interested in Duke, it would be impossible not to notice how the starched white material of his button-down strains across his chest and bulging biceps. Any moment, it'll burst at the seams. His presence is as intimidating as the permanent scowl etched across his face.

Here's the thing about Duke—he's always been kind to me. I think it's because neither of us belong at Hawthorne Prep and are just trying to navigate the shark-infested waters.

When Jasper waves for a second time, my shoulders droop, realizing that I have no choice but to join him. Not that I really thought otherwise. There would be questions if I chose to sit elsewhere. Even for a day. It seems less complicated to do what's expected while deciding how to handle Friday night.

"Looks like you're being summoned."

I immediately recognize the deep voice at my ear.

How did he manage to sneak up on me when I'm always so attuned to his presence?

His warm breath feathers across the delicate flesh of my neck as he steps closer until the heat of his body can radiate against my backside.

"Don't you ever get tired of it?"

I press my lips together, needing to keep the response buried deep inside. There's no way for me to admit the truth.

That I hate it.

And I'm starting to hate Jasper, too.

Or maybe I already do.

"What's the matter? You don't have an answer?"

"No," I whisper, barely moving my lips.

The urge to turn and meet his gaze pounds through me. Instead, my attention stays riveted to my boyfriend. His eyes are already narrowed, and from across the vast space that separates us, I see the storm clouds gathering on his face.

Jasper doesn't need an excuse to go after Austin, but this will definitely do the trick. And the boy standing much too close knows it. It's as if he's deliberately poking at Jasper to rile him.

Why can't these two just leave each other alone?

"I'm not afraid of him," he says.

That much is apparent.

I'm beginning to suspect Austin has a death wish.

Instead of commenting, I force my feet into movement, walking toward the center table with my tray. If my hands are trembling from his nearness, I do my best to ignore it and hope he doesn't notice.

What I know is that if I continue to stand here, looking as if we're engaging in a conversation, it'll only make the situation worse. Even though I don't glance over my shoulder, I'm unnervingly aware of Austin's towering presence shadowing my every movement. With each step, my heart picks up its tempo, thrashing painfully against my ribcage.

Once we reach the table, I settle on the bench next to Jasper. Austin drops down across from me with his lunch. A low growl emanates from within my boyfriend's chest as his body tenses like a tightly coiled spring. Any moment, he's going to leap across the space and a brawl will ensue. I can feel it brewing in the air.

Unwilling to chance eye contact, my gaze stays trained on my tray. It feels like the safest option.

"No one wants you here, Hawthorne," Jasper snaps. "Why don't you get lost? Better yet, go back to Chicago where you belong."

A heavy silence follows that comment as the tension continues to ratchet up.

I still, watching Austin from beneath the thick fringe of my lashes.

"Oh, I think there's at least one person who wants me here," he says almost conversationally, as if they're discussing the weather.

Air seeps from my lungs until there's nothing left.

Jasper's jaw locks and the muscle in his cheek twitches a mad beat as his arm snakes around my shoulders to haul me close. "Really? Who would that be?"

Austin's gaze flickers to me.

Oh god.

That's all it takes for the atmosphere to become oppressive as other people turn and stare. The last thing I want is for a fight to erupt. And I certainly don't want to deal with Jasper frothing at the mouth afterward.

What I can't figure out is why Austin is deliberately trying to piss him off. It seems shortsighted. Especially when he's already been suspended once this year. He's lucky he didn't get expelled when they got into a fistfight in the hallway the first week of school.

One more infraction and Austin will be tossed out of Hawthorne Prep. It doesn't matter if one of his ancestors founded the prestigious academy or that his father recently died of a heart attack. In fact, I'm pretty sure Mr. Pembroke, our headmaster, would be delighted to escort Austin off campus one final time.

"Me," Summer says, settling next to him with her tray in hand. "*I* want him here."

Jasper glares but wisely keeps his mouth shut. It's obvious from the way he smashes his lips into a thin, bloodless line that he wants to take her head off. If the slender, dark-haired girl weren't dating Kingsley, he'd probably rip her apart with his bare teeth.

No one wants to incur the wrath of Kingsley Rothchild. Not even the teachers. They pretty much give him free rein. He spears a penetrating look in Jasper's direction, almost daring him to step out of line.

Jasper's arm tightens around me until it becomes painful. Almost like he's trying to squeeze all the air from my body. Unable to stand another moment of the suffocating atmosphere, I shoot to my feet. The need to leave before the situation explodes into a mass casualty event thrums through me.

"Where do you think you're going?" There's an edge to his voice that's sharp enough to cut glass.

I blurt the first thing that comes to mind. "I need to talk with my mom."

When the edges of his lips curl down, a shiver creeps along my spine. "It can't wait? You need to take care of that right now?"

"Umm, yeah. I forgot to grab the spare set of keys before I left the house this morning. She's staying after school for a meeting or something."

He glances at my untouched tray. "You didn't eat."

My gaze flickers to the food. "Guess I wasn't very hungry." It's kind of hard to enjoy my meal when there's a giant pit taking up space at the bottom of my belly.

"After you grab the keys, come back and finish."

Yeah…that's not going to happen.

"I don't think there'll be enough time."

As I reach for the tray, Jasper says, "Leave it. That's what the staff is for."

There are times when I wonder if he remembers that my mother works at the school or if he's just being a passive aggressive asshole.

Although, let's face it…there's nothing passive about him.

"I don't mind dumping it in the trash," I murmur, heat burning the tips of my ears because I know everyone is watching our exchange.

The way Jasper treats people he perceives beneath him is yet another black mark against his character. Unfortunately, it's one of many. I wasn't born or raised with servants to wait on me hand and foot. And even if I were, I can't imagine believing that the status of my bank account somehow makes me a more valuable human.

Unwilling to argue in front of an audience, I swing away, darting from the sun-splashed room. As soon as I rush over the threshold into the large corridor, air escapes from my lungs.

With any hope, I won't run into him again for the rest of the day.

Once I leave the dining hall, my pace slows, and it takes a couple of minutes to wind my way through the hallways. Much like the cafeteria, there are wooden beams crisscrossing the high ceilings and elaborate chandeliers that hang suspended from the ceiling. More black and white photographs framed in gold strategically line the walls.

When I first stepped foot inside Hawthorne Prep, I was infatuated with the elaborate architectural features. I studied every photo and poured over the yearbooks, learning every detail of the history. I felt fortunate to be one of the chosen few accepted to such a prestigious institution. Someone who gets to walk these halls and sit in on lectures with guest speakers on a variety of interesting topics.

Three years later and the blinders have been ripped away. I've been forced to see this place for what it is. There's an ugly underbelly to Hawthorne Prep that no one talks about.

If I could do it all over again, I'd stay at the local public school. Maybe I wouldn't get the same top-notch education, but I wouldn't be made to feel as if I'm a second-class citizen simply because my parents don't preside over a multi-million-dollar company.

My feet slow as I reach the copy room where Mom can be found this time of the afternoon. The door is usually wide open, and I'll catch a glimpse of her standing in front of the machine from the hallway.

Instead, it's partially closed, leaving just a two-inch crack.

Which is...strange.

I step closer and push the thick wood just a bit before peeking inside. When I catch movement from within, the words gather on the tip of my tongue. I'm about to call out her name when I realize she's not alone. My voice dies a quick death as air clogs my lungs, making it impossible to breathe.

My eyes widen, bulging from their sockets. I give my head a little shake, needing to dislodge the image of her wrapped up in a man's arms. Even though I've only been staring for a few seconds, the mental snapshot has been singed into my brain for all eternity.

"Mmm, I've been waiting all morning to get you alone," he groans before his lips settle on hers.

My hand flies to my mouth as I falter a few paces before slamming into a hard chest. Strong fingers curl around my upper arms before I'm spun around to face the person who now holds me captive.

I'm almost afraid I'll find Jasper. His threat from earlier continues to echo in my brain. Instead, I find the dark-haired boy I've been unable to stop thinking about since he showed up two months ago.

It becomes necessary to lift my chin to hold his eyes. Even though I'm wearing my blazer, the tips of his fingers burn the flesh beneath the thick material as electricity sparks in the air. My mouth grows cottony as the woodsy scent of his cologne teases my nostrils.

It's so tempting to inhale a big breath of him and hold it captive in my lungs.

"Are you all right?"

That's when I remember what's going on in the copy room, and a jolt of panic slides through me as I jerk my head into a nod. "Yes. Sorry for bumping into you."

"It's not a problem."

When his grip tightens, I clear my throat before pushing out the words. "You should probably let me go."

His gaze bores into mine. "Is that really what you want?"

No.

But I can't say that.

"Yes."

As soon as the soft word escapes from me, his hands loosen before falling away. It's both a relief and devastating all at the same time. I don't understand how it's possible to feel so strongly about someone I barely know.

Once I've been set free, I slowly back away.

With a tilt to his head, he watches me. "There's only so long that you can run."

Goosebumps ripple across my flesh like a wave.

What does he mean?

From him?

Or Jasper?

I gulp. "That's not what I'm doing."

He takes a step toward me, eating up the distance between us. "Isn't it?"

"No."

"If you say so."

I straighten my spine. "I do."

"Seems like you're running from what you feel."

My step falters and my eyes widen. There are times when Austin stares at me that it feels like he can see straight down to my soul. I don't understand it. And if I'm being truthful with myself, he's right. It's why I've gone to such lengths to steer clear of him. He sees things that I'm not necessarily comfortable with.

I hold Jasper at a distance, but this is the boy I run from.

Instead of responding to the comment, I say, "I have to go."

With that, I flee down the corridor, putting as much space between what I witnessed in the copy room and the boy who makes me want things that aren't possible.

DELILAH

$\mathcal{A}$ chilly breeze whips through the football stadium as I climb the bleacher steps with a bottle of water from the concession stand. It's halftime and the Hawthorne Hawks are down by seven. You can feel the intensity of the cheering crowd as it rachets up with each second that ticks by on the clock.

Jasper is off his game. On the last play before the second quarter ended, he was sacked by a defensive end.

"Delilah!"

I rip my gaze away from the field as the team returns from the locker room for the second half and find Summer Hawthorne waving me down. She's sitting next to Everly Donahue. Much like the Hawthorne twins, Everly moved here at the beginning of the academic year. My guess is that these two have bonded over their newbie status. I know exactly what it's like to be an outsider at HP, so I'm glad they have each other.

Both are nice and seem down to earth. They're a breath of fresh air when compared to the other girls at this school. My gaze unconsciously slides to Sloane and her crew. I arrived at the same time as the girl gang and ended up getting swept along with them.

When I lift my hand to return the greeting, she signals for me to join them. I nibble my lower lip and chance another peek at Sloane. It's doubtful the blonde will notice my absence.

If she does, there'll be hell to pay.

Summer and Sloane are like oil and water. They don't mix. From the gossip I've heard swirling through the halls, they got into a fight in the girls' bathroom about a month or so ago. Apparently, there was hair pulling and claws. I give Summer a lot of credit for standing up to the popular blonde. She's a hell of a lot braver than I could ever be.

Instead of heading back to my spot, I detour to where the other two girls are hanging out. As I slide past a couple of other students, Summer pats the empty seat next to her.

"Join us."

"Thanks," I say with a grateful smile.

A loud buzzer rings throughout the stadium, signaling the start of the second half. Within the first two minutes of the third quarter, Jasper throws a pass that gets intercepted. The coach yanks off his ball cap before plowing his hand through his thinning blond strands and yanks the QB off the field.

When Coach Baker points to Austin, the dark-haired boy snaps his chinstrap into place and jogs onto the field.

Even though the stands have grown strangely silent, Summer rises to her feet and yells through cupped hands, "Go, Hawthorne! You got this!"

A few people turn and stare, including Sloane, who scowls before giving her the finger. Summer blows a kiss in the other girl's direction. It's difficult to contain the smile that trembles around the edges of my lips.

What's official is that Sloane has finally met her match.

Austin exchanges a look with his sister before his gaze shifts, touching upon mine. That one moment of connection is all it takes for my heartbeat to explode in my chest before sending it into overdrive.

Even though it's been a few days since I ran into him in the hallway, I still feel the burn of his fingers singeing the flesh of my arms through my clothing.

I'm forced from those thoughts when Jasper rips off his helmet before kicking over a jug of water. The coach doesn't spare him a glance. Like everyone else filling the stadium, he's focused on the game.

"Looks like someone's about to have a tantrum," Everly comments.

Yup.

There's no doubt in my mind that Jasper will be pissed off for the rest of the evening. The muscles in my belly pinch as a fresh wave of anxiety crashes over me. His attitude and behavior are the last thing I want to deal with. There's nothing I can do or say that will soothe his rage. My guess is that he'll drink too much at the party afterward and pick a fight.

Hopefully not with me.

His words from earlier this week ring unwantedly in my head.

I've given you more than enough time, and I'm done waiting.

The thought of Jasper forcing himself on me is enough to have bile rising in my throat. And the idea of him doing it while pissed off scares the shit out of me.

I wish it were possible to feign a headache and go home, but there's no way he'll allow it.

Summer nudges me with her shoulder. "Hey, are you all right? You look kind of pale."

I swallow down my nerves and force an anemic smile to my lips. "No, I'm fine. Guess I was spacing out for a sec."

She raises a brow as if she doesn't quite believe me. "Whatever you were thinking about must not have been very pleasant."

That's an understatement.

As tempting as it is to open up and confide, I keep the words buried inside. A deep sense of loneliness fills me. There is no one I can talk to about what's going on in my life. How ironic that I'm surrounded by a sea of people and yet, I couldn't feel more alone.

Then again, that perfectly sums up the years I've spent at this school.

I try to shake off the sense of foreboding that fills me by slipping the camera from my bag and adjusting the lens before bringing it to my face. Once I find Austin on the field, I snap half a dozen photos. The only time I feel like myself in this school and with these people is when I'm behind the camera, watching the world through the view finder.

The girls chatter throughout the game, including me in their conversation, but I can't shake the unease that continues to fill me. I feel every tick of the clock on the scoreboard as each second slips by. When the buzzer sounds at the end of the fourth quarter, the crowd in the stands goes crazy, cheering and yelling. The Hawks have managed to pull off a win, thanks to Austin.

As much as Jasper is loath to admit it, the other boy is a far more talented quarterback. Without Jasper's mother being a board member and their clout in the community, there's no way he'd be first string QB. Even though Jasper's teammates are loyal, they're desperate to win. Everyone wants a chance to go to state. And that won't happen unless Austin Hawthorne is given more playtime.

By the surly expression on my boyfriend's face, he realizes it as well.

DELILAH

"Good game, Hawthorne," someone shouts over the noise of the party. "Didn't think there was a chance in hell we were gonna pull that one off."

I wince as Jasper gnashes his teeth and hurls his half-filled cup of beer against the wall, soaking the people who have the misfortune to be standing in his line of fire.

"Hey!" Lucus Standish complains, swinging around and catching sight of an enraged Jasper. He immediately lifts both hands before carefully backing away. "Sorry, Morgan. Didn't realize it was you."

A second later, he vanishes through the sea of students. I stare after him, wishing it was possible to do the same. Instead, I'm stuck here at Jasper's side as he not-so-silently fumes. Even though it's his party, everyone gives him a wide berth. It's as if they can sense the volatility of his mood and don't want to get caught in the crosshairs.

Trust me, I feel the same. If it were possible to slink away, I'd do it in a heartbeat. Not even his closest friends or teammates want to be around him. The more people that congratulate Austin, the darker Jasper's mood becomes.

"I wish that guy would go back to wherever the hell he came from," he slurs, gaze fixated straight ahead.

Reluctantly, I glance in the direction he's glaring, knowing exactly who I'll find. If Austin were smart, he would have avoided this party altogether. But here he is, accepting compliments and congratulations with more dignity than Jasper ever could.

Once my attention is drawn to him, it's difficult to pull it away. A second later, his gaze fastens onto mine and tingles erupt across my skin.

No one—certainly not the boy at my side—has ever stirred these kinds of reactions within me.

The only thing Jasper instills is stark fear. If he didn't, I would have broken off this relationship after a couple of months when I realized what a mistake it was. I'm knocked from those thoughts when strong fingers wrap around my lower jaw and my face is jerked to the side. I wince as his fingers dig into my flesh.

"Stop fucking staring at him," he growls. "You belong to me and *only* me. That's the way it'll always be."

Embarrassment slams into my cheeks as people turn and stare. Even though I'll pay a price for it later, I bat his hand away. "I belong to myself and no one else."

As soon as his grip loosens, I take a quick step in retreat, trying to put space between us.

"Is that so?" The tiny muscle in his cheek twitches. That's always a bad sign of things to come.

I suck in a shaky breath before inching my chin upward. "Yes."

Before I realize what's happening, his hand snakes out and his fingers shackle around my wrist before dragging me through the thick crowd. Classmates scatter out of his way.

The music gets cranked up as I yell, "Let go!"

When I attempt to break the tight hold, his fingers clamp down on the slender bone. It's almost a surprised when it doesn't snap in half. Pain radiates through the area as he drags me from the living room down a dark hallway to his parents' master suite. Once I'm shoved over the threshold, he slams the door shut behind him.

"Jasper!" Shock spirals through me as I gape at him. "What the hell has gotten into you?"

His lips are a tight slash across his face as his nostrils flare. Even in the dimness of the spacious room, the red haze filling his eyes doesn't go unnoticed. Alarm bells explode in my head as he releases his hold.

I scramble backward, only wanting to get away. He's like a volcano on the verge of erupting. With him barring the only exit, my chances of escaping unscathed have dwindled to the single digits. My heartbeat thunders, turning painful. It's tempting to raise my hand and rub away the ache.

Instead of responding, he stalks toward me, eating up the distance I've put between us with a few long-legged strides. A burst of adrenaline rushes through me. Eyes locked on him, I retreat. Every step he takes forward has me stumbling in my haste. Too late do I realize that he's intentionally steering me toward the king-sized bed at the far end of the room.

"Jasper," I gasp, voice rising with panic, "*please.*"

As much as I hate to beg or plead, I need him to snap out of the rage that has taken hold and think about what he's doing. His dark intentions are written clearly across his expression, and they freeze the blood rampaging through my veins.

"I told you I was tired of waiting," he growls. "I wanted to have a good game and then celebrate between your prissy little thighs, but fuck that plan. Maybe it's better this way. I need something to take my mind off what happened on the field, and that's exactly what you're going to do." His fingers drop to the hem of his T-shirt, dragging it up his muscular chest and over his head before dropping it to the plush carpet.

My mouth turns bone dry, making it impossible to swallow down the fear that chokes me. "Not like this."

His lips lift into a smile. It's cruel around the edges and doesn't reach the hard glint that shines in his eyes. "Don't be such a damn baby. I promise, you'll enjoy every moment."

Even if he weren't drunk, it's doubtful that would be the case. Jasper isn't the type of guy to think about anyone else's pleasure but his own.

Before I can jumpstart my brain and formulate a plan, he lunges. His hard body slams into mine before we crash onto the bed. His heavy weight pins me to the mattress, making it difficult to draw air into my lungs. There's barely enough room to slip my hands between our bodies before flattening my palms against his chest and attempting to dislodge him.

"Get off!" I scream.

"Settle the fuck down," he snaps, shifting to subdue me.

"No! I don't want to do this."

Any minute, my heart will explode. Then again, maybe that would be for the best. I can't imagine living through something like this. The idea of him forcing himself inside my body—especially in anger—makes me want to vomit. Every time I look into my eyes and glimpse the hollowness, I'll be reminded of what he stole from me.

"Sure, you do. You're such a fucking tease."

He's delusional.

When I continue to fight, he reaches for my wrists.

I grunt, trying to buck him off, but nothing happens. He doesn't budge an inch. Jasper probably has a solid seventy pounds on me. He's not going anywhere. Tears of rage and disbelief prick my eyes.

Just as his fingers lock around one wrist, I slip my leg between his and bring my knee up, slamming it into his crotch with as much force as I can muster.

"Fuck!" he moans, rolling to the side. As soon as he hits the mattress, he curls up into a tight ball and groans.

The second his weight disappears, I suck a breath of fresh air into my lungs before scrambling off the bed. On shaky legs, I race to the door and yank the handle. Adrenaline rushes through my veins, making it feel as if I have the strength of a thousand men.

"Get your ass back here, you dumb bitch," he hisses.

Yeah...like that's going to happen.

"Fuck you," I spit, escaping over the threshold.

Once I step onto the marble tile of the hallway and I'm no longer trapped in the master suite, a tidal wave of relief crashes over me, nearly weakening my knees. It's tempting to slide to the floor and find my bearings, but I force my legs into movement. The need to put as much space between us as possible thrums through me like a steady drumbeat. It's all I'm cognizant of. My brain somersaults, unable to process what just happened, as I race through the echoing corridor, blindly passing by groups of drunk classmates.

I can't believe he tried to force himself on me.

The thought rings hollowly throughout my head until focusing on anything else becomes impossible. The acidic taste of bile rises in my throat, making me sick to my stomach. Would he have actually gone through with it?

Every instinct is screaming that he would have. He was drunk and angry. It's a lethal combination. He's been pushing me for weeks to finally sleep with him. Tonight turned out to be the perfect storm, and everything exploded.

Someone calls my name, but I don't bother glancing around. I can't. I just need to get the hell out of here. I'm terrified that Jasper will find me. By the time I reach the kitchen, the music is so loud that it vibrates in my skull and bones. With my head angled down, I weave through the press of people. Normally, this room feels large and spacious. That's no longer the case. Any moment, the walls will press in on me and I won't be able to breathe. A wave of dizziness overtakes me, attempting to drag me under. It's only when I reach the double story entryway that my heartbeat begins to slow.

When my name is called for a second time, I ignore it again, surging forward. My trembling fingers wrap around the brushed nickel handle before yanking open the door and stumbling onto the front porch, past the concrete balusters and potted mums. Cool night air rushes over my heated cheeks. I'm so relieved to be out of there that a fresh wave of tears stings my eyes.

I sprint down the driveway until I reach the paved road. The more distance I put between myself and the house ablaze with lights, the more secure I feel in my escape. Adrenaline leaks from my body with each step I take. It's only when I'm walking along the stretch of dark road that I realize I'll need to call Mom to pick me up. With a huff of breath, I slide my cell from the back pocket of my jeans as I walk past a long line of cars parked in the gravel.

Thank god I didn't leave my phone in my jacket.

Otherwise, it would still be inside the house, and I'd be shit out of luck.

I hit Mom's name at the top of the screen and wait impatiently for the line to connect. Now that I'm away from the stately mansion, the music fades and the sound of crickets surrounds me. A gust of wind rattles the tops of the trees and cuts through the thin fabric of my sweater. My footsteps echo off the pavement as darkness swallows up the light. When a twig snaps from somewhere behind me, fear slices through my body and I spin around, hoping Jasper isn't on the hunt.

I have no idea what he'll do if he finds me.

That's a lie.

I know *exactly* what will happen. I was lucky to avert disaster once this evening. It's doubtful my good fortune will hold out for a second time.

The phone continues to ring before Mom's voicemail bursts over the line. Frustration rises inside me as I hit end and immediately redial. That's our SOS code, signaling something important. Instead of picking up, I get a chirpy invitation to leave a message.

Damn it.

Where is she?

For a few seconds, I consider leaving a message before disconnecting and firing off a text, asking her to call me ASAP. Unsure what else to do, I shove the phone in my pocket and continue walking.

Who else can I call for a ride?

Sloane?

Ha!

I'd rather walk barefoot over crushed glass all the way home than ask her for anything.

And that's at least ten miles.

Jasper's house is situated in a subdivision of mansions outside the city limits and on the gently rolling hills of a golf course. Our houses couldn't be any farther apart if we tried. Ironically, it's the perfect metaphor to describe our lives.

Just as I'm about to turn onto the street that leads out of the subdivision and onto the main county road, bright headlights fall on me and my belly plummets to my toes.

DELILAH

For a moment, I consider diving headfirst into the trees and tall weeds that flank the sides of the road to hide, but whoever it is has already seen me. My muscles fill with paralyzing tension as the vehicle pulls alongside me and slows.

Please don't let it be Jasper.

There's no way I'll be able to fight him off for a second time tonight. Especially out here where no one will hear my screams.

The thought is terrifying.

Cool night air stings my lungs, getting clogged at the back of my throat as I swivel my head and peer through the open window. As soon as my eyes collide with green ones, my body wilts in relief.

Thank god.

I don't think I've ever been more grateful to see Austin Hawthorne.

"What the hell are you doing out here?" he snaps.

It takes a few moments to find my voice and force out a response. "Walking home."

His brows pinch together as anger rolls across his expression. "Why would you do that?"

I'm conflicted about telling him the truth. I know exactly what will happen if I do. He'll go back to that party and beat the shit out of Jasper. Even though I'm upset and angry, I don't want to drag Austin into my problems. It'll only escalate the simmering tension between them.

When he continues to stare, patiently waiting for a response, I say, "I didn't want to stay at the party."

It's not a lie.

It's just not the full truth either.

His lips press together as he studies me, seeming to peer beneath the surface. My heartrate kicks up its tempo. This time for different reasons. It would be so much easier to breathe if his attention wasn't focused solely on me.

"Where's Jasper?"

"Drunk."

Again, it's not a lie.

"So, for some reason, you thought it would be a smart move to walk home by yourself at night?"

Not really, but it's better than being raped.

When another breeze rattles the treetops, I wrap my arms around my middle and try to warm myself.

"Get in. There's no way I'm going to let you walk home alone."

I pause and consider my limited options. The last thing I want to do is put myself in another precarious situation. I was barely able to fight Jasper off and Austin is more muscular than my boyfriend. If he decides to attack me, there won't be much I can do about it.

A little voice inside my head tells me Austin would never behave that way.

When I don't immediately climb inside the SUV, he holds up my jacket. "You took off and forgot this."

I blink, surprised he would know which coat is mine. There was a giant pile on the couch in the living room. That's the moment I realize there's nothing coincidental about him finding me on the dark road.

Not once does he break eye contact as he leans across the passenger seat before grabbing the handle and popping open the door. "Get in, Delilah."

Air escapes from my lungs like a balloon with a slow leak as I chew my lower lip. I'm cold, tired, and emotionally drained. I can't take much more. Part of me is scared to take a gamble and be alone with Austin. But it's not for the same reasons I've shied away from being with Jasper.

Deep down, I know Austin is different.

I'm just not sure if I can trust my instincts.

"Come on, Delilah," he cajoles. "Don't make me come get you. Because I will."

As threatening as it should sound, terror isn't the emotion sliding through me.

Relenting, I make my way to the G-Wagon before settling on the buttery soft leather seat and closing myself inside the vehicle. My heart skips a beat when he leans over, takes hold of the belt, and drags it across my chest. As he clicks it firmly into place, our gazes fasten.

"Don't lock the door," I whisper.

He studies me for a long, drawn-out moment before laying the jacket carefully across my lap. "I won't."

My muscles gradually loosen as he swivels in his seat and pulls away from the side of the road, heading out of the subdivision. It's a relief that there's no longer a chance Jasper will find me.

For the time being, I'm safe.

I give Austin a sidelong glance and the muscles in my belly contract.

Well...as safe as I can be with him.

He stares straight ahead as he asks, "Are you all right? Did something happen at the party?"

The urge to blurt out the truth bubbles up inside me for a second time before I stomp it down. I'll deal with Jasper on my own. "No."

His gaze flickers to mine. In that moment of connection, it feels as if he can see straight through the lies.

"You sure about that?" A hard edge fills his tone.

With the fragile way I'm feeling, it wouldn't take much prodding for me to crumble.

"I'm sure," I murmur, pressing the back of my skull against the headrest and closing my eyes. I just want to shut down this conversation. Nothing good will come of it. "I was tired and wanted to leave, so I took off. End of story."

There's a moment of silence before he says, "If you belonged to me, there's no damn way I'd allow you to walk home alone."

The possessiveness filling his voice sends an avalanche of shivers cascading down my spine. It should be a turn off.

It's not.

Pleasure rushes through my veins before I can stop it.

Jasper's jealousy drives me crazy. He acts more like a spoiled brat set on guarding his toys so no one else can play with them. That's not the vibe I get from Austin. He's more concerned about my welfare.

When I remain silent, he growls, "Why are you with him?" His voice drops, sounding as if it's been scraped from the bottom of the ocean. "He doesn't treat you the way he should."

That's never been more apparent than this evening.

Whether Jasper realizes it or not, what we had is over. I'm not looking forward to that conversation, but I refuse to stay with him after the crap he just pulled.

My teeth rake across my lower lip before sucking the plump flesh into my mouth and chewing.

"You deserve so much better. I hope you realize that."

My gaze flickers to his, only to find him steadily watching me. Butterflies wing their way to life in the pit of my belly and the air gets sucked from my lungs. Everything I've secretly longed for with this boy is reflected within his eyes. It takes every ounce of self-control not to reach out and stroke his handsome face. Instead, I tighten my fingers and press them into my lap.

There's nothing I can do about the attraction I feel for him.

We turn out of the high-end subdivision and onto the dark county road that leads to the small town of Hawthorne.

Population eight thousand.

He jerks his head toward the ribbon of black pavement stretched out in front of us. "I assume you live this way?"

"Yes." I rattle off the address, giving him a few cursory directions before shifting on my seat.

I hate bringing people home with me. It's not that I'm embarrassed or ashamed, but next to most of the kids at HP, I live in a sad little hovel. Sloane's words from the one time she dropped me home from school last year echo unwantedly throughout my head.

Oh my god, you actually live in that?

Shock and disgust had weaved their way through her voice. The scrunched expression marring her pretty face had only driven home her genuine thoughts. I'd slunk from her fancy sports car with my tail between my legs and heat scorching my cheeks. She never offered me another ride and I refused to ask.

The memory is enough to have my belly tightening painfully as nerves explode inside me. Austin lives in the same wealthy subdivision as Jasper. His house is even bigger and more impressive than the Morgans'.

When my phone chimes, I slip it from my back pocket and glance at the screen, wondering if Mom is finally getting back to me.

Where the fuck are you?

Nope. Not Mom.

Another text quickly rolls in.

Are you going to answer me?

Absolutely not.

"What's wrong?"

"Nothing." I mute the sound as a third text flashes across the screen. Needing to change the topic of conversation, I blurt, "Congratulations on the game. That win had everything to do with you."

For the first time this evening, a smile curves his lips. Even when he was out on the field, turning the game around, there wasn't a hint of joy written across his features. The look of concentration etched there was palpable.

At the party afterward, I couldn't help but sneak furtive glances from beneath the fringe of my lashes. When classmates who had always gone out of their way to snub him were suddenly singing his praises, his stoic expression never faltered. I watched him nod in thanks before turning away and coolly dismissing them. Unlike Jasper, he didn't stand there, soaking up all the adoration.

As the slow smile moves across his face, tipping the corners of his lips upward, my breath catches almost painfully at the back of my throat, and I find myself unable to look away. If I'd thought he was handsome before, it's nothing compared to how arresting he is with pleasure lighting up his eyes.

"Thanks." There's a pause. "It felt good to be out there again."

"Hopefully now that you've shown what you're capable of, you'll get more play time."

What can't be denied is that Austin is talented and a natural leader on the field. Even guys loyal to Jasper followed the other boy's lead and played better under his direction.

"That would be nice." His deep voice turns wistful. "I miss playing like I did in Chicago. I've been a starter on varsity since freshman year. Moving here and sitting my ass on the bench every game is tough to swallow. Especially when..."

His jaw locks as his voice trails off.

It's so tempting to reach out and smooth my fingers over the grooves that line his forehead. I want to bring the lightness back into his expression.

Instead, I finish his sentence. "Especially when the guy you're second to isn't nearly as talented."

His thick brows furrow. "It's a lot to choke down. This team isn't nearly as good as the one I played on. We've won championships. And yet, I'm treated like someone who walked on without any experience. I've been playing since I was six years old."

I can't imagine how difficult that would be. It reframes Austin's entire experience in Hawthorne. He has every right to be angry. My heart constricts, going out to him.

He's been through so much in such a short period of time.

"You probably wish you'd never heard of the town of Hawthorne."

How could he not?

When he glances at me again, our gazes lock and hold. I feel the connection straight down to my toes. It's only when he rips it away to stare out the windshield that I become aware of the air trapped in my lungs.

"For the most part."

I don't realize that my hand has settled over his until the warmth of his fingers radiates against mine. Eyes widening, I still, wondering if I should pull away.

His gaze flicks to where we're now connected before returning to the road.

"There's only one good thing that's happened since we've been here. Everything else is shit."

A prickle dances across my skin, wondering what it is. I want to ask.

But I don't.

Can't.

"I'm sorry about your father," I murmur.

His shoulders are so broad and strong, only now do I realize that he carries the weight of the world on them. The way they slump forward shatters my heart into tiny, fragmented pieces.

It's so tempting to pull him close and stroke my fingers through his short, dark strands. I want to tell him that everything will be all right, even though I have no idea if that's the case. More than anything, I want to bring the smile back to his lips.

"I know what it's like to lose a parent. My dad died when I was seven."

His lips tighten into a thin line. "I can't imagine life ever returning to normal."

"It won't. But you'll find a way to make peace with it and move on. It'll just take a while."

He slows the SUV to twenty-five as we reach the edge of town and travel down Main Street. I've lost track of how many times Jasper has accelerated, reaching speeds of seventy and blowing through the three stoplights that dot the road. Even if the police caught him red handed, they'd turn a blind eye.

What's the point of ticketing or arresting Jasper when Benedict

Morgan not only owns one of the largest manufacturing plants in town but is the mayor of Hawthorne?

"You can always talk to me," I offer.

His hand slips from beneath mine before resettling over it. "I appreciate that." His voice softens. "It took weeks before Mom was finally able to get a grip and get out of bed. And now that Summer is back home where she belongs, it's better. Kind of like we're a family again."

My brow furrows as the odd comment replays in my head. "I don't understand. Where was Summer if she wasn't living at home?"

I can almost see the invisible shield falling into place. When he remains silent, I wonder if he'll bother to answer.

"Sorry, I shouldn't have mentioned anything. It's a long story. All I can say is that no matter how much I wish otherwise, my life is now in Hawthorne. We're not leaving. Not with Summer and Kingsley together."

"They could break up." Sure, they seem like they're in love, but feelings change.

He shakes his head. "Trust me, that's not going to happen."

I swivel in my seat until my body is angled toward his. Even though questions circle in my head, I get the feeling he won't reveal the answers. And since I'm someone who values their own privacy, I reluctantly drop the topic.

"Maybe now, everything will change. People will warm up."

He jerks his shoulders as if it doesn't matter, but I can tell, deep down, it does.

"I just need to make it through this year without getting kicked out of school, and then I can get the hell out of this town."

A small smile springs to my lips. "That's exactly what I've been telling myself, too."

Our gazes fasten as he searches my eyes in the darkness.

"Is it really that shitty for you?"

My throat closes up, making it impossible to swallow. Unable to speak, I shrug.

He takes my silence as an affirmative. "Tell me why."

I get the feeling he'd happily slay all my dragons if I gave him the least bit of encouragement, and it's difficult not to fall even harder for him. Just as Jasper wasn't what I assumed, neither is Austin.

I consider admitting the truth. It would be so nice to stop pretending and be truthful with one person, even if it's only for five minutes. Someone who knows what it's like to be an outsider at this school.

We have more in common than I ever allowed myself to believe.

"For starters, I'm here on scholarship, and everyone knows it." I force a smile and try to lighten the heaviness of my words. "They never let me forget it."

"Why is that something to be embarrassed about?"

Surprised by the question, I straighten my shoulders. "I'm not embarrassed about where I come from. It's more that people look at me differently and treat me like I'm less than."

I almost forget his hand is still wrapped around mine until his fingers tighten, strength radiating through both flesh and bone. The warmth travels through my veins until it pumps through my heart.

"You know," he says, turning onto my street, "I don't come from money. Chicago is expensive, and my parents were barely able to make ends meet. It's one of the reasons Mom and Dad decided that moving would be a fresh start for us." His eyes cloud. "Guess that didn't work out the way they expected."

A heavy silence falls over us as he pulls up in front of my house. His gaze settles on the tiny ranch that sits on a postage stamp sized lawn. Even though I told him seconds ago that I wasn't ashamed of our financial situation, heat claws at my cheeks.

"It doesn't change anything. Take it from someone who's gone from nothing to having more money than they know what to do with. Maybe Mom isn't worrying about our finances the way she was back home, but we're still the same." His gaze darts to mine, holding it captive. "You're the most real person I've met here. Everyone else has proven themselves to be arrogant assholes."

When I look away, his fingers settle under my chin, lifting it until I have no other choice but to meet the intensity shining within his eyes. Unlike Jasper's punishing touch, his is gentle. There's an unexpected tenderness to it as if he's taking great pains to be careful with me.

"I would never judge you, Delilah."

It's only when my muscles loosen that I realize how tense they've become. It takes effort to find my voice. "Thank you."

The attraction simmering beneath the surface intensifies, and it becomes necessary to fight my own instincts and hold myself back.

"There's nothing to thank me for. Isn't that the way it should be?"

"Not here."

"It's the way it can be between us."

When he gifts me with a slow smile, my heart lurches painfully.

Broody Austin is a sight to behold, but a smiling Austin?

That's enough to knock any woman on her ass.

"I bet the girls at your old school were devastated to see you go." As soon as the words slip free, my eyes widen, and I slap a hand over my mouth.

Horror floods through me, suffusing every cell.

Did I seriously just say that?

Out loud?

I want the plush seat to open up and swallow me whole before the situation can jackhammer to an all-new low.

His fingers curl around mine as the smile turns into a full-on grin. His voice dips, becoming husky. "Are you trying to tell me something?"

How is it possible for even more heat to burn my cheeks? Any moment I'll burst into flames. I think we can all agree that would be for the best.

"Absolutely not," I squeak, wishing there were a way out of this mess without humiliating myself any further.

He cocks his head. "I think you are."

A mortified groan gurgles up from my lips.

"Why are you so embarrassed?"

I roll my eyes and attempt to fight my way through the horror of this moment. "Because I didn't mean to blurt that out."

He shifts, moving closer. A serious light shines in his eyes, making them glow in the moonlight that slants in through the windows. "I like that you find me attractive."

"I'm sure that most girls do," I grumble.

How could they not?

He shrugs, acknowledging the truth of my words.

There's no way Austin doesn't understand his effect on the opposite sex. He might be a Hawthorne, but the girls here still eat him up with hungry eyes. I've overheard enough whispered comments about his finer attributes.

And trust me, there are many.

"I don't care what anyone else thinks." The intensity of his stare pins mine in place until it becomes necessary to fight for breath. "I only care about what's going on inside your head."

It's like a trapdoor springs open and the floor drops out from beneath me. Suddenly, I'm in free fall. I have no idea what to do with what he's telling me. As much as I want to keep drowning in his deep, soulful depths, I rip my gaze away and stare at our clasped fingers. His hand is so much larger than mine. It swallows it up.

That's exactly the way it feels.

Like he's swallowing me up.

"Would it make it better if I tell you something embarrassing?"

I glance up and raise my brows in silent inquiry.

It's doubtful anything he could say will rise to the level of what I've just blurted.

When he remains silent, my attention sharpens. I can almost see him internally debating with himself. Whatever he's wrestling with, it obviously goes much deeper than what I've just admitted.

Even though curiosity eats away at me, I murmur, "It's okay. You don't have to tell me anything."

He releases a gradual breath as his voice deepens. "It's just not something I talk about with many people. My family knows, but that's about it."

Concern prickles along my skin before erupting into gooseflesh. "Are you *sick*?"

My chest constricts at the idea that something serious could be going on with Austin. I honestly don't know how much more pain one family can withstand.

He shakes his head. "No, it's nothing like that. Maybe I'm making too big a deal of it." There's a pause. "I'm dyslexic."

Relief escapes from me in a rush of breath.

Thank god that's all it is.

For a moment, I was thinking the worst.

Now that he's revealed his secret, more pieces of the puzzle fall neatly into place. We have two classes together, English Lit and Pre-calculus. I've noticed that he struggles in our literature class. In the beginning of the year, when Ms. Pettijohn would call on him to read a passage out loud, a stubborn look would enter his eyes and he'd fold his brawny arms across his chest, refusing to do it. I've also caught glimpses of the homework he turns in. The handwriting is messy and there are always a slew of misspelled words littering the page.

Part of me wondered if he just didn't care about academics.

Obviously, that's not the case, and I feel bad for assuming the worst.

"You don't have anything to be ashamed of." The mortification I'd felt earlier drains away. It was stupid and fleeting. It doesn't mean anything when compared to what Austin struggles with.

I don't understand why he's entrusting me with something so private, but I'm grateful. It only strengthens the tentative bond forming between us.

His lips tug down at the corners as a flinty look enters his eyes. "Don't I?"

I shake my head, not wanting him to feel that way.

Especially where I'm concerned.

"Absolutely not."

He draws in a breath before gradually releasing it back into the atmosphere. "For a long time, I thought I was slower than everyone else. Not as smart. I had a hard time learning to read. And when you have a twin—one who's a brainiac and always did everything early—the comparisons suck. Even worse than that is when your classmates begin to realize that you can't keep up and it takes you longer than everyone else to grasp the concepts. They start to look at you differently."

"Yeah," I murmur. "I know what that's like but for different reasons. There's nothing worse than feeling singled out for something that's not within your control."

Some of the tension filling his shoulders drains away. "I guess you would."

"We have that in common."

Giving in to the urge that thrums through me, I reach out, running my fingers over the chiseled lines of his face. With his gaze fastened to mine, he sits perfectly still. When my fingers drift across his lips, his eyelids feather closed, and a tortured groan escapes from him.

"Do you ever think about me?" The way his voice deepens does funny things to my insides. "Because I think about you all the time."

The truth of the matter is that Austin's always there, lurking in my thoughts. No matter how much I try to shove them away, I can't.

Instead of answering, I jerk my head into a nod.

Our gazes continue to cling.

"So tell me, Delilah…what are we going to do about this?"

It's a good question.

One I don't have an answer to.

DELILAH

Bright sunlight streams through the window as I crack open an eye and stare at the digital clock on the nightstand. It's almost a surprise to discover that it's after ten o'clock. I refocus on the numbers just to make sure, unable to remember the last time I slept this late.

Then again, when was the last time I went to bed after two o'clock in the morning? We sat in Austin's sleek SUV and talked for what felt like hours before I realized just how late it was. Mom still wasn't home by the time I fell asleep. The thought of what she'd been doing—and who she'd been up to it with—is enough to make me groan as I turn over and curl up into a tight ball under the covers. Even though I close my eyes and try to slip back into slumber, it doesn't work. My mind is circling, trying to figure out when their affair started.

Unable to put off reality for another second, I toss aside the comforter and peel away my PJs before grabbing a cozy sweatshirt and jeans. Then, I throw my hair up into a ponytail.

As I open the door to the bedroom and step into the short hallway, I hear Mom puttering around in the kitchen. A large stone settles in the pit of my belly as I force myself into the sun-filled space. Mom and I have always had an open and honest relationship. It's been the two of us for so long. We rely on each other for everything. It's difficult to imagine that she's been keeping secrets from me.

Especially something of this magnitude.

I've come up with a hundred alternative scenarios for why she'd be hugging and kissing Mr. Pembroke in the copy room before discarding each one.

Her gaze locks on mine as she lifts the steaming mug to her lips and blows on it. "Morning, honey. Sleep well?"

"Yeah, I did."

When she falls silent, I realize her affair isn't something I can shove under the rug and ignore. I can't look at her without flashes of their embrace filling my head.

I clear my throat and force myself to say, "I tried calling you last night, but you didn't pick up."

Guilt flickers across her expression as her gaze drops to the ceramic mug in her hand. "You did? I'm so sorry. My ringer must have been turned off." Concern fills her eyes when they snap back to mine. "Was everything all right? Did you need something?"

For a moment, I toy with admitting the truth. But I'm not ready to talk about it. I need time to process what happened. Maybe afterward, we can have a conversation. As much as I hate to admit it, I'm afraid she'll downplay his actions and make excuses for his appalling behavior. She has it in her head that he's my ticket to a better life.

"No, everything's fine. I just needed to ask you a quick question."

"Oh?" Her expression smooths out as she takes a sip of coffee.

I wave a hand. "It wasn't a big deal."

"Are you sure, sweetie?"

"Yeah." I pause before blurting, "I didn't get to bed until two o'clock last night and you still weren't home."

My gaze sharpens on her, wanting to see every emotion that flickers across her face. A heavy silence blankets us as she averts her attention. The seconds that tick by are excruciating.

"Actually," she says, clearing her throat, "I was out on a date."

Even though it's been a little more than a decade since Dad died, a pang fills my heart. This is the first time she's mentioned going out with a man. There's always been too much going on and we were just trying to scrape by.

"Anyone I know?" I ask, forcing myself to remain calm.

"We're not ready to go public quite yet."

"Why not?" The small pit at the bottom of my belly grows until it's more of an unpleasant lump.

"It's a little complicated at the moment."

It would be all too easy to drop this awkward conversation, but I refuse to give in to the urge. I fold my arms across my chest and lean against the door frame. "What makes the situation difficult?"

Her eyes search mine before she forces out a brittle laugh that sounds nothing like her. "What's with all the questions? I'm a forty-year-old woman and entitled to my own life."

Air seeps from my lungs as my shoulders collapse. All Mom has done since Dad died is take care of me. There have been times when she's worked two jobs just to make sure I had everything I needed for school. When I decided to take up photography, she picked up a part-time job watching a neighbor's kid so she could buy me a brand-new digital camera.

The last decade hasn't been easy, and I'm the first one to admit that if anyone deserves to carve out a little piece of happiness for themselves, it's my mother.

"Of course I know that," I murmur. "I'm just surprised you haven't mentioned it before."

She tucks a stray lock of blonde hair behind her ear before releasing a breath. "I guess, in the beginning, I wasn't sure where it would lead, but now..." Her voice trails off, as if she's not quite sure how to explain herself.

When the silence continues to stretch, I prompt, "Are you saying this relationship is serious?"

"I think it might be."

I tilt my head, just wanting her to admit the truth so we can get it out in the open and talk about it. "But you won't tell me who this man is?"

"For the time being, it's not important."

My brows pinch as I shake my head. "I don't understand. If you like him and he feels the same, why does he have to remain a mystery?"

She purses her lips. "He's a very private person."

What's become obvious is that she isn't going to reveal his name. And maybe if I didn't already know, I'd let it go. But how can I do that?

I hate forcing the issue but don't see any other choice. "I stopped by the copy room during lunch the other day."

Confusion morphs across her features at the abrupt change in topic. "Oh? I don't remember seeing you. Wasn't I there?"

"No, you were." A beat of silence falls over us before I add, "Mr. Pembroke was in the room with you."

Her eyes widen as shock flashes in her eyes before it's quickly shuttered away. "The man is my boss. If I remember correctly, he stopped by with some papers that needed to be copied."

Disappointment swirls through me that she's lying. It's the first time I've felt this emotion where my mom is concerned. In fact, I've always been proud of her for keeping everything together after Dad died. She's the strongest woman I know.

"You were wrapped up in his arms and he was kissing you."

Her face turns ashen as she says in a clipped tone, "You're mistaken."

Slowly, I shake my head. "No, I'm not. The door was partially closed and when I pushed it open, I saw the two of you embracing. Stop lying. I know what I saw."

This conversation feels surreal. Have I ever spoken to my mother like this?

We stare silently for a handful of seconds before her shoulders slump and remorse fills her eyes.

"How long has this been going on for?"

A couple of weeks?

Months?

It can't be more than that.

With any luck, I'll be able to talk some sense into her before it goes any further.

"Two years."

I can only stare as if she's speaking a foreign language.

There's no way I heard her correctly.

Years?

My mouth crashes open as I gape.

"But he's married." The man is married with kids. Two of them attend Hawthorne Prep. The boy is a junior, and the girl is a freshman. I see both around school.

"I know," she admits quietly.

"Then why are you with him?" My voice escalates with each grounded-out syllable.

Years.

The word won't stop echoing throughout my head.

She jerks her shoulders defensively. "It's not like we planned for this to happen. We started talking at school, getting to know one another on a more personal level, and after a while, it led to more." Her expression turns earnest. "His wife doesn't understand him, honey. She doesn't get him the way I do."

A groan escapes from my lips.

Please tell me she's not that naïve. This is the same woman who's always steered me in the right direction. How could she be involved in something so wrong?

"None of that matters, Mom. The man is married!" When she freezes, staring at me with wide eyes, I raise my voice and repeat, *"He's married."*

"I know." Her voice is so low that I'm barely able to pick up the threads of it. "He's going to leave her."

It's so tempting to drag my hand through my hair before pulling it out. "Exactly how long has he been stringing you along with that line?"

I wince at the harsh question, almost unable to believe that it came from me.

The way she presses her lips together before slamming the mug down on the counter is all the confirmation I need to know that I'm right.

"Come on, Mom. You know better than this."

For the first time since the beginning of our conversation, anger flares in her eyes. "You don't know anything about our relationship, and quite honestly, you shouldn't be judging me. Don't we get that enough in this godforsaken town? I don't need to feel your condemnation too."

All of the emotion whipping through me like an impending storm drains, leaving exhaustion to take its place. "I'm sorry, that's not how I meant to come across. I'm just," my tongue slips out to moisten my lips, "I'm *concerned* that he's taking advantage of you." Even though I want to, I don't mention the married part again. "He's your boss."

"I know how it looks from the outside." Guilt flickers in her eyes before disappearing. "You probably think I'm a homewrecker, but trust me, nothing could be further from the truth. He and Pamela haven't been happy for years. They've stayed together for the sake of the children. Once they graduate from high school, he's going to divorce her. And then, after an appropriate amount of time, we can date openly. No one will ever know that we were having an affair."

My teeth sink into my lower lip as a fresh wave of anger crashes over me.

That guy really has it all planned out.

"I don't want to see you get strung along for years only to get hurt." Mom deserves so much better than...

To be some man's side piece.

I cringe as the ugly words flood my brain. If anyone were to find out about their affair, Mom would be forced to quit her job. There's no way around it. Neither of us could live through that kind of scandal.

Not in this town.

And it's highly doubtful he would stand by her side. He's always struck me as a weasel. Always kissing up to the parents and board members.

Does he actually plan to leave his wife?

Doubtful.

He has the perfect set-up.

An oblivious spouse at home, taking care of his children, and Mom at work, stroking his ego. A shiver of disgust slides through me.

"I promise that won't happen." A hopeful smile lifts her lips. "We love each other."

Before I can open my mouth to argue, there's a knock at the front door. Relief floods her expression as she races from the kitchen.

My mind spins, wondering how I'm going to get through to her.

"Morning, Ms. Robinson," a deep voice greets from the other room. "Is Delilah at home?"

I suck in a sharp breath.

Jasper?

What the hell is he doing here?

After last night, I can't believe he has the audacity to show his face.

What am I saying?

Of course he does.

There must be fifty texts on my phone. After I turned off my ringer, I shoved him from my thoughts and didn't think about him again.

"Sure is. She was a real sleepyhead this morning and just rolled out of bed." There's a pause before Mom pops back into the kitchen, "Jasper's here." She swipes the car keys from the counter. "I need to run to the store for a couple of things. I'll be back in about an hour."

Before I can beg her to stay, she escapes out the backdoor as if the hounds of hell are nipping at her heels, leaving me to face him on my own.

It takes a moment to gather my courage and force my feet into movement. It feels very much like I'm marching to my death as I walk into the living room and find Jasper loitering near the front door.

He looks terrible.

His eyes are bloodshot, and his hair is disheveled, sticking up at odd angles. If I'm not mistaken, he's still wearing the same clothing from last night. He looks rumpled. It's a far cry from his usual put-together self. It's highly doubtful concern for my welfare is what has him looking like this. If I had to guess, I'd say he probably partied into the wee hours of the morning.

His gaze locks on mine and I stutter to a stop, unwilling to get any closer.

"Where did you disappear to last night?" There's a beat of silence. "I texted a bunch of times and you didn't answer."

So much for an apology. I really should have known better. He probably doesn't even remember trying to maul me in his parents' bedroom. Disgust burns at the bottom of my belly and anger explodes inside me.

"I went home," I say in a clipped tone. Like I owe him any explanations after what he did.

He arches a brow when I don't elaborate. "How?"

"I walked."

"All the way home? That's at least ten miles."

"I got a ride," I grudgingly admit.

His demeanor changes as his eyes narrow. "From whom?"

"Does it really matter?" My voice sharpens as I cross my arms tightly over my chest. "Shouldn't you be relieved that I arrived home safely?"

When he explodes into movement, swiftly swallowing up the distance between us, I straighten, ready to run. I refuse to put myself in a position to be taken advantage of again by this guy.

Never.

Again.

"Yeah, it does. I want to know who gave *my* girlfriend a ride home."

That's not a title I plan on keeping for long.

"Austin." The name pops out before I can stuff it back inside. It would have been better if I'd pulled a random girl's name out of my ass. Then, we could have avoided the explosion that is sure to follow.

The muscle in his jaw tics as he grits his teeth and battles back his temper. "How many times do I need to tell you that I don't want you anywhere near him?" he growls, sounding like a rabid dog.

I draw in a deep breath before slowly releasing it back into the atmosphere. I need to pull the plug on this before I lose my nerve.

"This isn't working anymore. I want to break up."

For a long moment, he stares as if he didn't hear me correctly. With every beat of silence that slips by, my heartbeat thunders against my ribcage.

I tense, waiting for his reaction.

What I don't expect is the laughter that bursts from his lips as if I've just told him a hilarious joke.

He shakes his head as he continues to chuckle. "You don't get to break up with me."

I stare silently, unsure how to respond to that statement.

With a wave around the tiny living room, he says, "For fuck's sake, you live like a cockroach in a shithole." All amusement vanishes as his eyes sharpen until I can feel them clawing at my flesh, trying to rip me apart with his spiteful words. "Do you have any idea how lucky you are that I lowered my standards to date someone who can't even afford to pay for their own tuition and shops at secondhand stores?"

The beat of my heart turns agonizing. Any moment, it'll burst free from my chest. It's tempting to lift my hand and rub the area.

"If that's how you truly feel, then this shouldn't be a big deal. Kind of sounds like I'm doing you a favor."

Fury flashes in his eyes, and I scramble back a step.

Instead of responding to the comment, he growls, "Here's what you need to do—pull your head out of your damn ass, because I'm getting real tired of your bullshit."

My mouth falls open when he swings away and storms out the front door before slamming it shut so hard that it rattles on its hinges.

As the eerie silence settles around me, I stare in shock, unsure where that leaves us.

DELILAH

As I grab my backpack, there's a honk from the driveway. My muscles freeze as my belly drops. After our conversation Saturday morning, I'd assumed that Jasper wouldn't be picking me up for school on Monday.

I mean, we're not together…right?

"Honey," Mom calls from the kitchen, "Jasper's waiting for you. Better hurry."

It blows my mind that he's parked outside after the shitty things he said to me. It's tempting to whip out my phone and fire off a text, telling him that there's no way I'm getting into the car with him.

"Delilah?" Mom calls again.

"I know." My head continues to spin as I leave the bedroom.

Doesn't he think I was serious?

I told him I wanted to break up and he laughed before hurtling insults at me. If he needs to be set straight, then that's exactly what I'll do.

"See you at school," Mom calls from the kitchen as I head for the door.

"Yup."

Once on the front stoop, I pause, and my gaze fastens on Jasper.

Even though he's wearing mirrored sunglasses that shade his eyes from view, I feel the second his attention settles on me. That's all it takes for a chill to slither across my flesh.

Fifteen minutes.

I just have to put up with him for fifteen minutes.

And then I'll be free.

As soon as I slide onto the seat, the words shoot out of my mouth. "I haven't changed my mind. It's over."

Everything inside me goes whipcord tight, waiting for an explosion to rock the Porsche. If it becomes necessary, I'll jump out of the sleek sports car and hitch a ride with Mom. I'm almost hoping that's what happens. It would be so much easier to contend with.

Instead, he says in a subdued tone I've never heard before, "I'm sorry about what I said yesterday. I didn't mean any of it."

Shock reverberates through my entire being as my wide gaze jerks to his. The last thing I was expecting—especially after his ugly tirade—was an apology.

I rack my brain.

Has Jasper ever conveyed regret for his bad behavior?

Nope.

He yanks off his sunglasses, and I'm equally stunned to find what can only be described as a look of contrition marring his expression. The usual smugness he wears like a badge of honor is nowhere in sight.

Yet another first.

My muscles gradually loosen. "Really?"

His lips wilt at the corners as he nods. "Yeah."

"What you said yesterday was hurtful," I admit in a low tone, unsure how far I can push him.

"I know." He scrubs a hand over his face as if trying to erase the memory. "I feel like shit about that. I lashed out and it was seriously messed up. I don't know what got into me."

Holy crap. Who is this guy and what has he done with the real Jasper Morgan?

My mouth works a couple of times, but sound remains elusive.

I'm at a total loss.

"Look," he says, pulling out of the driveway at a speed that doesn't give me whiplash, "I won't try to talk you into staying with me."

I release the pent-up breath held hostage in my lungs. "Good, because I won't change my mind. You and I don't mesh well, and we shouldn't be together." It's a relief to release the truth into the atmosphere. And the fact that he's not arguing makes it even better.

As we drive through the sleepy town, his demeanor becomes even more subdued.

"I get it. We're over." His attention stays pinned to the windshield. After a few minutes of silence, he says, "I hate to ask this of you, but can we hold off on breaking up," he glances in my direction, "officially that is, until after the school fundraiser next weekend? My mom's been planning it for the past six months and she wants everything to be perfect. She'll go off the deep end if we split up right before the event."

Now that I'm this close to being done with him, I just want to snip all ties and move on with my life. I don't want to wait another week. And I sure as hell don't want to pretend that we're still a couple and go through the motions in front of everyone.

I shake my head. "Jasper, I don't know..."

"Please?" His voice softens. "In hindsight, I realize I was a shitty boyfriend, and I took you for granted, but I'd consider it a huge favor if you'd just do this one thing for me. After that, there'll be no hard feelings. I promise." He gives me a small, lopsided smile. "Maybe we can even be friends."

He won't hear any arguments from me about being a crappy boyfriend, it's just shocking that he has enough self-awareness to realize it.

When I remain silent, his tone grows pleading. "I wouldn't ask if there wasn't a reason."

Turning away, I stare out the window as the scenery flies by and contemplate my options. I'm aware of how vindictive Jasper can be, and it's something I'd like to avoid at all costs. If staying together for an extra week will make our breakup more amicable, then maybe it's worth it.

Plus, Mom is really looking forward to the event. She's already purchased fancy dresses that cost an arm and a leg. She'll be crushed if we break up beforehand, making the situation awkward with his parents.

I seriously can't believe I'm going to say this but…

"Just until after the charity event, then we're officially over."

I wait for Jasper's trademark smugness to flash across his face and make me feel like I've made a tactical error in judgment.

It never happens.

He inclines his head before pulling into the school parking lot. "I know. For what it's worth, I'm sorry about Friday night. I was a total asshole. After getting pulled from the game, I drank too much, and everything spiraled out of control. It's my fault and it shouldn't have happened. I really need to get a better grip on my emotions."

I blink, thrown off by not one, but two apologies uttered in the same conversation.

Who is this person?

"Thank you." Maybe he's right and there's a possibility for us to remain friends in the future.

All right, maybe we'll never hang out together and be besties, but it would be so nice not to have to worry about him making my life a living hell, which is exactly what I was anticipating.

Is six more days spent pretending we're together worth peace until graduation?

Yeah, it is.

He slides into a parking spot in the first row. "My behavior is why you left the party in the first place and hitched a ride with Austin. I'm just glad he got you home safely, and I should have told you that the other day."

You'd think after the first couple of apologies, it wouldn't be so shocking to hear contrition weaving its way through his voice.

"He did." What I won't mention is that we sat in his SUV and talked for hours, getting to know each other on a deeper, more personal level as we discovered how much we have in common. It's the first time I've really connected with someone at Hawthorne Prep.

It was nice.

"Good." He gives me another slight smile before killing the engine.

We grab our bags and exit the vehicle.

"Thanks for the ride," I say, heading toward the front entrance of the school. "I'm glad we got a chance to talk."

In a shocking twist, I actually mean it.

"Me, too. If you don't mind, I'll pick you up for the rest of the week. If people find out we've split, it'll spread like wildfire. Then it'll only be a matter of time before my parents find out. Like I said, Mom's already stressed out with the caterers and event planner. She's like a bridezilla without the wedding part."

My lips lift at the description of Kristina. Honestly, I don't know her very well. Whenever I've been forced to interact with his parents, I always got the feeling she thought I was beneath her son. But Jasper has been really cool about this, and I'm appreciative of his maturity. It'll make the rest of the school year bearable.

"Sure, I guess that's fine."

"Great." Instead of hanging around and prolonging the conversation, he jerks a thumb toward his teammates loitering in the parking lot. "I'm going to hang with my friends. I'll catch you later?"

I nod, relieved that I don't have to stick by his side until the bell rings.

As much as I wish this were a clean break, I'd rather we part on friendly terms. So, if that means I need to paste a smile on my face and stand by Jasper's side for a little longer, then I'll do it.

In the end, it'll be worth it.

DELILAH

"Would you mind copying these papers before you leave for the afternoon?" Ms. Pettijohn sets the thick stack at the edge of the desk I'm working at.

I rise to my feet. "Sure, I'll take care of it right now."

"Thank you. That would be helpful."

I scoop up the pile. "Not a problem."

"Were you able to get through all the freshman quizzes?"

"I finished third and fourth hour. I'm halfway through fifth hour. Then I'll enter the scores in the grade book."

Her lips bow into a slight smile.

With Ms. Pettijohn, that's akin to a full-blown grin.

"I'm going to miss you when you graduate. In all my years at Hawthorne Prep, you're the best TA I've had. Your attention to detail is impeccable."

Pleasure floods through me. "Thank you. I've really enjoyed the experience. What I've learned from you has only solidified my decision to become a teacher."

Her lips curve just a bit more as she nods. "You'll make an excellent one. Perhaps you can come back and student teach here."

Yeah…there's no way in hell that's going to happen. But I would never tell her that. She's been wonderful.

"Maybe," I say lightly.

She glances at her slim wristwatch before shooing me toward the exit.

Since it's sixth hour and everyone is still in class, the hallways are silent. The soles of my shoes echo off the shiny black and white checkered marble floor as my mind replays the past few days.

If I thought Jasper would quickly revert to old patterns of behavior, he's managed to shock me yet again. It's reminiscent of how he acted when we first got together.

During lunch the other day, one of his friends cracked a joke at his expense and instead of blowing up, he laughed it off. Yesterday, he showed up at my house before school with a cup of my favorite coffee and a scone from a little shop in town.

Had he behaved like this during our relationship, we probably wouldn't be breaking up. But as pleasant as he's being, it doesn't alter my decision. Once Sunday morning rolls around, we're parting ways.

Even though he hasn't mentioned anything, I suspect he's trying to win me over.

Why else would he be so nice?

As I turn the corner and the copy room comes into view, my pace automatically slows. A tiny part of me is concerned that I'll stumble across Mom and Mr. Pembroke making out again.

After our awkward conversation Saturday morning, neither of us has brought up the subject. Mom's pretending like it never happened, which is annoying. I get that she's embarrassed, but maybe she needs to think about the reason for that. She shouldn't be sleeping with her boss who is a married man.

It's just…wrong.

No matter what her excuse, my stance won't change.

I stare at the door that's been left slightly ajar. It's like my feet are frozen in place as the sound of my heartbeat thumps in my ears until it's as loud as the roar of the ocean. When everything remains silent, I force myself to press against the thick wood and push it open. The creaking of the hinges has me jumping before I cautiously peek inside.

Air rushes from my lungs and my body deflates when I find the space empty. I didn't realize how anxious I'd become until this moment.

Normally, I'm happy to run into Mom at school.

Unfortunately, what I caught a glimpse of last week is still there, buzzing around in the back of my head. It's going to take a while for me to forget about it.

If that's even possible.

My muscles loosen now that I know I'm not walking into an embarrassing situation. I step inside the room before glancing at the digital clock on the wall. There's less than twenty minutes for me to get all this done. Standing at the machine, I set the number of copies that are needed before feeding the first page. A loud humming noise fills the space before duplicates are spit into the tray. After a neat stack forms, I start the second sheet. I've done this so many times that I could probably do it with my eyes closed.

It doesn't take long for my mind to wander and my thoughts to drift to Austin. My belly trembles as I replay our conversation from Friday night in my head. As much as I hate it, I'm back to keeping my distance. I promised Jasper I wouldn't tell anyone we'd secretly broken up.

I've never been one to go back on my word.

And I won't start now.

Even if it's to him.

But I feel terrible. Anytime our gazes collide across a crowded room, I see the confusion flickering in Austin's green-flecked eyes. He doesn't understand why I've pulled back.

Five more days and I'll be able to tell him everything.

Hopefully then…I don't know.

Maybe we can go out?

Spend more time together?

I'm unsure what the future holds for us, but I'm excited to find out.

I'm halfway through the stack of copies when the fine hair at the nape of my neck prickles with awareness and I swing around, only to find the very person dominating my thoughts leaning against the doorjamb, silently watching me.

"Hi." My voice comes out sounding breathy, even to my own ears. It's tempting to press my palm against my lower abdomen to quell the nerves that flutter around like a horde of butterflies.

"Hey." Almost casually, he pushes away from the doorframe and stalks closer. That's exactly what it feels like…being stalked.

His movements are lazy and graceful, as if he has all the time in the world. The moment he steps inside the space, it shrinks around him, making the room feel more cramped than usual.

That's all it takes for my heartbeat to pick up speed and pound a steady tempo that vibrates throughout my body. When he's no more than a few feet away, I take a hasty step in retreat until my spine hits the wall. The intensity lurking in his eyes makes me feel as if I'm prey trying to evade a predator.

The difference is that I don't want to escape him.

Instead, I want to drag him closer until the woodsy scent of his cologne teases my senses and makes my head spin. I want to feel his warm breath drifting over my lips.

When I flatten against the wall, his wide palms settle on each side of my head until I'm caged in and there's nowhere for me to run. I crane my neck in order to hold his steady gaze. Within the green depths, I see all the questions vying for precedence.

"You've been avoiding me."

There's no way I can answer that without lying.

Confusion flickers across his face as his voice softens. "I wasn't expecting that after our conversation."

He lowers his mouth just enough for his minty breath to waft over my lips. I have to bite back the whimper that tries to escape.

"Are you ever going to leave him?"

Yes!

My mind screams the answer. I hate that I have to lie just to have a future with him.

"You deserve better. You realize that, right?"

My mouth turns so cottony that swallowing becomes impossible.

"He doesn't treat you the way you deserve."

His lips ghost over mine without ever quite touching. It won't take much more of this sweet torture for me to lose my mind.

Maybe…

Maybe I should tell him what's going on so he understands that he's the only one I'm thinking about.

When I angle my head, he draws away. "You have to know that I'm not going to touch another dude's girl. Even if that guy happens to be Jasper." He bites out the last part.

With that, his hands fall away from the wall as he backs up, putting more distance between us.

The truth sits perched on the tip of my tongue.

"Austin…" My voice dies as Jasper steps into the room.

"Hey."

He glances at me and then Austin. The dark-haired boy straightens to his full height as if expecting a fight to break out. If I'm being honest, I'm bracing for it myself. Especially after what happened Friday night at the game. But instead of going off the deep end and losing his shit, Jasper actually smiles.

My mouth falls open in surprise before I snap it shut.

He shifts, his gaze settling on Austin. "Thanks for making sure Delilah got home safely the other night. I was acting like an asshole, and she had every right to take off."

Austin's dark brows slide together as uncertainty flickers across his face. Like me, he's thrown off balance by Jasper's strange reversal.

"It wasn't a problem. Guess I was just in the right place at the right time."

"I'm glad you were." There's a pause as Jasper plows a hand through his short blond strands. "I know it's a little late, but I'm sorry for how I've treated you. Instead of welcoming you to HP, I went out of my way to make you feel like you didn't belong. Hawthornes get a bad rap in this town, and I allowed my preconceived notions about your family to dictate my thoughts and feelings. It was crappy on my part. You're not your ancestors. At least, not the ones who founded the town or company. And you're certainly not your grandmother either." He glances away as if embarrassed by his own behavior before looking Austin square in the eye. "If you're willing, I'd like the chance to start over."

This time, when my mouth crashes open, there's no shaking off the shock. I can't believe I'm hearing all this. By the stunned expression marring Austin's face, he feels the same.

When the other boy remains silent, Jasper forces out a self-deprecating laugh. "After all, we're on the same team and have a lot of friends in common. We should probably try to get along and let the past stay where it belongs—in the past." He thrusts out his hand. "What do you say, Hawthorne?"

Austin's narrowed gaze drops to Jasper's outstretched arm. For a long, silent moment, he remains still. My heart pounds a painful staccato against my ribcage as air gets clogged at the back of my throat.

Just when I think Austin will tell him to go to hell, he grasps the other boy's hand and gives it a firm shake. "I'd like that."

"Cool." Jasper grins.

My gaze flickers from one guy to the other before sliding back again. No matter what I thought might happen, this wasn't it.

Not only am I at a loss for words, it feels like I've entered a parallel dimension.

One where nothing makes sense.

Jasper's undergone a total personality transplant, and Mom is having a secret affair with the headmaster of my school.

The only thing I know for certain is that I can't take any more weirdness.

DELILAH

om keeps up a steady flow of chatter as we drive from our house to Jasper's palatial mansion where the Hawthorne Prep annual charity function is held each year. There's a mile-long line of expensive cars parked along the street outside the estate.

"It's such a shame that Jasper didn't have a good game last night," Mom says, breaking into the whirl of my thoughts. "I feel bad for the poor guy."

Much like last week, Jasper made several errors that cost the team both yards and points. The coach yanked him out before halftime, sending Austin in to take his place.

And just like the previous game, the other boy turned things around within the quarter and they won by a field goal. It doesn't matter if it was by the skin of their teeth. A win is a win in everyone's book. As soon as Jasper was pulled from the game, I held my breath, waiting for him to lose it on the sidelines.

It never happened.

In fact, he clapped and cheered when Austin threw a touchdown to one of the receivers. It's like an internal switch has been flipped and his behavior is the complete opposite of what it's always been. And not just with Austin, but me as well. He's been sweet and considerate this entire week. At lunch on Friday, he even joked around with Austin.

It was bizarre.

"He seemed to take it in stride."

She nods before peering up at the stone mansion that's lit up like a Christmas tree as we crawl up the weathered brick drive.

"I can't believe how gorgeous their house is," she murmurs as if the occupants might overhear her whispered comments. "I can't imagine what it would be like to live in such a huge place." A wistful edge creeps into her voice.

I reach out and settle my hand over hers. "I like ours better. It's cozy."

She rips her gaze off the ten thousand plus square foot mansion long enough to meet mine before snorting.

"Come on, honey...you can be honest. It won't hurt my feelings. Living here would be a dream."

It's funny, I used to think the same thing, but not anymore. A lot of these people are self-absorbed jerks. They don't care about anyone or anything but themselves. It took me a while to realize the kids behave that way because they've learned it from their parents. In this instance, the apple doesn't fall far from the tree.

Wanting to lighten the mood, I wave a hand toward the property. "Can you imagine what a nightmare that place is to clean? It probably takes days."

"Do you honestly think they do it themselves? They probably have an army of help."

Not that I'll admit it to her, but she's right. There's a housekeeper who lives full-time at the residence and another woman who comes in daily to cook meals.

It takes another ten minutes to finally make it to the front entrance. As soon as we roll to a stop, a valet springs into action and opens Mom's door. I almost wince when a loud creak fills the air. If the younger man notices or doesn't think we belong, his expression remains impassive.

Another valet in matching black pants and a white shirt opens my door before offering a hand to assist me from the compact vehicle. As soon as they drive away, Mom flashes a bright smile, and we walk arm in arm up the wide stone stairs that lead to the front door.

Mom's hand flutters before smoothing the front of her dress. "I hope Jasper's parents remember me. It's been a while since we've seen each other."

I don't tell her that they entertain almost every weekend and not once has an invitation been issued. It's probably never occurred to them to offer one or get to know her on a more personal level.

"I'm sure they will." My gaze sweeps over her length. "You look beautiful. The dress is really pretty, and I like the way you styled your hair."

She beams before pressing a kiss against the side of my face. "Thanks, sweetie. I watched a tutorial on YouTube. It's amazing how much you can learn there." Excitement fills her voice as she drops it to a whisper. "And I didn't cut the tag off the dress. My plan is to return it tomorrow. It's just too expensive to keep. I mean, where else am I going to wear something this fancy?"

"You know, we didn't have to attend. It's not mandatory or anything."

Her blue eyes widen. "Are you kidding? I wouldn't have missed this for the world. When else am I going to get a chance to look around the Morgan mansion and rub elbows with the elite of Hawthorne? Tonight, we're like Cinderella at the ball."

I give her a tight smile, wishing she wasn't in such awe of these people. Most aren't worthy of her admiration.

The front door swings open and a tall, thin man gives us a quick once over before stepping aside and allowing us entrance into the spacious foyer. It's probably as big as our entire ranch.

"Good evening." He extends an arm toward a woman dressed in a simple black outfit carrying a silver tray filled with a dozen flutes.

"Feel free to help yourself to a glass of champagne. There's a bar set up in the dining room and all the silent auction items are on display in the music conservatory."

"Thank you." Mom beams, brimming with pleasure as she helps herself to a glass of bubbly liquid before bringing it to her lips and taking a delicate sip. "Mmm. Delicious."

As we step farther inside the monstrous house, her gaze bounces around the room, trying to take in everything at once. It would be impossible not to be awed by the sheer amount of wealth on display. From the gorgeous, crystal chandelier that hangs suspended from two stories above to the intricate iron banister that curves along the sweeping staircase and the arched doorways that boast detailed plasterwork. It all drips old, established money.

"This place is even more beautiful inside than I imagined," she says, voice filled with awe.

Unlike Mom, I've been attending parties in mansions like this since freshman year. A good number of the girls I've gotten to know at HP live in similarly sized homes. Maybe not this grand, but affluent by anyone's standards.

"And look at how beautiful everyone looks. The gowns are gorgeous, and the jewels so sparkly." She leans closer and whispers, "It's doubtful they bought their dresses at Rothchild's. I had to scour the racks just to find this one."

Jasper mentioned that his mother and a few of her friends flew to Chicago for a long weekend. These gowns didn't cost a couple hundred dollars, they were more like thousands.

Her hand flutters to her hair as if to make sure every strand has been sprayed into place.

"You look lovely, Mom. Don't worry."

"It's hard not to feel self-conscious." She shifts from one foot to the other and takes another quick sip of her drink. "I feel so out of place."

"We could always leave." A hopeful note enters my tone. "Maybe pick up a pizza on the way home, get into our pajamas and watch a movie."

I'd much rather be cozied up on the couch than here with a fake smile plastered across my face.

She gives me an *are you crazy* look before shaking her head and dismissing the suggestion. "That would be incredibly rude. Maybe we don't have the kind of bank accounts that most of these people do, but we still have class and manners."

I force a smile through the disappointment. "You're right."

She slips one arm around my waist before giving me a squeeze. While searching the sea of people, she takes another drink of champagne before craning her neck. "Oh, there's Edmond!"

Edmond?

Before I can ask who she's talking about, she takes off across the room, teetering on sky high heels until reaching Mr. Pembroke. He's deep in conversation with Kristina and Benedict Morgan.

Oh god.

Edmond Pembroke?

My heartrate accelerates as my gaze stays fixated on her, watching as she leans in to kiss the slim blonde's cheek before doing the same with Benedict. Her expression softens as she shakes Mr. Pembroke's hand. If I didn't know they were anything but employee/employer, I probably wouldn't read too much into her behavior.

That, unfortunately, is no longer the case.

The wattage of her smile increases. She's practically glowing as she stands beside the headmaster. I watch in horror as her fingers settle on his forearm.

"Wow, you look gorgeous."

Knocked from my thoughts, I swing around only to find Jasper. He's holding a flute of bubbly in one hand and a crystal tumbler of amber colored liquor in the other.

"Thank you." My fingers drift over the pale pink gown with its sweetheart neckline and tulle skirt. "So do you."

He flashes an easy grin. "I look gorgeous?"

Actually, he does. From his perfectly style blond hair to the crisp white shirt beneath a custom black tux, he looks like he could be an expensive model.

"What I meant to say is that you look handsome," I correct, feeling foolish.

"Thanks." He extends the glass of alcohol. "I thought you might want something to dull the pain. I have a feeling it's going to be a long night."

"Oh." I glance at the delicate flute. "Thank you."

Under normal circumstances, I don't drink. That's not to say I've never had a beer or two at a party, but I've found that it's far safer to stay sober and keep my wits about me. Especially when running with this crowd.

But…Jasper makes a good point.

It's going to be a long night, and taking some of the edge off wouldn't do any harm. One visual sweep of the room shows that most of my classmates have flutes or tumblers in hand. This might be a school function, but none of the adults seem to care.

Some of my wariness dissipates as my fingers wrap around the fragile stem and bring the rim to my lips for a taste.

Mom's right.

It's delicious.

The effervescent liquid slides smoothly down my throat.

Jasper takes a healthy swallow of his liquor. "Where's your mom?"

Still chatting with Pembroke and his parents.

A kernel of fear blooms in my belly as I remind myself that the two work together and there's nothing odd about them engaging in conversation. No one is going to look at them and realize they're having an affair, even though I feel like there's a neon sign flashing over their heads.

Shifting his body, he leans closer. "Did you tell her what happened?"

My heart stutters a couple of beats. "No."

His eyes sharpen. "She doesn't know that we're broken up?"

I shake my head, wondering why it would matter. In a couple of hours, the charade will be over.

There's a moment of silence before he clears his throat. "Is there any chance you'll change your mind?"

Just as he asks the question, Austin snags my attention from across the space. He's here with his mother and sister. This is one of the few times I've seen Mrs. Hawthorne since the funeral. The brittle smile plastered across her face tells me that she's trying to be strong and doesn't want to be here. I recognize it because I've forced the same smile to my lips hundreds of times. When my attention returns to Austin, I find his stare already fixated on me. A shiver of desire dances down my spine as our gazes cling.

He's ridiculously handsome in his tux.

The magnetic pull I feel is so intense that I have to stop myself from swallowing up the distance between us.

After this evening, I'll be free to do whatever I want. I can finally stop holding myself back from the person I truly want to be with. That's been the hardest part of this week.

"Delilah?"

I give myself a quick mental shake and refocus on the boy at my side.

"Sorry," I mutter, heat stinging my cheeks. "No, there's not."

Jasper spears a look in the same direction and finds the person who has captured my attention. My fingers bite into the delicate stem of the flute as I steel myself for his reaction. Even though he's done a complete one eighty this week, I can't help but expect something small and innocuous to shove him over the edge.

With a shrug, he flashes a smile. "You can't blame me for trying."

That's all it takes for the tension filling me to dissolve. "I really do hope we can remain friends."

His smile widens as he opens his arms. "How about one last hug?"

Relieved that he's handling our breakup like an adult, I step into his embrace as he presses a kiss to my cheek.

"Of course, we'll always be friends," he says, hands trailing up and down my back.

Just as I grow uncomfortable, his arms fall away, and he takes a step in retreat.

"I should probably go. Dad wants me to make a speech about how the funds raised tonight will benefit the students…blah, blah, blah."

Relief floods through me that not only is this conversation over, but so is our relationship.

"No problem. I'm sure you'll kill it."

"That's the plan."

With a wink, he saunters away, disappearing through the thick crowd.

DELILAH

"*H*ello everyone and thank you so much for joining us tonight."

Benedict's voice booms into a microphone on the makeshift stage situated at the far end of the living room in front of the floor-to-ceiling windows. He's flanked on one side by his wife, Kristina. She smiles adoringly at him before glancing over the crowd and waving to a few friends. Jasper stands with one hand shoved casually into the pocket of his pants on the other side. All three resemble blond Barbie dolls with perfect hair, skin, and bodies. Behind them is Mr. Pembroke in a rumpled suit along with the board members of Hawthorne Prep.

I slip my phone from my little black purse and sneak a peek at the screen. We've been here for almost two hours and it's after ten o'clock. I glance around for Mom, hoping she'll be ready to leave as soon as the speeches are wrapped up. Although, who knows when that will be. These are people who enjoy listening to themselves talk.

"You look really beautiful," a deep voice says near the outer shell of my ear.

That's all it takes for a shiver to dance down my spine as his warm breath feathers across my skin.

"Thank you." I twist just enough to meet his burning gaze. The intensity shining from within his eyes sends my belly into freefall.

Benedict's voice fades to the background as we continue to stare.

After a minute or two, he shifts his attention to the stage. "Looks like your boyfriend is about to speak."

Boyfriend.

Not anymore.

So badly do I want to blurt out the truth and clear the air between us.

But how can I do that when I made a promise to Jasper?

A few more hours and I'll be free of this.

Of him.

An idea takes root inside my head. Instead of leaving the event with Mom, maybe Austin and I can go somewhere quiet and talk. I can explain everything that happened this week, and we can figure out where we go from here.

I want to move forward with him. The week I spent avoiding Austin has only made me crave his company more. I don't think I could hold out past this evening.

I lift a finger to my lips. "Shhh. What he's about to say is important. You'll want to hear this." I'm joking, of course.

When he snorts, a smile simmers around the edges of my lips. It takes everything I have inside to contain it.

"Like my father mentioned, we'd like to thank everyone tonight for their generous donations. Every little bit makes a difference." Jasper places a hand against his chest as he casts a sweeping glance over the silent crowd. His voice projects to those in the back. "As a student who's had the great privilege of attending Hawthorne Prep, I'm able to see firsthand how these funds enrich the lives of both the students and staff."

"Don't you think he's laying it on a bit thick?"

My soon-to-be ex has always been an amazing public speaker. He probably didn't write a single word, just got up there to wing it. The guy has a lot of great qualities, and I really hope the change I've seen in him this week is permanent.

"If you asked any student, former student, or staff member, they'd tell you that one of the most unique things about Hawthorne Prep is that at the heart of it, we're one big, happy family. Once you've walked through those hallowed halls, you become a part of the tradition and the institution itself. A little piece of you will always remain there, and I'd like to think that our beloved Hawthorne Prep will live on within us long after we walk through the doors on graduation day for the last time. It's the solid foundation our futures will be built on. This year, we were lucky enough to welcome back two members of the Hawthorne community whose descendants founded both the town and the school."

There's a smattering of applause as the audience cranes their necks and glances around. Mrs. Hawthorne inclines her head toward those who meet her eyes. A blush suffuses Summer's cheeks as Kingsley stands sentinel behind her, hands resting protectively on her slender shoulders. It's obvious from the expression on his face that he'll rip anyone to shreds who dares to even look at her wrong.

Austin looms so close that I feel the way his muscles coil as tension radiates from him in thick waves. What I've discovered is that he's only comfortable in the spotlight when on the football field.

"Since I know everyone here is a Hawks fan, my guess is that you've all been in the stands each Friday night, cheering us on."

A burst of clapping breaks out.

Jasper waits for the crowd to settle before glancing down at the stage and clearing his throat as if he's about to confide something deeply personal. I can almost feel the crowd surge forward, not wanting to miss a word.

"If I'm being honest, those wins come down to one player. I don't think anyone would disagree that he's become a vital member of our team. And if I do say so myself, we're damn lucky to have him." Jasper searches the sea of people until it lands on the boy behind me. "Come up here, Austin."

A smile lifts my lips as I glance over my shoulder and meet his wary gaze. The muscles in his jaw tense. His attention flickers to me before he gives his head a quick shake.

When he takes a step in retreat, Jasper chuckles. "Come on, don't be shy. Get up here!" When Austin doesn't budge, the other boy's voice booms throughout the spacious room, "Let's show our new QB that he's not only an important part of the Hawks team, but an integral part of Hawthorne."

Thunderous applause erupts, becoming almost deafening. I glance at Mrs. Hawthorne and find the first genuine smile I've seen from her this evening. Crystal-like tears shimmer in her eyes as she claps along with the crowd. Summer slips an arm around her mother before resting her head against the older woman's shoulder.

I can't resist thinking that their family has been through so much in such a short period of time. Moving to Hawthorne hasn't been easy. This evening and the friendship Jasper is extending feels almost like a turning point in their story. For the second time tonight, I'm blown away by this newfound maturity on display.

Where was this guy during our entire relationship?

I can only marvel at this improved version of Jasper.

Even though Austin doesn't want the attention, I think this is exactly what he needs in order to gain more acceptance in this town.

With an encouraging smile, I meet his gaze. "You should go up there."

"Why? I hate this kind of stuff," he grumbles. "I'd much rather stay here. Near the exit in case a quick getaway becomes necessary."

"I know, but everyone is clapping, and they're not going to stop until you give them what they want." I turn before poking my finger into his hard chest. "And what they want is you."

His brows lower. "I refuse to give a speech."

"Then don't. Just wave and say thank you for the kind words. Tell them how happy you are to be in Hawthorne."

A glint of humor ignites in his eyes. "So…what you're saying is that I should lie?"

I grin. "Pretty much. I think this is Jasper's way of extending an olive branch. It's important to meet him halfway."

"Fine." He huffs before adding reluctantly, "But be warned, if this goes sideways, I'm holding you personally responsible."

I nod and squeeze his arm. "Fair enough." Although, that's not going to happen, so I have nothing to worry about.

With one final look, he steps around me before reluctantly making his way through the crowd toward the narrow stage.

Jasper flashes a grin as he walks up the short staircase to the platform. As soon as Austin is within striking distance, the other boy throws an arm around his brawny body, tugging him close.

"I'm going to let you all in on a little secret," he says, voice ringing out as the audience grows silent.

It's almost impressive, the way Jasper can command the crowd. Then again, maybe I shouldn't be so surprised. This is how he's always been with his peers. I just didn't realize his charisma extended to grown adults.

"When Austin first arrived at Hawthorne Prep, I'm ashamed to admit that I was reluctant to give him a chance both in school and on the field."

I glance around and realize that almost everyone is paying attention. A tremor slides through me and I run my hands over my bare flesh.

"It might have taken a while, but I think the two of us have finally come to a place of understanding. I'm confident in saying that with Austin on the team, there's no way he won't lead us through playoffs and then on to the state championship game next month!" He pats Austin on the chest. "Have you seen this guy in action?"

Another rousing burst of cheers explodes through the crowd. Even though the school and town are small, most are diehard football fanatics.

As Austin loosens up enough to smile, Jasper adds in a joking tone, "Now we just have to make sure this guy keeps his grades up, so he's eligible to play. He won't be able to help anyone sitting on the bench. Unfortunately for Austin, Ms. Pettijohn's English Lit class is getting the better of him."

My grin falls away as I glance at the laughing crowd. It's as if someone has wrapped a fist around my heart and is squeezing it until breath becomes impossible.

Why would he say something like that in front of everyone?

Austin's gaze slices to mine as any hint of happiness vanishes and an icy veneer slips over his expression.

Jasper lowers his voice as if confiding a secret to the hundreds of people gathered at his estate. I can almost feel the crowd surge forward so as not to miss a single word.

"Most of you probably don't know this, but our superstar QB is dyslexic." Jasper nods, making eye contact with the audience as if they're having an intimate conversation. "How sad is it that he struggles to even read at grade level? A learning disability is no joking matter."

I blanch, unable to believe my ears.

Oh god...what's he doing?

When Austin attempts to leave the stage, Jasper tightens his hold so he can't escape without making a scene.

"In the months that Austin has been here, I've heard plenty of my fellow classmates laugh and talk about this guy being all brawn and no brains, but what they don't understand is the struggle he goes through on a daily basis. Especially at Hawthorne Prep, where the academics are rigorous. This isn't Chicago, after all. These teachers aren't going to hand out passing grades simply because someone is a football player. So, even though we're lucky to have the Hawthornes back home where they belong, maybe they're lucky to be here as well. Every single one of us can assist Austin in overcoming his challenges in the classroom. If we all work together as a team, we can make sure Austin passes his classes and graduates from this amazing academy."

I raise my hands to my mouth in horror.

The crowd grows so silent you could hear a pin drop. The pity on their expressions makes me sick to my stomach.

When the room remains quiet, Jasper chuckles. "I probably shouldn't have said anything, but this guy has impressed me so much, and I want everyone in Hawthorne to understand the reasons for it. Let's hear it for Austin!"

Another round of thunderous applause erupts. The noise is so deafening, it rattles the windowpanes. Austin's face has turned ashen as his nostrils flare. He stands rooted in place, looking like he wants to melt into the stage, all the while gritting his teeth. As soon as Jasper releases him, he stalks away with his hands tightly clenched.

Instead of returning to where I stand frozen in place, he slips out the set of French doors that lead into the velvety darkness. As the audience continues to clap, Jasper returns the microphone to his father.

"That was a very touching story, son. Thank you so much for sharing it with us. You're absolutely right about Hawthorne being one big happy family. And around here, family takes care of its own."

Jasper nods as his gaze slices to mine and his lips lift into a malicious smile.

DELILAH

My hand flutters to my belly as if the firm pressure is enough to stifle the nausea roiling like a storm inside as I swing away and race for the same door Austin escaped through a handful of seconds ago.

I...can't believe Jasper publicly humiliated him in front of all those people.

Classmates.

Teachers.

Teammates.

The entire town.

He won't be able to go anywhere in Hawthorne without whispers dogging his heels. I don't know Austin well, but I realize that it'll kill him to have people gossiping about something so painful and private.

As Benedict rambles about the fundraiser, I reach for the handle with trembling fingers before pushing it open and stepping outside into the cool night air.

For all I know, he's taken off.

I certainly wouldn't blame him for it.

Instead, I find him standing on the stone balcony that overlooks the vastness of the backyard. In the distance are the gently rolling hills of the golf course. From here, I see the stiff set of his shoulders and can feel the thick tension radiating off him in suffocating waves.

I bite my lower lip, unsure what to say or how to make the situation better.

"Austin," I whisper.

When he swings around, the barely suppressed fury simmering in his eyes steals my breath and has me shrinking back a step.

A long, painful heartbeat passes as we stare. The glower on his face is unmistakable.

"It's funny that I actually thought you were different from the rest of these assholes." He releases a humorless bark of laughter into the atmosphere. "Guess I was wrong. You're so much worse."

My mouth falls open.

Oh god...he thinks I told Jasper about his dyslexia.

I shake my head almost violently. "I never said a word. I have no idea how he found—"

"Baby, there's no longer a reason to lie," Jasper says, stepping out of the shadows and snaking a muscular arm around my waist. I can only gawk as he hauls me close. "It was all a joke. I mean," he cocks his head as pity flashes across his face, "you get that, right? You're not actually *that* stupid, are you?"

A muscle twitches in Austin's jaw.

Hushed whispers echo in my ears and I realize with a sinking heart that we're no longer alone. People have filtered out from the party and are crowding around us.

Jasper's eyes widen. "Holy shit! You actually thought she was interested in you? Fuck, dude...I can't decide if that's hilarious or just pathetic." He pauses as if giving the question serious consideration. "Nah, it's definitely pathetic. Like Delilah would ever be interested in Hawthorne trash." He shakes his head as his voice escalates with each word. "Especially trash who can't even read a fucking book."

Snickers erupt from the press of people on the balcony. I glance around in horror as more classmates pour through the door. The ones in the back crane their necks, not wanting to miss a single word.

A growl emanates from deep within Austin's chest as his hands tighten at his sides. Just as I open my mouth to tell him not to do it, he springs forward. Jasper shoves me aside and I stumble in my heels before steadying myself and swinging around.

"Austin, no!" I scream.

Doesn't he realize that Jasper has been baiting him?

A fight is exactly what he's angling for.

But it's much too late. It's doubtful Austin can hear me through the red haze shimmering around him like a living, breathing entity as he draws back an arm and slams his fist into Jasper's face. Instead of retaliating, the other boy staggers a few paces, his hands fly to his nose as blood gushes from it, dripping onto his starched white shirt before puddling at his feet.

Kingsley leaps forward and grabs Austin, dragging him away as he whispers harshly in his ear. His attempts to defuse the situation don't work. Austin's narrowed gaze stays pinned to Jasper as he continues to growl. His lips are peeled back in a snarl. When he continues to struggle against Kingsley's hold, Duke Carmichael jumps in to offer assistance.

"Austin, stop!" Summer cries.

But still, he doesn't spare her a glance as he tries to break free and get to Jasper.

"What's the meaning of this?" Mr. Pembroke barks, shoving his way through the throng of students that fill the outdoor space. His gaze bounces from a bloodied Jasper to Austin, who continues to struggle against the boys holding him.

Kristina sweeps onto the balcony. Her eyes widen as she gets a good look at her son. "Jasper! My god, who did this to you?"

Benedict pulls a snowy white linen handkerchief from his breast pocket and hands it over to stymie the blood that continues to flow.

"Austin attacked me."

My mouth tumbles open at such a blatant lie.

Mr. Pembroke's icy stare settles on Austin. "It would appear that trouble follows you everywhere you go, young man."

"Just ask Delilah," Jasper says in a nasally voice. "She saw everything. She'll tell you what happened."

The older man turns his considerable bulk toward me before raising a brow. "Is that true, Ms. Robinson? Did Mr. Hawthorne strike Mr. Morgan?"

My teeth sink into my lower lip as I try to phrase my answer without implicating Austin. "Technically, that might—"

"Perhaps I should have been more specific," he interrupts before snapping, "did Mr. Hawthorne strike Mr. Morgan first?"

I press my lips together, not wanting to answer.

"Ms. Robinson," the headmaster growls, growing more irritated by the second "please don't make me repeat myself."

My gaze cuts to Austin. An icy mask has fallen over his features. Beneath it, barely leashed fury and pain seethe, attempting to break free.

"Yes, but—"

Mr. Pembroke slices an arm through the air. "A yes or no response is all that's required. Did Mr. Morgan then retaliate and assault Mr. Hawthorne in return?"

My shoulders collapse beneath the heavy weight of the question.

When his bushy brows rise, I force myself to whisper, "No."

Leaning forward, he cups a hand to his ear. "I'm sorry, Ms. Robinson. You must project your voice louder in order to be heard."

The hushed murmurs filling the crowd turn silent.

My cheeks flood with heat as I glance around and find everyone's attention pinned to me. My stomach spasms as my mouth turns bone dry. "No."

"Hmmm." He nods as if he suspected this answer all along. "It would seem the situation is fairly cut and dry."

Before I can protest, Mr. Pembroke swings to Austin. "I'd like to see you and your mother in my office at seven o'clock sharp Monday morning. Failure to report will result in an automatic expulsion."

Mrs. Hawthorne elbows her way through the crowd until she can reach her son. Tears shine in her eyes as she wraps a protective arm around him.

"Rest assured, we'll be there," she says in a clipped tone.

"It would probably be best if you took your son home now. He's disrupted quite enough of the evening."

Not bothering to wait for his mother's reply, Austin stalks toward the French doors that are wide open. As he strides through the throng, it parts like the Red Sea, creating a direct path to the exit. Whispers follow, increasing in volume with every step he takes. When he's no more than a handful of feet from where I stand, frozen in place, his furious gaze locks on mine. The hatred swirling through his green depths is enough to make my blood run cold and have me recoiling.

Just as he's about to pass, he grinds to a halt. His lips ghost over mine without ever quite touching. A shudder slinks down my spine as the fine hair on my bare arms prickles with unease. I rack my brain for the words, something that will make this better, but they refuse to be summoned.

Before I can utter a sound, he walks away, disappearing inside the illuminated mansion. The buzz of conversation explodes with his departure, swirling around me as the past ten minutes is rehashed. Classmates throw inquisitive glances in my direction and talk amongst themselves.

Now that the show has ended, everyone returns to the party that is in full swing. I can almost see the gossip spreading from one person to another until it's all anyone is able to discuss.

The thought of stepping inside Jasper's house makes me sick to my stomach.

I have no idea what to do or where to go.

I'm frozen in place.

Unable to move.

Unable to suck a full breath into my lungs.

I squeeze my eyes tightly shut and feel the painful hammering of my heart. It continues to grow in intensity. Any moment, it'll explode from my body.

I'm knocked from the anxiety gripping me by the throat when someone slams their shoulder into mine. Eyes flying open, I gasp and stagger before catching myself on the stone railing, only to find

Summer Hawthorne scowling at me. Her hands are balled so tightly at her sides that her knuckles have turned bone white.

"How could you do that to him?" She pauses. "What the fuck is wrong with you?"

I wince at the fury that whips through her voice. Any possibility of a friendship between us has now been destroyed.

Thick emotion rises within me and it takes effort to summon my voice. "Summer, it's not—"

"Save it," she growls. "You're a real bitch, you know that? I don't understand how I could have been so wrong about you."

Her words hit me like a physical blow. I have no idea how I remain upright when all I want to do is double over and sink to my knees.

When tears spring to my eyes, she advances. "Don't you dare cry after the shit you just pulled! If he gets expelled, it'll be your fault!"

I shake my head.

No…

When she takes a menacing step forward, her boyfriend grabs her, tucking an arm around her shoulders before steering her away. If there's one thing I've learned about Summer Hawthorne, it's that she'll go to battle to protect her brother. Their connection is unbreakable.

Kingsley's dark eyes lock on mine, and what I see within them makes my bones quake. If I thought my life was hell at Hawthorne Prep before tonight, it's nothing compared to what I have to look forward to Monday morning.

Before I can blurt out the truth, they disappear inside the mansion. I swing away, turning my back to the house as I stare blindly into the darkness. Shock spirals through me as everything that just happened replays in my head like a slow-motion picture show until I want to sob.

My freshly painted fingernails dig into the cement baluster. It's only when I hear the crickets chirp in the yard that unease prickles the back of my neck and I realize that I'm not alone. I swing around and find Jasper loitering a few feet away. Splotches of blood decorate the snowy whiteness of his shirt.

Our gazes lock and hold.

I shake my head and croak, "Why would you do that?"

A smug smile lifts his lips as a spiteful glint fills his eyes. It's a look I've become intimately acquainted with. A fresh wave of nausea crashes over me.

"Did you think I was just going to let you walk away?"

The question explodes in my brain but for some reason, it doesn't compute.

"What?"

His upper lip curls with disdain. "You heard me." There's a pause as he carefully dabs at his nose. "You should have felt honored to be my girlfriend. Instead, you're like a bitch in heat, panting to spread your legs for Hawthorne trash." He shrugs. "Now you can have him."

All at once, it hits me.

Oh my god.

My mind tumbles back to Monday morning and his abrupt change in behavior. It was so out of character that I should have realized it was nothing more than an act. Instead, I'd stupidly believed he felt bad. I could kick myself for being so gullible and falling neatly into his trap.

He shifts, leaning closer. "Except it's doubtful he'll want you now." Venom floods his voice, turning it gleeful.

It would be a lie to say that I never suspected Jasper could be so cruel. It's the reason I allowed this relationship to linger instead of breaking it off.

Deep down, I realized *exactly* what he was capable of.

But this…this is on a whole different level.

When I remain silent, he continues, "Just remember that you brought this on yourself. Now, there's no one to protect you. We both know how dangerous it can be to walk the halls of Hawthorne Prep without allies. Contrary to what I said earlier, we're not one big happy family. It's more like a shark-infested tank, and you're fresh blood, sweetheart."

My chest constricts, making it difficult to suck in a shuddering breath. What he's saying is true. I've witnessed the depravity with my own eyes over the past three years.

Unwilling to let him see how much his threats have affected me, I straighten my spine and force my chin upward. He's like a rabid animal, and the smell of my fear will only incite him.

"See you on Monday." With a grin, he saunters away as if he doesn't have a care in the world. The soles of his wingtips strike the concrete before fading as he disappears inside.

Once the door closes, I hold my breath captive in my lungs until my vision swims. Just as my head grows light, a burst of air explodes from my lips. There's no doubt in my mind that Jasper will turn my life into the stuff nightmares are made of. The months stretched out ahead of me now feel like a prison sentence. The thought is enough to have tears pricking the backs of my eyes.

I have no idea how long I stand outside staring into the velvety darkness. When the French doors open and there's a soft click of heels, I steel myself, unsure who else I'll have to deal with. I no longer have the energy for it. Mental and physical exhaustion has set in, draining me.

"Delilah?"

My shoulders falter at the sound of Mom's hesitant voice.

"Are you all right?"

I turn enough to meet her gaze before shaking my head. Even that miniscule movement takes a herculean effort. "No. I'd like to go home now."

Mom's lips flatten into a thin line as she nods and opens her arms to me. That's all the encouragement I need to fly into their comforting strength. And then I'm cocooned in the familiar scent of her perfume. The one she's worn forever.

When I was a kid and something was wrong, she'd wrap me up in her arms and the soothing floral scent would envelop me. Back then, it was easy to believe that everything would work out the way it was supposed to, and life would carry on in much the same way it once had.

With a sinking heart, I realize that's no longer possible.

DELILAH

Nerves prickle along my skin as Mom grumbles from the seat beside me and I sneak another peek at my phone.

It's quarter to seven in the morning.

"Can you drive a little faster?" I ask, wishing she would press the pedal to the metal.

She shoots me a bleary-eyed look that borders on sour. "Why did we have to leave so early? I didn't get a chance to make a cup of coffee."

I nibble my lower lip. "I need to talk to someone."

"School doesn't even start until half past seven."

Instead of meeting the questioning gaze she spears me with, I stare straight out the windshield at the passing scenery as the gated property of Hawthorne Prep comes into view. I don't want to tell her about my plan to speak with Mr. Pembroke before Austin arrives for their meeting.

They must have talked on the phone at some point yesterday, and he filled her in on all the ugly details, because she told me to stay away from him. She reminded me that this wasn't the first time he'd gotten into a fistfight with Jasper. Even though we'd been alone in our house, she'd dropped her voice to a hushed whisper and told me that he would probably get expelled, since this was his second offense in a matter of months.

I can't allow that to happen.

Still muttering under her breath, she parks the Civic at the back of the lot. Before she can kill the engine, I grab my bag and jump out before racing toward the entrance. The sun is just rising over the stone structure, bathing it in incandescent light. From the outside, it's a gorgeous, three-story building with beautifully detailed architecture. Inside, however, it's a veritable nightmare except for those at the very top of the social food chain.

"You're not even going to wait for me?" Mom calls out, raising her voice.

I whip around. "Sorry. I'll see you later, okay?"

She waves me off in irritation.

Once I reach the set of double doors, I yank the handle and jog through the corridor. The soles of my shoes echo off the black and white marble tile. It's not a surprise to find the halls deserted at this time of the morning. The only students here are the kids on the swim team, and they're probably finishing up in the Olympic sized pool.

As soon as I reach the main office, I scan the interior. Austin and his mother aren't here yet. Mrs. Baxter glances up from her desk in surprise. A friendly smile wreathes her weathered face when she catches sight of me. She's a grandmotherly type and one of the few genuinely nice people here. She doesn't treat anyone differently based on their income bracket. It doesn't matter to her if you're at HP on scholarship or your parents bought a seat on the board.

"My goodness. You're here awfully early."

"Yes," I huff, heart still pumping from my sprint. "I was hoping to speak with Mr. Pembroke."

She spears a quick glance at his closed office door before leaning toward me and dropping her voice to a conspiratorial whisper. "Now's not a good time. He's preparing for a meeting."

"I know." Impatience spirals through me as I hop from one foot to the other. "There's important information I need to share with him."

Her brows pinch together as her lips sink at the corners. It's an odd look on her normally smiling face. "I'm afraid he asked not to be disturbed."

Everything inside me plummets. "Please, Mrs. Baxter? It's important. I don't want Austin to get expelled." I pause before adding desperately, "Especially after what he's been through."

Sympathy floods her expression as her hand flutters to her ample chest. "Oh dear, I know. What happened to Griffin was so tragic." A faraway look fills her eyes. "I remember when he used to walk these very halls."

Just as I steeple my hands, ready to plead my case, she capitulates. "All right. I'll see if you can pop in for a minute or two. That's all the time he can spare, Delilah. I hope you understand."

I nod, grateful that she'll at least speak with him.

She rises to her feet before smoothing down her rumpled blouse and skirt. "I don't want you to get your hopes up. He's extremely busy."

With that, she pads to his office before tentatively wrapping her knuckles against the thick wood and stepping inside the room. The door remains cracked open and from inside I hear the low babble of voices. I tilt my head, hoping to eavesdrop on their conversation. When that doesn't work, I inch closer until I'm able to catch the low rumble of his words.

"That's not necessary. I spoke with more than enough witnesses at the fundraiser. Please tell Ms. Robinson that I don't need another account of the situation. I think we can all agree that Austin Hawthorne is a loose cannon. I was against the board giving him a second chance after the last incident."

He's going to expel him.

That knowledge is all it takes for me to burst into movement. Before I realize it, I've crossed the carpeted space. As I reach the door, I shove it open and step inside the office. His words fall away as they both swing their heads toward me.

Before he can say anything, I blurt, "Please, Mr. Pembroke? All I'm asking is that you hear me out. You didn't give me a chance to explain what happened before the fight."

His scowl becomes even more ferocious. "I believe Mrs. Baxter asked you to wait outside."

"I apologize for interrupting, but you need to know all of the information."

His lips thin. Even though I try to hold myself perfectly still, it's hard not to squirm beneath his icy glare. It's obvious that he's already made up his mind and isn't interested in hearing the other side of the story. But still…how can I walk away without trying to sway his decision?

"I know how valuable your time is," I say, gulping down my nerves. "And I wouldn't be here if it wasn't important."

Silence stretches to the point of uncomfortableness before he finally huffs out a breath. "Fine. You have exactly two minutes."

Relief escapes from me in a rush and nearly weakens my knees. Without another word, Mrs. Baxter slips from the office, closing the door softly behind her until the lock clicks.

I take a quick second to collect my thoughts. It's important I get this right. If not, Austin will be expelled. No matter what his feelings are toward me, I don't want to see that happen.

The older man lifts a brow as he bristles with impatience. "I'm waiting. What was so important that you had to burst into my office without an appointment before the start of the school day?"

"I realize the situation looks bad, but there's a reason Austin hit Jasper."

He crosses his arms over his barrel like-chest. "Are you trying to tell me that there's an acceptable justification for resorting to violence?"

I blink and attempt to backtrack. "Of course not. I—"

"I'm relieved to hear that. If there's one thing that will not be tolerated at this school, it's fighting in any shape or form. High standards are set at Hawthorne Prep for a reason and are strictly adhered to. Physical aggression is never a satisfactory alternative to discussion and the need to find common ground. This is not the first time Mr. Hawthorne has been sanctioned by the board for fisticuffs. One would have thought that after his last disciplinary action, he would have learned his lesson. Unfortunately, that has not turned out to be the case. It's a pity really." He glances impatiently at his chunky silver wristwatch. "If you'll excuse me, there are still a few loose ends I need to tie up in preparation for this meeting."

"You saw what happened! Jasper embarrassed Austin in front of the entire school."

His brow furrows as he cocks his head. "I have no idea what you're talking about, young lady. I remember no such thing."

"The speech."

"I found nothing wrong with it. In fact, it would seem as if Jasper was extending a peace offering, attempting to be both inclusive and welcoming." His expression turns wintery. "And what did the poor boy get in return?" Before I can open my mouth, he snaps, "A punch in the face. It's as if the Hawthornes were raised without manners."

"Jasper had no right to disclose such personal information. Can you not understand why Austin would feel humiliated?"

His face scrunches. "Exactly what is there to be embarrassed about? There are a number of students here who struggle with academic challenges. What I can tell you is that a positive outcome cannot be achieved through violence. I'm sorry, nothing you say will change my mind on the topic. A decision has already been reached. I think it's in the best interest of the student body for Mr. Hawthorne to find an alternative school that will better suit his needs. What's become glaringly apparent in the past month or so is that he does not belong here. I've taken it upon myself to speak directly with the principal of Hawthorne Public so his transition will be as smooth as possible."

"But Mr.—"

He adjusts the lapels of his suit before striding past me. It only takes a handful of steps for him to reach the door. "Please don't waste any further breath. This conversation is over. You should have saved us both time and energy by not coming here and trying to intervene on Mr. Hawthorne's behalf. While your passion is commended, it's gravely misplaced."

Just as his sausage-like fingers wrap around the handle, I blurt, "I know you're sleeping with my mother. I doubt that's something you'd want your wife or the school board to discover."

As soon as the words escape from my lips, I want to snatch them from the air and shove them back inside my mouth where they belong.

By the widening of his eyes and the stillness of his body, he's in just as much shock as I am. That's all it takes for the atmosphere to turns suffocating.

"Excuse me?" When I remain silent, his eyes narrow and his lips flatten into a grim line. "What did you just say?"

Swallowing past the thick lump that has wedged itself in the middle of my throat feels impossible.

Oh god. Am I really doing this?

"You're having an affair with my mother," I force myself to repeat.

"I don't know where you got such a ludicrous idea," he blusters, face growing splotchy.

"I saw you kissing in the copy room two weeks ago."

He straightens to his full height, which is only a handful of inches taller than me. "I don't know what you think you saw, young lady," he growls, "but you're mistaken."

"I'm not. If word of your affair gets out, your career and reputation will be ruined. You'll have to resign from Hawthorne Prep." I let that sink in before adding, "If they don't fire you first."

He pales and asks stiffly, "What is it that you want?"

Even though it feels like my heart is on the verge of exploding, the constriction loosens just a bit.

"I don't want Austin to be expelled. Whether you believe me or not, Jasper is the one who started the fight. He knew exactly what buttons to press to push Austin over the edge. But you're right," I say hastily, "Austin shouldn't have hit him. That was a mistake."

Sweat springs to my palms as he continues to glare. Unease grows in the pit of my belly, and I shift beneath the relentless intensity. It takes everything I have inside not to cower before him and apologize.

"You're playing a very dangerous game," he says softly.

"That was never my intention."

"Then you should drop this immediately, and we'll both forget you ever waltzed in here and threatened me."

If only that were possible.

"I can't. The Hawthornes have been through enough already."

"They don't belong here," he snaps, voice rising. "They would be better served by the public school system."

I shouldn't be surprised by his candor or attitude. He would be singing a different tune if their family carried any clout in the community.

When I remain silent, he asks snidely, "Are there any other demands you'd like to make while you're here?"

I shake my head.

His beady gaze stays pinned to mine as he rips open the door. "Then it's high time you leave."

I jerk my head into a nod and force my feet into movement. It's only as I cross over the threshold that I realize he never gave me an answer. I have no idea if he'll expel Austin. What I do know is that I've done everything possible to help the situation.

More than I probably should have.

The moment I step over the threshold, tension leaks from my muscles, leaving me to feel shaky from the confrontation. I've never so much as received a detention, and now I'm blackmailing Pembroke?

Nausea explodes in the pit of my gut. If I don't get to the bathroom, I'm going to—

With my head bent, I hasten my pace and slam into a hard body. Strong hands lock around my upper arms to hold me in place when I stumble back a step. As I lift my chin and meet the gaze of my captor, I realize that I've crashed into the very person I've come to rescue.

The hatred that blazes from his narrowed eyes is enough to freeze the blood running through my veins. The anger that had radiated from him on Saturday night doesn't hold a candle to this.

"Mr. Hawthorne," our headmaster snaps, "remove your hands from Ms. Robinson at once. You're in quite enough trouble as it is."

Instead of following the demand, his fingers tighten, digging into my flesh beneath the thick wool blazer as he drags me closer. My feet shuffle forward as pain shoots through me. Unable to look away, I wince as his warm breath drifts across my parted lips.

"I hope you and Jasper had a good laugh at my expense. When I'm done with you, you'll wish you'd never heard my name."

Dread floods through me and my mouth snaps open.

"Save it," he growls, unwilling to hear me out.

"In my office immediately, Mr. Hawthorne!"

With that, he shoves me away. I stagger before catching myself. If I thought my heart was hammering from my meeting with Mr. Pembroke, it's nothing compared to the way it now thrashes in my chest, struggling to break free. He gives me one final glare before stepping inside the small room. The moment he's gone, I wilt against the counter, clasping the edges as if holding on for dear life.

Austin Hawthorne has never frightened me.

But in this moment, he does.

DELILAH

My feet drag as I head to the cafeteria for lunch. The morning started out brutal and has only gone downhill from there. People I've known for years now stare at me like I'm chewed-up bubblegum stuck to the bottom of their expensive shoes.

Every step through the richly paneled halls was followed by a loud ripple of whispers and laughter in my wake. Classmates who I once thought were my friends have quickly turned on me. It's exactly what I suspected would happen if Jasper and I broke up. But even I couldn't have foreseen the lengths he'd go to humiliate Austin and destroy me.

The guy isn't just a conceited asshole, he's diabolical.

As much as the situation sucks, it's a relief to no longer be with him.

It's the only silver lining I'm able to find.

My spine stiffens as a few giggles erupt from behind me. As difficult as it is to deal with Jasper, the girls are almost worse. Most would turn on their bestie with the least bit of provocation. And I was nowhere near that status.

"Hey, Delilah. Wait up." Sloane's voice rises above the din.

I squeeze my eyes tightly closed for a second before hastening my step. Not that I'm in any great rush to reach the caf, but I'd prefer not to get stuck in a conversation with her. She's the female version of Jasper, and that makes her dangerous.

When I fail to respond, a slender arm gets looped through mine. "How are you doing, girl?" She makes a frowny face as her voice fills with faux sympathy. "Seems like you've had a rough morning."

I paste a plastic smile in place and shrug. "Nope, everything's fine."

Even though she's being all sweet and nice, I don't trust her as far as I can throw her. Everything with the popular blonde is pretense.

I give her a sidelong glance and watch her sculpted brows rise. "Really? That's not what I heard. Rumor has it that Jasper dumped you Saturday night because he found out you were screwing Austin behind his back." She gives me a speculative look.

Without going into detail, I say, "If you want me to confirm that we're no longer together, it's true."

"Wow. I didn't think you had it in you to be such a ho. Congrats."

When my brows jerk together, she laughs. "Oh, don't take offense. We all know there's a double standard. No one even bats an eye when these guys fuck around or get blowies from other girls. But the moment we step out, we're the cheats." She shrugs. "So…tell me about Austin. I'm dying to hear all the juicy details."

"We're not together."

"Hmmm. Seems like you got the raw end of the deal. Lost your boyfriend and side piece at the same time. I'm sure if you beg Jasper, he'll consider taking you back."

"That's not going to happen."

"Seriously? You don't want to get with him again?"

"Nope."

"No one would blame you for crawling back on your hands and knees." Her voice drops several octaves as she gives me a penetrating look as if capable of hypnotizing me with her baby blues. "So what are you going to do now?"

I shrug.

Just get through the day the best I can.

And then tomorrow, I'll get through that one as well.

"Just remember that if you ever need a shoulder to cry on, I'm here for you."

I almost stumble over my feet at the comment. There's no way I'd tell her anything of a personal nature, because I know damn well that she'd use it against me. Whatever juicy tidbit I confided would be spread through the halls of HP by the end of fifth hour.

I give her another tight smile as the drone of voices increases and we reach the spacious dining hall. "Thanks, I appreciate the offer."

Pursing her shiny lips, she pats my arm. "You're being so brave about this whole thing. Especially since you've practically committed social suicide and you're basically a pariah."

Better to be an outcast than in a relationship with Jasper.

As we step inside the double story space, Sloane slips her arm free. "Well, it was super nice chatting with you. The girls and I are going to head to our usual table. I'd ask you to join us but," she shoots me another sad face, "it would be awkward, considering that we're sitting with your ex."

"No worries. I'll be fine."

"Of course you will, sweetie." She turns to her group of minions who trail after us. "Come on, girls. Lunch awaits."

Most send pitying looks my way from beneath mascara-laden lashes as they flip their extensions on their way past.

Aubrey is the only one who stops before pointing to the far end of the room. "If you're looking for a place to eat, there's a table over there in no-man's land. I'm sure the rejects won't mind you joining them."

With a wave of her two-inch acrylic nails, she skips away, leaving me to stand alone in a crowd of hundreds. As my gaze roves over the sea of unfriendly faces, I regret my decision not to hide in the photography studio. It's tempting to slowly back out of the room before turning tail and running. Except...that would make everything worse. These people are like rogue sharks. As soon as they smell a drop of blood in the water, there'll be a feeding frenzy. There's no other choice but to face it head on. Even if I have to do it on my own.

I should be used to this feeling of isolation.

But the truth is that it never gets easier.

A burst of laughter rings out and my gaze automatically slides toward the sound. Slone is perched on Jasper's lap with her arms locked around his neck as he grins. She leans closer, whispering something in his ear before they both turn and glance at me.

Heat floods my face as I force my feet into movement.

Heads swivel, gazes locking on me with each table I walk by. The babble of voices follows, growing stronger with each step I take. The snippets of conversation I catch make it difficult to hold my head up high.

By the time I reach the table on the outer edge, I wish the floor would open up and swallow me whole. This is so much worse than I anticipated. Last night, as I laid awake in bed, I tried to tell myself that Saturday night wouldn't be a hot topic of conversation.

I couldn't have been more wrong.

It feels like that's all anyone can talk about.

Even a few teachers gave me curious looks.

Like Mr. Pembroke, no one is blaming Jasper for outing Austin's secret. Somehow, everything has been twisted up until it no longer reflects reality, and I'm the cheating whore who has been dumped by her boyfriend. My heart plummets, knowing that Jasper will continue to fuel that particular fire. And there's nothing I can do to shut it down.

No one will listen to me.

Air seeps from my lungs as I drop down at a table on the outermost ring. I stare at the brown paper bag and realize I don't have much of an appetite. The thought of consuming even a bite makes me sick to my stomach. Unsure what to do, I pull out the bottle of water and twist off the cap before lifting the container to my lips and taking a small sip.

As soon as the cool liquid hits my belly, it threatens to revolt. I have no idea how I'm going to get through this without falling to pieces. I will away the tears that threaten the backs of my eyes.

Just when I consider the merits of rushing from the cafeteria, two guys wander over before stopping. I keep my gaze averted, hoping they'll move it along. The last thing I want to do is acknowledge their presence.

My heart sinks when one says, "Hey, Delilah."

The laughter that lurks beneath the smug tone tells me everything I need to know about how this conversation will go.

I suck in a deep breath and force myself to meet their gazes.

Recognition dawns.

Both are on the football team, but I don't remember either of their names. We've never said much to one another. There's never been a reason to. What I do know is that the one who spoke is a loud, obnoxious guy who laughs at his own jokes. I've also seen him go out of his way to pick on and belittle other students. Especially ones he perceives as weaker.

That knowledge has my muscles turning rigid and the small pit at the bottom of my belly growing in size. It takes concerted effort to keep from folding in on myself with the need to be a smaller, less visible target. Although, I can already tell from the malicious glint in both of their eyes that it's much too late for that.

Their sights are locked on me, and there's no escaping.

When I fail to respond, loudmouth takes a step closer, forcing me to crane my neck to hold his gaze.

"I just wanted to put it out there that I'd be more than happy to slide into Jasper's place now that you two are splitsville. He's told all the guys how much you like sucking cock." When he drops his hand, my gaze unconsciously follows the movement as he grabs himself. "You've probably already heard that I've got a pretty big one. It would be a real pleasure to watch you choke on it."

His friend grins and they nudge each other like he just said the funniest thing ever.

Before I can tell them to go away, a deep voice says from behind me, "Get the fuck out of here, Wendt. Otherwise, we'll see how flexible you are when I ram that giant dick you were just bragging about down your throat."

Right.

Aiden Wendt.

It doesn't take long for the smirk to fall from Aiden's face as he straightens to his full height, which is still a good six inches shorter than Duke. "What's the problem, Carmichael? I'm just offering my services in case she gets restless now that Morgan isn't banging her on a regular basis."

"You're the last person she'd want looking in her direction. So do us both a favor and get lost."

"What?" His upper lip curls. "You already claim the bitch? That was pretty damn quick."

Duke's nostrils flare as his eyes narrow. "I'm gonna count to three, and if you're dumb enough to still be standing here when I reach three, I'll give everyone in the caf dinner and a show." One brow slinks upward. "Understand?"

"Who the fuck—"

"One."

"Jesus—"

"Two." Duke tosses his bagged lunch on the table and cracks his knuckles. The movement makes his biceps pop beneath the white button-down he's wearing.

Aiden grumbles before stalking away without another word. His friend scurries after him.

The tension gripping me gradually dissolves as I track their movements from the corner of my eye to the table in the center of the dining area. Before I can look away, Jasper snags my gaze and a vicious smile spreads across his handsome face. It's enough to send a chill slithering down my spine.

Whatever my ex has planned, this is only the beginning.

It takes every ounce of strength to rip my attention away before refocusing on the blond boy now parked across from me.

"I hope you know that I never liked him," he says conversationally, as if discussing the weather.

The unexpected comment has a burst of laughter escaping from me. "I can't imagine why."

One side of his lips quirk.

This is what a full-blown smile looks like on Duke Carmichael.

If I'm being completely honest, it's pretty dazzling.

The guy is ridiculously handsome.

Even though most of the girls at HP enjoy looking at him, very few are brave enough to venture too close. He's like a feral dog. One that could turn at any moment. Since we've known each other for so long, I don't feel that way. I'm pretty sure we're friends.

At least, I think we are.

"It probably has something to do with the guy being a self-absorbed prick."

"You're right." If only it hadn't taken me so long to figure it out. I could have saved myself a lot of grief. "Thanks for shutting Aiden down."

He shrugs. "It was my pleasure. Us scholarship kids gotta stick together, right?"

"Yeah." When the nape of my neck prickles, I spear another reluctant glance in Jasper's direction, only to find him watching me with narrowed eyes. I know that look all too well. I also understand what it means. My voice drops. "You don't have to sit here. The last thing I want to do is involve you in this mess."

He reaches into his brown paper bag and pulls out a sandwich. "You didn't involve me. I involved myself."

"It's not that I don't appreciate—"

"If anyone has a problem with it, they can talk to me." He takes a huge bite of the bread, meat, and cheese before chewing methodically and swallowing. "Got it?"

I could argue, but I realize it won't do a damn bit of good. Duke is stubborn to a fault.

"Thank you." I give him a slight smile filled with gratitude.

"There's no reason to thank me." He points to my untouched lunch. "Now eat."

Even though I can't bear the thought, I stick my hand inside the brown paper bag and pull out a fruit snack.

He stares at it with a frown. "Is that all you got in there?"

"No."

"Then show me. A fucking fruit snack isn't enough to fuel you for the rest of the afternoon."

Spoken like a true athlete.

When Duke stares expectantly, I roll my eyes and pull out the small bag of pretzels. "You're kind of bossy, you know that?"

He snorts and stares at the baggie. "You're seriously killing me here. How does your mom let you walk out the door with that garbage?"

"My mother considers me an adult who can pack her own lunch."

"Clearly you've proven her wrong."

I reach into the paper sack again and pull out the sandwich before flattening the bag and setting it on top. "Happy?"

His expression never falters. "Ecstatic."

"Great."

He points to the food. "Now eat."

We engage in a silent stare-down before I huff out an exasperated breath and remove the sandwich from its plastic wrapper before lifting it to my lips and taking a nibble.

Unlike me, Duke demolishes his in less than two minutes.

It's almost impressive.

As I lower it to the table, he shakes his head. "You need to finish. Don't you dare give that prick the satisfaction of seeing how much he's upset you."

"My lack of appetite has nothing to do with him," I mumble, gaze dropping to the table. "I'm just not hungry."

"Bullshit. Now eat."

My wide gaze snaps to his. "Duke—"

"And look happy while doing it."

"Happy?" I echo in disbelief.

"Yeah. You know…smile. Maybe even laugh. Look like I'm the best damn company you've ever had."

A reluctant smile tugs at the corners of my lips as I nod toward our classmates. "That wouldn't be a lie."

His expression lightens, losing some of its severity. "There you go. Was that so difficult?"

I draw in a breath before releasing it. "No." Then, I bring the sandwich to my lips again and force myself to take another bite. Once I've swallowed it down, the words tumble from my mouth before I can stop them. "Have you seen Austin this morning?"

"Nope. Heard he got suspended."

My heart sinks like a bolder. "He did?"

"For three days. The guy's lucky he didn't get kicked out of school or off the team."

Suspended. Not expelled.

My shoulders slump in relief. Football is everything to him.

Without it...

I don't even want to think along those lines.

There's a moment of silence before he adds in a serious tone, "I'm shocked that Pembroke didn't pounce on this opportunity to get Austin out of here."

He would have, if I hadn't barged into his office this morning. But I keep that tidbit to myself.

"Guess he got lucky this time," he muses, looking thoughtful.

"I wouldn't go that far." With a grimace, I swallow down another small bite before lowering the sandwich to the table. If I attempt to force down any more, there's a good chance the masticated pieces will make an encore appearance.

His attention stays locked on me as he lifts his Gatorade and takes a swig. "Heard you were in Pembroke's office before school started."

I glance away and lie through my teeth, "I needed to speak with my mom."

"Hmm."

Before he can give me the third degree, the bell rings, signaling the end of lunch, and the cafeteria erupts into chaos. There are only two more periods left, and the last one is my TA hour with Ms. Pettijohn. After the day I've had, it'll be a relief to hide away in her empty classroom and lose myself in test corrections.

DELILAH

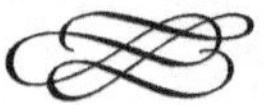

By the time I walk into Ms. Pettijohn's room, I'm on the verge of falling apart. There's not much more I can take. Fifth hour was the worst of all of them. Jasper waited for me to show up and made sure to cause a scene. It was so embarrassing that I wanted to melt into the floor. A few of his friends dropped notes on my desk with lewd suggestions.

Even though Duke sat with me at lunch and I'm appreciative of that, I've never felt more alone. If I thought begging Mom to transfer to Hawthorne Public for the rest of senior year would do any good, I'd fall to my knees in front of her and plead my case. But there's no way she'll allow that to happen.

The woman cried actual tears of joy when she opened my acceptance letter during the spring of eighth grade. For some reason, Mom doesn't see the kids at school for what they really are—spoiled brats who think they can do whatever they please without consequence.

And there's zero point telling Pembroke about the bullying. After the way our conversation played out this morning, he'd probably be thrilled by the news.

So...I'm stuck.

Ms. Pettijohn glances up from her computer. "Good afternoon, Delilah."

I force a smile. Even though I like the older teacher and she's always been kind, there's no way I can confide in her. In fact, there's no one I can talk to about this. It only makes me feel more isolated than I already am.

"Hi. Should I finish up the test corrections from last week?"

Fifty minutes of mindless work is exactly the kind of distraction I need. If she wants, I'd be happy to take papers home with me. My social life has just become nonexistent. Which is fine. It's not like I enjoyed hanging out with Jasper and his friends anyway. Or constantly fighting off his advances.

"No." She leans back in her chair and pulls off the black-rimmed glasses that sit perched on the bridge of her slender nose. "Something's come up that I need your assistance with."

"Oh?"

"I have a student who needs extra help in English. Honestly, he could use support with most of his subjects."

Hmm...sounds interesting.

For the past couple of years, I've volunteered my time after school to tutor some of the younger students. Since I plan to become a teacher, it's an activity that will look good on college and scholarship applications.

"Is this person free during sixth period, or will we need to work after school in the library?"

She hesitates before saying, "Actually, you'll be working with him during sixth period at his house."

I blink, thrown off by the answer. "At his house?"

"I know it's a little unorthodox, but this particular student has just been suspended for three days. So, I'll need you to start this afternoon."

My belly drops to the bottom of my toes. It feels like I've just thrown myself off a cliff and am plummeting to my death.

"Suspended?" I echo faintly.

"Yes. I believe you know Austin Hawthorne."

Oh god.

"I do."

"Good. Then this arrangement should work out perfectly."

That's the last thing it will be.

The thought of spending time alone with Austin sends a burst of panic rushing through my veins as icy cold tendrils of fear wrap themselves around my heart before squeezing painfully. The look of retribution that had blazed from his green depths this morning is enough to make my body tremble. My brain whirls, trying to come up with an excuse as to why this arrangement won't work.

There's no way I can be alone with him. It would be like throwing a lamb to a wolf. An image of him wrapping strong fingers around my throat and squeezing the slender column flashes through my head.

Slowly.

He would do it slowly to draw out the pain.

With a gulp, I blurt, "I don't think I'm the best person to work with Austin."

Her eyes sharpen as she tilts her head. "Why would that be?"

Unable to hold the steeliness of her gaze, I glance toward the window before sucking in a harsh breath. It feels as if the bright and sunny skies are mocking me. "I just think there's someone else better—"

She doesn't allow me to finish my thoughts.

"I'm afraid there isn't anyone else available during sixth period." An uncomfortable silence ensues. One that leaves me fidgeting beneath the intensity of her scrutiny. "I must say that I'm surprised by your attitude, Delilah." The disappointment that fills her voice leaves me wincing. "I wasn't expecting this from you. You're always so positive and willing to work with any student, no matter how challenging. If you think as a teacher, you'll be able to handpick your pupils, allow me to kindly disabuse you of that notion." There's another pause. "Perhaps you should reconsider your future endeavors."

The last thing I want is Ms. Pettijohn thinking I'm not serious about a career in education. She wrote several glowing recommendations to include with my college applications, and I'll need more for the scholarships I plan to apply for in the spring.

Indecision spirals through me. "Forget I said anything," I mumble. "It won't be a problem."

She raises a brow. "Are you certain?"

Nope.

I nod, realizing there's no other option.

She swivels in her chair. The moment I'm released from her penetrating stare, my body wilts.

She gathers up a stack of papers before thumbing through them and then passing the pile to me. "I've taken the liberty of collecting Mr. Hawthorne's work from his other instructors. Your job will be to go over each assignment in detail and help with a couple of problems should they arise. If there are concepts he's unable to grasp after a thorough explanation, he should email the specific teacher for more direction."

I take the books and paperwork, clutching the stack to my chest as if it has the power to protect me. "All right."

When I stand rooted in place, she clears her throat and glances at her wristwatch before tapping the small face. "You should probably get moving. There's no need to check out at the office. I've cleared you to leave after fifth hour for the next three afternoons."

"Okay."

With no other recourse, I head to my locker.

Each step feels like I'm walking to certain death.

If there's one thing I know, Austin Hawthorne will be even less thrilled to see me on his doorstep than I am to be there.

DELILAH

I park Mom's old Civic on the weathered brick driveway and stare up at the two-story monstrosity that looms before me. After a second or two of silence, I twist the key and kill the engine. A pit the size of Texas has taken up residence at the bottom of my belly, and nothing I do helps to dislodge it.

My fingers twitch to restart the vehicle and speed from the driveway. After everything that happened, I can't imagine what it'll be like to come face to face with the tall football player. There's no erasing the hostility that had shined brightly in his eyes from my memory. That image has me inhaling a deep breath before forcing it out again. It does nothing to calm the nerves that are currently eating me alive.

Left with no other choice, I swipe the books and paperwork from the passenger seat and open the door before stepping onto the brick drive. The portico is just as impressive as the rest of the sprawling stone residence. Once at the front door, I glance through one of the glass side panels and peek inside. A few seconds tick by without movement.

Maybe Austin isn't home.

Everything inside me tentatively lifts at the possibility.

I glance toward the driveway again and realize my vehicle is the only one parked there. My hand trembles as I reach out and press the bell. The sound echoes throughout the cavernous first floor. If anyone is home, there's no way they didn't hear that.

A fresh burst of anxiety explodes inside me as I tap my foot against the concrete.

One second slowly slips by.

Then another.

Hope rises within me like a soaring phoenix.

When a full minute ticks by and there's still no answer, I consider swinging around and hightailing it from the premises. I can return to school and tell Ms. Pettijohn that I tried. It's tempting to whip out my phone and snap a pic just to prove that I'm not a liar. After the way she stared at me fifteen minutes ago, I'll probably need it.

Instead of giving in to the urge to run, I stab the button for a second time before peeking through the beveled glass panel.

It's official. Austin's not here.

A tidal wave of relief crashes over me, nearly bringing me to my knees.

Just as I turn away, ready to scamper back to my car, the door swings open. My spine stiffens as I grind to a reluctant halt and throw a glance over my shoulder. What I find is enough to stop my heart mid beat.

Austin stands in the entryway with athletic shorts that are slung low around lean hips and nothing else. Not even shoes or socks. A bead of sweat mars his brow. My guess is that he's in the middle of a workout.

By the time my gaze lifts to his, a scowl has taken up residence on his face. That's the moment I realize I've been standing on the porch, silently gawking. Heat stings my cheeks.

"What the hell are you doing here?" he barks.

My mouth turns bone dry as I squirm beneath the harsh intensity of his stare. I'm not used to him looking at me with such a potent concoction of rage and resentment.

It takes effort to clear my throat and summon my voice. "Ms. Petti- john arranged for me to tutor you during sixth hour while you're suspended." He continues to glare, crossing thickly corded arms against his bare chest. The movement makes the muscles of his biceps bulge with a roadmap of veins that stand out in sharp relief.

Unconsciously, I take a step in retreat. "If you'd prefer to work alone or with someone else, I totally—"

"Get inside."

Those two words settle like heavy stones at the bottom of my belly, and I stay frozen in place, chewing my lower lip with indecision.

A feeling of foreboding suffuses every cell of my body. Somehow, I just know that if I step foot inside this house, it'll lead to my utter ruin and destruction.

Before I can formulate an excuse and carefully back away, he snaps, "Now, Delilah."

"Umm…"

Instead of waiting for me to vomit out the rest of the words, he swings away, stalking up the sweeping staircase.

My heart jackhammers a painful staccato against my ribcage as I track his movements with my eyes.

"Where are you going?" I call, voice wavering throughout the cavernous space.

"Up to my room."

My gaze darts around the foyer. From the silence that surrounds us, there doesn't appear to be anyone else home. "Do you think we could work in the kitchen or maybe the study?"

"Nope."

Once he reaches the middle of the elegantly curved staircase, he stops and scowls. Sparks of fury fly from his eyes. Even from this distance, it's almost a surprise when I don't find myself burned to cinders.

"Should I call Pettijohn and tell her that my tutor can't be bothered to tutor me? I'm sure that'll go over well."

A steady puff of air escapes from me as I reluctantly cross the shiny marble floor and follow him to the second floor. By the time I reach the third riser, he swings forward again and ignores me.

Privately, I admit that staring at the wide expanse of his bare back isn't a hardship. I've never caught a glimpse of Austin when he wasn't wearing either his school or football uniform. When I've laid awake at night, thinking about him, I couldn't begin to imagine what lurked beneath his perfectly pressed shirt and blazer.

Now, the chiseled V of his lower abdomen will forever be scorched into my brain.

He swings a right at the landing and disappears. By the time I reach the top of the stairs, there's no sign of him. I pause, staring down the long stretch of hardwood dotted with plush area rugs. Nerves flutter at the bottom of my belly.

I only have to be here for forty minutes.

We'll go over the assignments and I'll make sure he understands the directions. Maybe start a couple of problems. Once that's done, I can take off.

Tomorrow, we can meet at the public library in town. Or even a coffee shop. Anything would be better than being alone with Austin.

In his room.

Now that I've given myself a silent pep talk, I straighten my shoulders and force my feet into movement. It takes eight steps to reach the first door. I hesitate, steeling everything inside me before cautiously peeking around the frame. I find Austin with navy-colored headphones covering his ears and heavy black weights in both hands. His back is to me as he curls each one to his chest. I hover in the doorway as his muscles ripple with each exertion.

Riveted by the movements, I can only stare.

After a few minutes trickle by and he continues to ignore me, I shift. "Austin."

Nothing.

There's not even a glance over his shoulder to tell me that he's aware of my presence.

"Austin," I say again, raising my voice.

More crickets.

I huff out an irritated breath before ripping my gaze away and glancing around the spacious interior. There's a queen-sized bed shoved against the far wall and a long dresser that sits opposite of it.

Nothing more.

With no other options, I cross the room and settle on the edge of the mattress.

This is ridiculous.

Why am I here?

The guy is intent on ignoring me.

I pull out my phone and check the time.

Now we're down to thirty-five minutes.

Well…whatever.

If Austin wants to waste his tutoring time by working out, that's fine with me. The less we interact, the better off we'll be. As soon as school is released for the day, I'm out of here. No one can say that I didn't hold up my end of the bargain. And that's all that matters.

My gaze reluctantly drifts to Austin before licking over his sculpted muscles. It's crazy how buff this guy is. He must spend hours a day working out in addition to football practice.

Jasper plays the same sport but looks nothing like him.

This is the first time I've been in Austin's presence, and he's made a point of ignoring me. Normally, when we're near one another, even in passing, his gaze is firmly locked on mine. It's obvious that he holds me responsible for what happened Saturday night. If he'd just give me a chance, I'd explain that I had nothing to do with it. I was as shocked and appalled by how Jasper humiliated him in front of the school.

My ex played both of us.

I should have realized something was up by his abrupt change in behavior, but I was too relieved by his agreement to break up amicably to inspect his motivations more thoroughly. Now, I'm paying the price.

I glance at Austin.

We both are.

My mind tumbles back to the night he pulled up alongside me on the road. That was the first time we'd delved beneath the surface and really got to know one another. If there was any chance for us to move forward with a relationship, it's been blown to smithereens.

Austin Hawthorne despises me.

And I can't blame him for it.

I snap back to the present when he sets the weights on the floor and rips off his headphones, tossing them onto the nightstand next to the bed.

His cheeks have a slight pink stain to them, and his breathing is labored. Intensity fills his eyes as his attention locks on me. That's all it takes for a punch of arousal to hit me square in the gut.

"I need to hop in the shower."

I jerk to my feet. "That's fine. I'm going to take off. There's no point in me sitting here and wasting more time."

It's obvious from the past ten minutes that he has no interest in working together. I'll talk to our teacher tomorrow morning and see if there's another student who can tutor him.

"I'll be back in five minutes and then we'll get to work."

Before I can argue, he disappears inside the private bathroom attached to his room. When he doesn't bother closing the door as he strips and steps inside the shower stall, I spin away so I won't be tempted to take a peek.

It's like he's doing everything in his power to make me squirm.

My gaze slides over the sparseness of the room before I gravitate to the antique dresser. There are three framed photographs interspersed with a handful of trophies on the polished-to-a-high shine surface. The first picture is of him, Summer, and his parents.

If I had to guess, I'd say this was snapped a year or two ago. He's not as well-defined as he is now. They're all wearing summery clothes while posing with a lake in the background. After studying it for a handful of seconds, I set the frame down and move on to the next one.

It's a picture of Austin in his football uniform. There are dark smudges beneath each eye and his shoulders look ridiculously broad with the thick pads beneath the black and red jersey. He's grinning at the camera with a trophy raised in one hand. Unable to help myself, I drag a finger across the glass, as if it's possible to touch him in this happy moment.

Rarely have I seen Austin smile.

The one in the photograph makes my insides clench.

"And here I thought you might have taken off and I'd have to chase you down," a deep voice says near my ear.

I jolt and nearly drop the frame before setting it carefully on the dresser and swinging around to face him. Air leaks from my lungs and my eyes widen when I find all that brawny strength standing less than a foot away.

Without a stitch of clothing to cover it.

I swallow before squeaking, "What are you doing?"

He arches a brow. "Attempting to get dressed. Kind of hard to do when you're in my way."

Instead of stepping aside and giving me room to maneuver, he moves closer, hemming me in with his big body.

Alarm bells trill in my head as I flatten against the dresser. If I could crawl on top of it to escape his overwhelming presence, I'd do it in a heartbeat.

"You need to back off," I say, trying to keep the quaver from invading my tone.

His eyes darken. "Do I?"

I hate myself for the way my knees weaken at the sound of his gruff voice. "Please."

His pupils dilate as he continues to stare. "I always imagined what it would be like to hear that word on your lips."

Air gets clogged in my throat. It feels as if my heart is on the verge of exploding. "Austin…"

He retreats enough to give me a bit of breathing room. "Is that better?"

"Yes." Unconsciously, my gaze slides down the length of his hard body before settling on his erection.

My eyes widen.

The longer I stare, the harder it becomes.

Holy.

Crap.

There's a voice inside my head shouting that I need to stop gawking, but following the directive is impossible. It's like a traffic accident

I'm powerless to look away from. I'd be lying if I didn't admit that it's tempting to study him more thoroughly.

How's it possible that he looks both soft and hard at the same time?

I jerk out of the mental fog that has descended when he grips his thick shaft in the palm of his hand.

"What's wrong?" His voice is deep and guttural. "Haven't you ever seen a cock before? Because I gotta be honest, that's not what Jasper's been telling everyone. According to him, you love being on your knees."

My wide gaze darts to his. "He's a liar," I choke out.

After what happened at lunch, that no longer surprises me. I'm kicking myself all over again for giving Jasper the time of day. It feels like a mistake I'll spend the rest of the year paying for.

He tilts his head as his hand continues stroking the hard length, squeezing it until the tip turns a purplish hue. "Is that so?"

I straighten my shoulders and inch my chin higher. "Yes."

"Interesting. Exactly what part is a lie?"

"All of it."

His lips lift into a mocking smirk. "Are you actually trying to tell me that you're a virgin?"

"That's none of your business," I say primly as another wave of heat slams into my cheeks.

Fire leaps into his eyes. "That's where you're wrong, sweet girl. Everything about you is now my business."

The rough edge that fills his voice as he bites out the endearment sends a thousand shivers racing down my spine.

When his strokes grow faster, my attention reluctantly drops to the harsh movement. It shouldn't be this fascinating, and yet I'm powerless to rip my eyes away.

"I have an idea. Why don't you drop to your knees, open real wide, and we'll see what kind of aim I have."

My lower jaw turns slack.

"Yup, just like that."

I do the only thing I can and dart for the door.

DELILAH

I make it three steps before he catches me. Strong fingers curl around my bicep before I'm spun around and dragged against the hard length of his naked body. A gasp slips free from my lips as his hot flesh singes mine through my blouse and skirt.

Any moment, I'm going to go up in flames.

"Austin..."

Fury dances in his eyes as he steers me toward the bed. It takes everything I have inside to stay upright and not trip over my own feet. Just as I try to reason with him, the back of my knees hit the edge of the mattress and I find myself falling. Before I can roll away, he follows me down, his bigger body pinning mine in place.

For just a second, my mind tumbles back to the party with Jasper. Panting breaths escape from me as I stare up at him with wide eyes.

"Where do you think you're going, Delilah? My time isn't up yet. I still have another fifteen minutes."

Adrenaline spikes through my veins, making it impossible to think straight. "I'm supposed to be tutoring you."

A wolfish grin slides across his lips. "Oh, you'll definitely be tutoring me. Just not in English."

To punctuate the words, he rolls his hips, and I feel the thick slide of his erection against my core. The fear I expect to spike through my blood turns into something altogether different. A million little shudders reverberate outward until the sensation reaches the tips of my fingers and toes. It doesn't make sense that I have to bite back the pleasure blooming in my core and keep the sound trapped inside. The urge to meet his thrusts head on pounds through me.

"You like that, don't you?"

The words might be arranged in the format of a question, but it's not one. By the knowing look that fills his eyes, the answer is written clearly across my face.

Although that doesn't stop the lie from tumbling out. "No."

He snorts as his warm breath drifts across my lips. The last thing it should be is intoxicating. I shouldn't want to gulp him in, holding him captive in my lungs.

"Liar," he whispers, flexing again. "I bet your pussy is sobbing." There's a beat of silence and his tone deepens. "Maybe I should find out for myself."

My breath hitches painfully in my chest as I shake my head. "Please, don't."

I'm terrified that he's right. I can feel the growing wetness between my thighs. Being this turned on is a new experience. In the beginning, the thought of Jasper touching me was exciting, but the pushier he became, the less I wanted to be around him until, in the end, he repulsed me.

The sensations coursing through me aren't like anything I've ever felt before. As much as I want to hate what he's doing, part of me likes it and is curious to explore it in more depth.

"Mmm, I like that word on your lips." His voice drops as he rubs the tip of his nose against mine. "My new mission in life is to make you beg."

Anger spirals through me, because that's all this is to him. A game. "I will never beg you for anything." I only hope it's a promise I can keep.

His lips lift into a smirk as a throaty chuckle rumbles up from deep inside him.

"That sounds suspiciously like a challenge. And there's nothing more I enjoy than one of those. Especially if it involves bringing you to your knees."

There's just enough room for my palms to slip between us so they can press against his chest.

"Why are you doing this?" My tongue darts out to moisten my lips. "This isn't you."

Storm clouds gather in his eyes as he snarls, "How can you say that when you know next to *nothing* about me?"

"That's not true."

When he grinds against me again, arousal detonates inside my core. This time, dousing the desire set ablaze is impossible. It's like a wildfire burning out of control.

As soon as the whimper escapes, his eyes sharpen and a predatory look flares to life within them. One hand snakes up the bare skin of my leg, leaving a rush of shivers in its wake. When I attempt to shift, he holds me in place, anchoring me with his larger body. There's no way to escape his touch.

"Austin..."

"What, sweet girl? You want me to stroke that pretty little pussy of yours? Is that what you need? Jasper's not giving it to you anymore and you're already lonely?"

I'm deathly afraid that he'll touch me in a way no one else ever has. I'm more turned on now than I've been in my life, and that scares the shit out of me.

Especially when all he's doing is lashing out.

His despicable behavior should disgust me.

I should be fighting him tooth and nail.

Clawing at his face.

In that moment of clarity, I realize there must be something very wrong with me.

What other reasonable explanation could there be?

"I've already told you," flames lick at my cheeks as I force out the rest, "Jasper never touched me like that."

His hand inches upward, moving dangerously close to the apex of my thighs.

"Doubtful. All he did was brag to anyone who would listen about how much you enjoyed him banging you. How you begged to be filled." By the end of his tirade, his voice is nothing more than a snarl as if he detests the thought of Jasper defiling me almost as much as I do.

"They're all lies."

"Ah, right. I forgot. You're as pristine as the freshly driven snow."

The moment his fingers stroke across the seam of my panty-covered pussy, my teeth sink savagely into my lower lip to keep the moan trapped inside. I'll be damned if I give him anything else to wield against me. His warm breath rushes across my mouth, making me dizzy with the ferocious need attempting to claw its way out.

"Just like I suspected—you're fucking soaked through."

Instead of acknowledging the truth, I turn away. The last thing I want to see is the triumph filling his eyes.

"Tell me, sweet girl, are you owner specific or does it even matter who touches you?"

A harsh laugh escapes from him as I jerk my head until my gaze can refasten on his.

"Fuck you."

His fingers pause over my entrance before slowly pressing against it.

"I bet you'd enjoy it if I did."

I smash my lips together until they feel bloodless and shove at his chest, wanting only to dislodge him. He doesn't budge. Instead, his fingers fall into a steady rhythm that makes me want to scream as arousal crashes unwantedly through me.

Any moment I'm going to—

The heavy weight crushing me to the mattress vanishes as the intense sensations throbbing an insistent beat dissolve, leaving me feeling achy and unfulfilled. It's disturbing to realize that it actually wouldn't take much to make me beg.

Without a word, he swings away before sauntering to the dresser. My gaze tracks his movements as my heartrate gradually settles. Even though my brain is firing off a slew of messages, nothing is being received. All I'm capable of is lying on the bed, limbs akimbo, trying to find my bearings.

My gaze falls to his naked backside as he yanks open the dresser drawer.

Why does he have to be so gorgeous?

So perfectly built?

That's when I realize he's way more dangerous than Jasper.

I've spent the last month pining for Austin. Even though I denied it to myself, he's fascinated me since we were first introduced at Hawthorne Prep. And that longing has only grown over time.

With fleeting touches.

Simmering looks.

Quietly spoken words I coveted like something precious.

"You ready to get to work?"

I blink, only to find him looming over me. He's wearing athletic shorts, but his chest is still bare.

I clear my throat and pray he's done messing with me for the day. I don't know how much more I can take. "Can we go downstairs now?"

"Nope. Here's just fine."

His gaze slides down my body. That's all it takes to make me aware that I'm still sprawled out on his mattress. I jerk upright before combing my fingers through my mussed hair.

"It would be easier if we worked at a desk or table."

"Nah. I like seeing you in my bed." He tilts his head. "Although, it would be better if you were naked. Any chance of that happening?"

"No."

"You sure about that? Seems like you enjoy me touching you."

I shake my head and force my gaze away. It's so much easier to think straight when I'm not staring full on at him. He's just...too much.

Too masculine.

Too sexy.

Too angry.

Pull it together, Delilah.

You have to get through this.

I inhale a deep breath before steadily releasing it back into the atmosphere.

As I reach for the stack of papers, I realize that my fingers are trembling. Actually, my entire body is shaking. No matter how many cleansing breaths I force myself to take, my body refuses to settle.

It vibrates like a livewire.

I pick up the first sheet and stare at the words, trying to make sense of them as they swim before my eyes. Why is it so impossible to concentrate?

Austin settles close enough for our thighs to brush. When he strokes a finger along the curve of my jaw, I nearly jump off the mattress.

"What's wrong, sweet girl? Are you distracted?" Before I can force out a response, his voice drops, turning smoky. "I know exactly how to fix that problem."

"I'm fine." I chant the mantra over and over in my head, needing it to be true.

His fingers drift along my cheek.

"Can you stop that?" I keep my attention focused on the paper in my hands and will them not to tremble.

"No. Touching you helps me concentrate." His silky voice turns steely. "You of all people should know I have issues. You were quick enough to blab all the details to your asshole boyfriend."

My shoulders collapse under the weight of his accusation. "I didn't tell Jasper anything."

He snorts, disbelief ringing throughout his tone. "Oh yeah? What a coincidence that he found out about my dyslexia and shared it with the entire fucking school right after we had a convo about it."

It sounds unbelievable even to my own ears.

"I know it looks bad, but I swear that I didn't say a word."

Rage blazes from his eyes as he pushes into my personal space. "I don't care how much you swear, I won't believe a damn word that escapes from your lying lips."

"I'm sorry about what happened."

"You're sorry?" His voice escalates as he parrots the words back.

With a flinch, I steel myself. "Yes."

"Then you shouldn't have a problem helping me get back at him."

A kernel of unease blooms in the pit of my belly. "I don't—"

Before I realize what's happening, he snaps his teeth and bites my lower lip. A gasp escapes from me as I sit rooted, frozen in place. The metallic taste of blood hits my tongue. When a pitiful whimper escapes from me, he tugs at my flesh before releasing it.

My fingers fly to my mouth, grazing the abraded flesh as my gaze stays fastened to him. When I lift my fingers away, I find a smear of blood.

I can't believe—

His hand snakes around the nape of my neck to drag me closer as his tongue darts out to lick at my lip. "I don't give a fuck what you want. You're going to help me get back at Jasper."

I wince, scared to ask but more frightened not to know. "How?"

"From now on, you belong to me. To do with as I please. Understand?"

When I attempt to shake my head, his grip tightens, turning painful. There's no getting away from him.

"I don't want any part of this."

His features remain unyielding. "Guess that's tough shit, isn't it?"

"You can't force me to go along with your plan."

His smile turns vicious. "Wanna bet?"

Unease slithers down my spine as I fight my way free of his grasp before popping to my feet and slowly backing away. It's a surprise when he remains seated, not bothering to come after me.

Even though I'm reluctant to take my eyes off him, I slip my cell from my pocket and glance at it, continuing to creep toward the door. "I need to pick my mom up from school."

Once I reach the threshold, relief crashes over me. The first thing I'm going to do tomorrow morning is tell Ms. Pettijohn that I can't work with Austin. She needs to find someone else.

There's no way I can do this again.

Just as I step into the hallway, he says, "I know your mom is fucking Pembroke."

A strange paralysis takes hold as air gets wedged at the back of my throat, making it impossible to breathe. My wide gaze flies to his just in time to see the triumphant smile flash across his face.

"It'd be a real shame if that got out."

"You would do that?" I croak.

One dark brow slinks upward. "What? Expose a secret you didn't want anyone to know about?" There's an uncomfortable beat of silence. "Damn right I would. I told you this morning that I'd make you pay, and that's exactly what I intend to do. Did you really think you could fuck me over and get away with it?"

"I told—"

His hand slices through the air. "Save it. You've been exposed for the liar you are."

Now that I'm no longer running away, he rises leisurely to his feet. I remain in place, powerless to move. My heartbeat picks up tempo as he eats up the distance that separates us.

When we're standing toe to toe, his fingers slip beneath my chin.

"Do you have any idea how crazy it'll drive him to see you with me?"

"You don't have to do this," I whisper.

The hard glint grows in his eyes. "Actually, I do." There's a beat of silence. "Were you serious about Jasper never fucking that sweet pussy?"

Heat scorches my cheeks as I glance away.

"Eyes on me," he growls, tightening his grip.

My gaze snaps to his.

"I want an answer."

It takes effort to force out the word. "Yes."

His white teeth flash in the sunlight that slants in through the window. "All the bragging he did and here the guy couldn't even close the deal." His voice dips. "Can you imagine how fucking much it'll kill him to think that I got to you first? That I'm enjoying what he'll never have?"

The thought makes me sick to my stomach. "Austin—"

My voice dies away as his mouth ghosts over mine. His warm breath inundates my senses, making it impossible to think straight. Like a magnet, my body unconsciously sways toward his. I jerk away before we can collide.

That's all it takes for shame to flood through me.

His lips quirk at the corners as if he's aware of the internal battle being waged within.

"I'll see you tomorrow, Delilah," he says, taking a step in retreat.

My fingers rise to my lips, feathering over them in disbelief.

What's wrong with me?

How can I long for his kisses when I'm nothing more than a pawn in his game?

My heart slams painfully against my ribcage as I force my feet into movement and race through the hallway and down the stairs before flying through the heavy front door to the car.

Even from the driveway, his soft chuckles echo darkly in my ears.

DELILAH

My fingers shake as I fumble with the key. It takes three attempts before I'm finally able to steady my hand enough to slide the thin metal into the ignition and start up the engine. Air rushes from my lungs in relief as I stomp on the gas pedal and speed from the driveway. It's only when I leave the subdivision behind in the rearview mirror that my heartrate settles and rational thought once again prevails.

I can't believe he's blackmailing me into helping him get revenge on Jasper.

There's no way I can go through with this. No matter what he threatens to do. I'd rather live with the consequences than be his puppet.

When I see Austin tomorrow, I'll tell him that I refuse to get sucked any further into this game he's intent on playing. He can threaten all he wants. When it comes down to it, he can't force me to do anything. Even though the thought of everyone at school finding out about Mom and Pembroke is humiliating, it's better than being a pawn used to inflict damage.

At the end of the day, that's all I am to either of these guys.

I won't allow them to use me this way.

By the time I drive through the stately iron gates of Hawthorne Prep and arrive at the front entrance, I've concocted a plan for moving forward. If that means everyone finds out about Mom's relationship, so be it. That's the risk they took when they decided to have an affair. I'll just have to keep my head down for the remainder of the school year and hope it blows over at some point.

What other choice is there?

I'm knocked from those thoughts when I catch sight of Mom stalking from the stone building. My brows pinch together as I study her ashen features.

If I didn't know better, I'd think she'd been crying.

A bad feeling settles over me as the muscles in my belly contract.

She jerks the handle of the passenger side door before dropping onto the fabric seat and clutching her brown leather purse to her chest. I'm almost afraid to ask what's going on because it's clear from her demeanor that something is gravely wrong.

The tension ratchets up in the atmosphere as I silently pull out of the parking lot. Just as I work up the courage to ask what's wrong, she turns and glares.

"How could you?"

Eyes widening at the barely concealed fury that simmers in her voice, I give her a sidelong glance before focusing straight ahead. The brief look is more than enough to see the sparks of fury flying from her narrowed eyes.

When I remain silent, unsure what to say, Mom snaps, "You threatened the poor man? *Really, Delilah?*"

My mouth drops open. "What? I didn't…" My voice trails off as my earlier conversation with the headmaster explodes in my brain. At the time, it hadn't been my intention to coerce him into doing what I wanted, but I suppose that's exactly how it came off.

As a threat.

Blackmail.

Precisely the same thing Austin is doing to me. Using information —*the same damn information*—to secure my cooperation.

Oh, the fucking irony of it all. If I didn't want to cry, I'd be tempted to laugh hysterically.

It seems impossible that my life has become such a tangled mess. I stare blindly through the windshield, unsure what to say or how to make the situation better.

"And for what?" Her voice escalates with every word that falls from her lips. *"That troublemaker, Austin Hawthorne?"*

"He's not a troublemaker," I murmur before wincing as the previous hour spent in his company rushes back to haunt me. "I didn't want to see him get expelled. What happened Saturday night wasn't his fault. Jasper provoked him."

"Who cares!" she screams, eyes turning wild. "You realize that if anyone finds out that Edmond and I have been seeing each other, it'll cause a huge scandal and we'll both be out of our jobs?" There's a pause. "What will we do then? How will we pay the mortgage, buy groceries, or put gas in the car?"

"You can get another—"

"No, I can't! It's not that easy. This job is high paying, has excellent insurance, benefits, as well as a pension. I don't want to lose that. There's no way I'll find anything else like it in Hawthorne." A mirthless laugh escapes from her. "I'm forty years old. What will I do? Start over at my age? Should I ask Jasper's father to give me a job in his factory?"

Sickness churns in my belly. Any second, the bile will rise up and spew all over the place.

"I don't know," I whisper.

Her body slumps as if all the air has been released from it. "No one else can find out about this, do you understand? There can be no mention of it."

"I didn't mean for any of this to happen. I just didn't want Austin to get expelled."

"Oh my god! Who cares about that boy?" Her upper lip curls with scorn. "All he's done is cause trouble since arriving in town. He should have been sent to public school where he belongs with the rest of the lowlife losers."

"Mom." My eyes widen, swinging to her for a heartbeat. "They're not lowlifes or losers. I still have a lot of friends who attend Hawthorne Public."

Her shoulders hunch as she sniffs and swivels to stare out the window. "The best thing I ever did was get you out of that hellhole. Now you have every opportunity open to you because of the sacrifices *I* made. Don't you dare ruin it."

I open my mouth before snapping it shut again. There's no point in arguing when she's this worked up.

"You stay away from that boy." When I don't immediately respond, her voice sharpens. "Do you hear me, Delilah?"

My teeth rake across my lower lip, and I wince, tongue darting to the place Austin bit me. "I can't do that."

"Why not?" A steely note enters her voice. It's not a tone I'm used to hearing from her.

I gulp. "Ms. Pettijohn asked me to tutor him while he's out on suspension."

Mom crosses her arms against her chest. "I'll speak to Clarissa. Someone else can tutor that animal."

"No." The answer slips out before I can stop it.

From the corner of my eye, I see her stare at me like I've lost my mind.

"Excuse me?"

"There's no one else who can do it." I gulp. "It's only for two more days. And then…"

"And then *what?*"

"There won't be any reason for us to talk," I lie.

Even though I know that won't be the end of it, I decide not to enflame her temper any more than it already is. Hopefully, she'll calm down in a couple of days and be more reasonable.

"Better not be," she grumbles.

The pit that has taken up residence at the bottom of my belly continues to grow as I attempt to navigate a way out of this mess.

But there isn't one.

I'm stuck.

What I know is this—I can't allow Austin to divulge her secret. The price would be too steep.

Whatever he demands, I'll have to give.

DELILAH

A huff of relief escapes from me as I push through the door to the photography studio. If I thought yesterday was bad, today has been ten times worse. There weren't just curious stares accompanied by whispered comments aimed in my direction, it was full-on glares and poisonous remarks meant to inflict damage. More than one guy asked if they could take Jasper's place in my bed.

Apparently, all my ex did was run his mouth and lie about our relationship. I spent the first part of the morning denying the accusations, only to realize that it didn't matter what I said.

In fact, trying to address the lies only made it worse.

By noon, I'd decided there was no way I was heading to the cafeteria for lunch. The new plan is to hide out in the studio until graduation.

Hesitating over the threshold, I glance around the space and find it empty. Normally at this time of the day, Mrs. Chambers is here, developing film or working with students, but she's nowhere to be found.

Maybe that's for the best.

I'm not sure how much longer I can hold this mask of indifference in place before totally falling to pieces. My shoulders slump as I beeline for a table and set my lunch down. Then I drop onto a chair before staring at the brown paper bag as I fight back the hot prick of tears that stings my eyes. How am I going to make it through the rest of the school year like this?

After dinner last night, I broached the subject with Mom about transferring schools just to feel her out. It hadn't gone well. She shot me a scowl before saying that she'd made too many sacrifices to see me graduate from public school. She abruptly ended the conversation by turning away and finishing the dishes.

So…I'm stuck.

My belly growls, breaking the silence that has settled around me. Even though I should force myself to eat, the thought of food makes me nauseous.

Instead of unbagging my lunch, I shove it aside and glance around the room at the photographs that decorate the space. A number of them are mine. Every spring, the school holds an art exhibit for the students to display their creative endeavors. My freshman and sophomore years, my pictures took second place. Last spring, I won a first-place ribbon. Even though it's only October, I'm already thinking about what photos I can enter.

I'm knocked from my thoughts when a deep voice says, "Whatcha doing in here all by your lonesome?"

My head snaps to the door and a prickle of fear skates across my skin when I find Jasper blocking the only exit. His hands are shoved into his khaki pants and the predatory gleam that fills his eyes has a burst of nerves exploding in my belly.

"Eating lunch."

He saunters closer before settling on the edge of the table and clucking his tongue. "Poor Delilah, all by herself."

It becomes necessary to crane my neck to hold his gaze. If I've learned anything about this boy, it's that it can be dangerous to take your eyes off him for even a second.

"What do you want?" It takes effort to keep my voice steady and not allow the fine tremble to work its way through it. The worst thing I can do is allow him to glimpse my fear. It would only feed the hungry beast that lives inside him.

He shrugs. It's a careless gesture that belies the excitement radiating off him in suffocating waves. The delight etched across his expression is barely contained. He's like a child on Christmas morning. Only now do I understand how much he enjoys the hunt. The thrill of the chase. That's all I ever was to him. Our entire relationship was about wearing me down, trying to take something I was unwilling to give.

"Just wanted to know if you missed me yet."

Is he seriously crazy?

Instead of bursting into laughter, I press my lips together and shake my head.

"You know…I could make it all stop."

My eyes widen.

Duke was right. He really is a prick.

When I remain silent, one side of his mouth hitches. "It must be hell to walk through the corridors and hear everyone whispering behind your back, talking about what a slut you are. All I'm saying is that if you got on your knees and begged prettily, I *might* consider taking you back."

The thought of being anywhere near Jasper makes me violently ill.

I still as he reaches out and sweeps his index finger along my lower lip before pressing the thick digit into my mouth and down my throat until tears spring to my eyes and I'm gagging.

"Of course, there'll be a price to pay."

I knock his hand away before shoving back from the table and coughing.

A chuckle falls from his lips. "Only this time, we'll do things *my* way. I'm tired of waiting. I want inside that virgin cunt." He smirks as his gaze drifts lazily over me. "Other places as well."

I shoot out of the chair and stumble back a few paces, attempting to put more distance between us. "Get the hell away from me. There's *nothing* you can do to make me consider dating you again."

His eyes narrow as he rises to his feet. "Is that so?"

I straighten my shoulders and stiffen my spine. There's no doubt in my mind that I'll regret this little show of defiance in the not-too-distant future. I can see it in his eyes.

"Yes."

When he stalks closer, I retreat until my back hits the wall and I realize there's nowhere else for me to go. I'm trapped and at his mercy. It's the last place I want to find myself. The direness of my predicament is slammed home when he stalks close enough to cage me in before pressing his firm body against mine until I can feel the rise and fall of his chest.

"Whether you give it to me of your own free will or I have to wrestle it away, I don't give a shit," he says in a deceptively soft voice that belies the steel in his eyes. "I plan to take what belongs to me." His lips sweep over mine. "Understand?"

"I will never give you anything." Where I find the bravado when I'm shaking in my shoes, I have no idea, but I'm glad it's there.

A wolfish smile spreads across his face as his gray eyes take on a predatory gleam. "Good. I appreciate things more when I have to fight for them. And nothing will give me more satisfaction than when you bleed for the first time." He grins. "And then the second and third."

His words turn my stomach, because I know they're true. He's no longer hiding the ugliness of his personality. It's all out in the open.

A voice clears their throat and my gaze flies to the art teacher. I don't think I've ever been so relieved to see someone in my life.

"Mr. Morgan and Ms. Robinson, as seniors, I'd think the two of you would know better. Empty classrooms are no place for cavorting. If you're not here to work on a project, perhaps you should return to the cafeteria."

Jasper's gaze never deviates from mine. "Sure thing. Delilah had something in her eye, and I was helping to get it out."

"She seems perfectly fine to me," the younger woman says dryly.

My ex takes a few steps in retreat, giving me room to breathe.

"Think about what I said," he whispers in a voice meant only for my ears.

Before I can tell him to go to hell, he flashes an easy smile at the teacher and strolls away. As he disappears through the door, the sound of his whistling can be heard from the hallway. The relief that floods through me is enough to weaken my knees as I sag against the wall.

Mrs. Chambers' eyes soften as she holds my gaze for a long moment. "Is everything all right?"

No, it isn't and I'm beginning to doubt it'll ever be again.

It's so tempting to vomit out the truth, if only to get it off my chest, but what good will it do?

No one can help me.

I'm on my own.

DELILAH

Much like yesterday, fifth hour turns out to be the worst. And considering the nasty comments and looks I received throughout the morning, that's saying something. Tears of frustration simmer beneath the surface. It takes effort to suck them in and keep them buried deep inside.

I'll be damned if I give Jasper the satisfaction.

My mind keeps tumbling back, combing over our relationship with fresh eyes. How didn't I see him for the monster he is? How did I ever believe he had a single kind bone in his body?

My gullibility is almost laughable.

And clearly, Jasper is howling with laughter. He's like a cat toying with a mouse. He watches me, biding his time, while his minions do his dirty work, incessantly pecking at me until I want to curl up in a ball and cry. I have no doubt that he's waiting for me to crawl back to him and beg for his forgiveness. His words from earlier ring unwantedly in my head.

I appreciate things more when I have to fight for them. And nothing is going to give me more joy than making you bleed for the first time. And then the second and third.

Bile rises up my throat.

Yesterday, I dragged my heels, not wanting to leave school after fifth hour. Today, it's the opposite. I can't get out of here quick enough. Even if it means spending time alone with Austin. As much as he frightens me, it's not in the same way Jasper does. There's an evilness to him I was blinded to.

That's no longer the case.

My eyes are now wide open.

Of the two boys, I'll take Austin any day of the week.

My muscles loosen as I drive through the imposing gates of Hawthorne Prep and turn onto the county road that will lead to his subdivision. As I roll down the window, a crisp autumn breeze assaults my senses. I love everything about this season, from the cozy sweaters, caramel apples and Halloween decorations strewn around town, to the scent of smoke from burning leaves and chimneys that permeates the chilled air.

I glance at the cloudless cornflower colored sky. It's a perfect fall afternoon and yet, there's not an ounce of pleasure to be found in it. My life has imploded, and I have no idea how to fix it. Jasper has turned the school against me and won't be happy until I'm back under his control. Mom is still pissed at me for bursting the fragile bubble she'd cocooned herself in. Even though I've apologized, she's giving me the cold shoulder. Mr. Pembroke scowled at me outside the main office when I passed by him this morning. And Austin wants me to pretend that I'm his in order to get back at Jasper.

What I don't know is if he'll demand more.

My mind unconsciously drifts to yesterday and what it felt like when he laid his hands on me. It was nothing like when my ex touched me.

There's something about Austin...

Maybe I didn't want him to arouse my body, but that's exactly what happened.

Not wanting to dwell on those disturbing thoughts, I shove them from my head and turn onto the main road of his sub. As I drive further into the high-priced community, each house grows in size until I reach the Hawthorne mansion. A burst of nerves explodes in the pit of my belly as I stare at the palatial residence through the window.

Just like yesterday, there aren't any cars parked in the drive.

A tremor slides through me. I was really hoping his mother would be at home so we wouldn't be alone.

I give myself a silent pep talk before exiting the vehicle and dragging my feet to the portico and then up the wide stone stairs to the front door. My hand trembles as I reach for the bell. The sound echoes throughout the cavernous space. Minutes tick by, and it only feeds my restlessness. Just as I'm about to press the bell for a second time, the door swings open and much like yesterday, Austin stands before me in low-slung athletic shorts and nothing else.

My mouth dries as my gaze dips. There's a smattering of dark hair across his chest before it arrows to the center of his ribcage, past his bellybutton before finally disappearing beneath the thick waistband.

He leans casually against the doorframe. "Just give the word and I'd be more than happy to lose the shorts."

My gaze slices to his smirking expression and the knowing look that glints in his green eyes. That's all it takes for heat to flood my cheeks.

Oh my god…

I can't believe I did that.

What's wrong with me?

Why does the sight of his nearly naked body make me go a little bit stupid?

After the way he forced himself on me yesterday, nothing about the guy should turn me on.

And yet…

I swallow down the painful realization.

That's not the case.

"No thanks, I'm good."

He arches a brow. "You sure about that?"

When his hand drops to the waistband of the shorts, my gaze tracks the movement. Air gets clogged in my lungs as he shoves the thick strip down enough for me to see the dark curls at his groin.

I throw out a desperate hand. "Please stop."

"There's that word again. Although, I think we both know that stopping is the last thing you want me to do."

Self-loathing fills me as I silently acknowledge that he's right.

It takes effort to swallow past the lump of wet sawdust that has settled in the middle of my throat. "Can we just get to work?" My tongue darts out to moisten my parched lips. *"Please."*

With a snap, he releases the band. "You want to work? Then that's what we'll do."

The pent-up breath held hostage in my lungs leaks from me as my knees weaken.

When he swings toward the staircase, I blurt, "Can't we study on the first floor?" Lord knows it's big enough with plenty of space.

He stops on the second tread before throwing a glance over his shoulder. The intensity of his gaze pins mine in place. "What's the matter? Are you afraid to be alone with me?"

Deathly.

His voice drops, becoming so low that it scrapes something deep inside. Something I'm terrified to inspect more closely.

"Afraid of what might happen?" There's a beat of silence as his eyes search mine, seeming to pick through my thoughts. "And that you'll enjoy it?"

That's a resounding affirmative to both questions.

But there's no way I'll admit that to him. Can you imagine what he would do with that kind of information?

I straighten my shoulders and lie through my teeth. "Of course not."

"Then there's nothing for you to be concerned about."

I press my lips together, irritated that he's caught me neatly in a trap. I'm damned if I do and damned if I don't.

His shoulders shake with silent mirth as if he can hear the thoughts running rampant through my head. As he continues up the staircase, I'm treated to the broad expanse of his back. His shoulders are the widest part of him before tapering to a narrow waist.

I jerk my gaze away before reluctantly following.

By the time I reach the second-floor landing, Austin has disappeared inside his room and the door has been left wide open. I draw in a deep breath before steadily releasing it into the atmosphere and propelling myself forward. Once outside his personal space, I pause. The woodsy scent of his cologne lingers in the air and assaults my senses. It's so tempting to inhale a big breath. Instead, I carefully peek inside, only to find it empty. That's when I hear the shower from the bathroom running.

My muscles loosen in relief.

Maybe he isn't going to torment me like yesterday.

Since there aren't any seating options, I drop the stack of books on the bed before gingerly settling next to them.

There's no way I'll bring it up to Austin, but I did a little research last night on dyslexia to see if there were any tips or tricks I could use to make working with him easier. I remember him admitting that Summer helped him a lot. It was so tempting to text her, but I didn't think she'd answer. Or, if she did, it would be with a barrage of names and accusations.

His sister has always been kind to me, but after the fundraiser, she refuses to meet my gaze. Like everyone else, she believes I was Jasper's willing accomplice.

Just as I grow restless, Austin saunters out of the bathroom. My gaze darts to him long enough to see that he's naked. The cottony feeling returns to my mouth as I yank my attention away and force myself to stare at the landscape beyond the windowpane.

It doesn't work.

"I see you watching me from the corner of your eye. It's all right if you want to check me out. I don't mind."

He strolls close enough for me to feel the heat emanating from his body in suffocating waves. I release a shaky breath and attempt to ignore him. He's like a child seeking out attention.

It doesn't matter if it's positive or negative.

His voice drops, becoming low and husky. "Last chance to get your fill."

The snap of material against firm flesh makes me jump. Muscles tightly strung, I glance just in time to see him pulling up his athletic shorts. My nerves settle now that he's clothed.

Somewhat.

"Maybe you could put a T-shirt on?" I suggest.

"Nah."

"How about being showered and changed by the time I get here tomorrow?"

"But then you wouldn't get to see my cock, and I know how much you enjoy that."

Heat rushes to my face until self-combustion feels imminent. He's—unfortunately—not wrong. I find his body ridiculously fascinating.

Especially that part of him.

"I barely looked at you today," I mumble.

"I know, and I'm feeling seriously neglected by your lack of interest. Want to change that?"

I clear my throat and try to redirect this conversation. "Can we please get to work? I need to pick up my mom by three."

"Sure." He drops down next to me on the bed. "After you admit you enjoy staring at my naked body."

"Austin…"

"All you have to do is admit the truth. Is that really so difficult?"

"I'm indifferent."

His hand slips beneath my jaw before gripping it tightly and turning my face until there's no other choice but to meet his steady gaze. It's hot enough to singe me alive from the inside out. Carefully, he searches my eyes. It's as if he can see all the secrets I keep locked away. It's a disconcerting feeling.

"Liar." He cocks his head. "Are you embarrassed by the truth?"

One hundred percent.

"I'm not attracted to you at all."

A chuckle rumbles up from deep within his chest. "Hmmm." His voice turns silky. "Should I prove what a little hypocrite you are?"

I shake my head, knowing there's no way I'll be able to withstand his touch before folding like a cheap house of cards. Already, I'm teetering on the brink. Before I realize what's happening, he shoves me against the mattress and hovers over my upper body until his mouth can ghost over mine. The mintiness of his breath feathers against my lips. It's just as intoxicating as the masculine scent of his cologne.

My head spins with his nearness as the intensity of his gaze holds mine captive. It wouldn't take much to drown within their green depths. His lips drift across mine. The movement is unexpectedly tender. When I open, he slides downward, sharp teeth nipping at the point of my chin. Lower still and he's moving along the slender column of my neck.

Mmmm. His mouth feels amazing.

Nothing like Jasper's.

The difference is night and day.

Where my ex would instill panic and fear, Austin instills...

Need.

Desire.

Arousal.

As much as I don't want to feel it, there's no stopping the heady mix of sensations as they rush through my veins.

And he knows it.

Knows exactly how he's able to affect me with just one touch.

His teeth scrape against my collarbone before continuing his descent until he reaches the first button of my starched blouse. My breath catches as he separates the material and places a kiss between the swell of my breasts.

With a lift of his head, our gazes collide. "Ready to admit the truth, or should I keep going?"

"You win." Barely has he touched me and already my breathing has turned labored.

My body stills as he slips the first pearly button from the loop before tugging the fabric apart.

"What have I won?" he asks, gaze focused on the skin he's intent on bearing.

"Austin, please..."

"There you go again—begging. One of these days, I'm going to give you exactly what you're pleading so prettily for."

When his fingers hover over the second button, I blurt, "I like looking at you, all right?" The words tumble from my lips in a rush. "Are you happy now?"

"Not really." He slips the second button through the hole so that even more flesh is displayed. "What exactly do you like looking at?"

My jaw locks. It's obvious he won't be satisfied until he completely humiliates me.

When I remain silent, trying to figure out a way to fight him, his fingers drift over the bare skin above my bra. Goosebumps rise in their wake. Back and forth he strums until I can't stop myself from shifting restlessly beneath him, hungry for more of his touch.

It's demoralizing to realize that Austin is capable of turning me against myself and reducing me to a quivering mass of hormones.

"Everything," I gasp.

"Be more specific."

I gulp and force myself to admit, "Your biceps."

"Is that it?" His finger dips beneath the material, moving dangerously close to my nipple.

"Your chest," I blurt.

When the blunt tip of his digit brushes over the stiffened peak, a whimper escapes from me.

"Anything else?"

"Your backside."

"You mean my ass?"

"Yes," I whisper.

He caresses the stiff little bud for a second time, sending a thousand little shivers reverberating throughout my body.

"What about my cock?" His gaze lifts, fastening onto mine as if he'll never release it. "Do you like looking at that?"

More heat pools in my cheeks but part of me no longer cares. The only thing I can focus on is the pleasure he's sparking to life inside me. It's not like anything I've ever experienced before, and as much as I want this madness to stop, I want it to continue.

I've never felt more at odds with myself. It's the strangest sensation.

His hand slips from my shirt, leaving me to feel bereft. A moan of protest almost breaks free from me when his mouth settles over the stiffened peak through the fabric of both my shirt and bra. The moan turns into more of a cry as the taut bud is surrounded by warmth. Even though it's not skin-on-skin contact, I feel the tug of his lips to my very core. Unconsciously, my fingers tunnel through his hair, attempting to shove him away.

Or maybe I'm trying to drag him closer.

I don't know.

Or maybe I do, and it's that knowledge which frightens me most.

Where is the line?

What *won't* I let Austin Hawthorne do?

He nips at me before repeating, "Do you enjoy staring at my cock?"

"Yes," I gasp. "I like looking at all of you."

"Good girl."

And then he's sucking my nipple into his mouth with a greediness that has my back bowing off the mattress. This goes on until I'm crying out and my core is pulsing with a shameless amount of need. I have no idea where this girl writhing on the bed has come from. She's not someone I recognize.

With one final tug, he releases me. Disappointment takes up residence at the bottom of my belly. Or maybe it settles lower.

Much lower.

"Don't ever lie to me again." He nips at the sensitive peak and a burst of pain streaks through me before exploding into something that resembles pleasure. "Understand?"

The potent mix of sensations is confusing.

How can something that hurts feel so good?

When I remain silent, he bites me again and the same feelings ricochet through me.

"Yes!"

With a quick burst of movement, he rolls away before settling at my side like nothing happened. As if he didn't just open a door and usher me through it. The way he's able to swiftly switch gears leaves me feeling like I have whiplash. Unlike him, it takes me a handful of seconds to find my bearings. My fingers drift to the buttons on my shirt to refasten them when he knocks my hands away.

"Leave it open."

I swallow and consider arguing, but the likelihood of it doing any good is slim to none. The best thing I can do is focus on the assignments and get the hell out of here.

Using my elbows, I lever myself into a seated position.

"Should we start with English?" I wince at how low and breathless my voice sounds.

"Sure." He shrugs. "You're the one in charge."

I almost snort. We both know that's a lie. Austin is the one who holds all the power. I'm nothing more than a plaything to be used at his discretion.

Now that my heart is no longer racing and the synapses in my brain are back to firing, I fish out the assignment Ms. Pettijohn included in today's bundle before passing it to him.

That's all it takes for the smugness in his eyes to dissolve.

"Have you finished *The Kite Runner* yet?"

His stoic gaze flickers to me. A shield falls over his eyes, making it impossible to guess his thoughts.

When he fails to respond, I ask, "How far are you into the story?"

"A couple chapters. It's boring as fuck."

My mouth falls open. "Really? Once I started, I couldn't put the book down."

"What do you want me to say? I'm just not into it."

I nibble at my lower lip before hesitantly admitting, "I have an idea. Something that might help you."

He lifts a brow in curiosity.

At least, I think that's what it is.

It's tough to tell.

I glance away before forcing out the words. "I thought it might be easier to listen to the book instead of reading it yourself."

The change in his demeanor is immediate. A crack of anger flashes across his face as he snaps, "You don't think I know how to read?"

I quickly shake my head as a thick wave of tension rolls over me and my muscles stiffen. "No, of course not. I just thought it would be easier for you to listen to the story, so you don't have to concentrate on decoding the words."

"Because I'm slow?"

"I don't think you're slow. I think you have a learning disability that makes school more of a challenge. It's nothing to be ashamed of."

"Who said I was ashamed?" he growls, anger growing.

A fine tremble works its way through my body. On the inside, I'm shaking like a leaf. "No one."

He smashes his lips together as his glare turns ferocious.

"It was just an idea," I mumble, only wanting to drop the subject. "I don't know how you'll complete the assignments if you haven't made it at least halfway through the book."

"I suppose you've read it already."

"Yes." Actually, I checked it out from the library and read it a couple years ago.

But I don't add that.

His expression turns pinched as he sneers, "Let me guess, you read it for fun in your spare time."

Unable to hold his gaze, I glance away. "Maybe."

"Then you can fill out the answers for me. See? Guess I'm not such a dipshit after all."

My wide eyes fly to his as I shake my head. "I'm not going to cheat. You need to do the work yourself. I can help if you want, but that's it."

The glower returns. "Fine, have it your way. We'll listen to the stupid book."

I release an unsteady breath and attempt to calm my frazzled nerves. Getting him to agree to this feels like a small victory. In all honesty, I thought he would fight me much harder. Before he can change his mind, I grab my cell from the pocket of my blazer and pull up the audio version before pressing play. We listen to the narration for all of five minutes before Austin scoops up my phone and stops it.

"Why did you do that?"

"The voice is putting me to sleep."

Seriously?

I roll my eyes. "You either need to read the book or listen to it. There aren't any other choices."

"Not true."

When I lift a brow, he says, "I'd prefer you read it to me."

"That wasn't one of the options."

"I don't find your voice boring at all." He cocks his head. "You want to make this work, don't you?"

Of course.

But…

"I can't read the entire book to you." I have zero desire to spend that much time alone with him.

All right, so maybe that's not entirely true.

"Why not?"

"Because…it'll take too long. I've been assigned to tutor you while you're out on suspension. Once you return to school, you won't need me anymore. You can work with your teachers."

When his lips lift into a slow smile, my belly hollows out. Whatever he's going to say next, I won't like.

"Did you really think this was going to end tomorrow?" He shakes his head. "Oh no, sweet girl. We're going to be spending a lot more time together. How else am I going to rub you in Jasper's face?"

I shake my head. "I don't want to be involved—"

"Too fucking late for that. You're up to your eyeballs in it."

When I open my mouth to argue, he says in a silky voice, "I mean, unless you want everyone at school to find out that Pembroke is boning your mother."

His threat makes my heart stutter before pounding painfully into overdrive. "You know I don't."

He flashes a grin. "Yeah, I had a hunch that would be your answer."

When I continue to stare, he points to the book on the bed. "You gonna get to it or what?"

Resentment rises inside me as I glare. "You're forcing me to do something I don't want."

"Yup. Sucks to be powerless, doesn't it?"

I gnash my teeth together before picking up the paperback and opening it.

"What chapter are you on?" I grumble.

"Just start at the beginning."

I suck a deep breath into my lungs before gradually releasing it. This is for the best. Reading to Austin is by far the safest way to spend time together. I won't have to worry about him laying his hands on me.

As I thumb through the pages and find chapter one, he scoots further up the bed until he's able to fully stretch out. His hands get tucked behind his head. The movement makes his biceps swell and the veins running beneath his sun-kissed skin bulge, becoming more prominent.

It's a challenge to not get distracted. After a quick mental slap, I refocus my attention and begin reading.

Just as I turn the page, he pats the space next to him. "Come over here."

I shake my head. "No, I'll—"

"If you don't move your ass, I'll be forced to retrieve you." Even though he doesn't budge from his spot, his deep voice holds the dark promise of a threat. One I know he'll make good on.

Another burst of nerves explodes in my belly as I tentatively scoot backward until we're side by side. We're so close that the sleeve of my arm brushes against his bare skin. With a stack of pillows behind me, I sit ramrod straight as apprehension churns in my gut.

"Lay back. It'll be more comfortable for both of us."

I glance at him, prepared to argue. When he gives his head a slight shake, I snap my mouth shut and do as he insists.

My body turns rigid as I glance at him from the corner of my eye. "May I continue now?"

"Is there someone stopping you?"

When I bare my teeth, his lips quirk and a chuckle rumbles up from his chest.

"You're adorable when you're angry. Like a kitten with claws."

I huff out an aggravated breath before finding my place again and focusing on the words. It only takes a page or two before I'm slipping inside the story and forgetting that Austin has forced me to lie beside him. As I start chapter two, I peek at him to see if he's paying attention and find that he's turned onto his side and has his head propped up on his hand. His concentrated stare leaves me mentally stumbling.

"Don't stop," he says softly. "Keep going."

I clear my throat and refocus. Only this time, I'm unable to get wrapped up in the characters like before. I'm much too aware of Austin's hot gaze fastened to me. It's like a physical caress. I string together syllables to make words, but they don't hold much meaning. Especially when he strokes the pads of his fingers along my bare thigh. When he reaches the hem of my skirt, he shoves the thick material up my leg.

My gaze jerks from the book. "What are you doing?"

"Touching you. It helps me concentrate. We'll just think of you as my very own human fidget toy."

"Are you being serious?"

"One hundred percent." His expression remains solemn as his fingers dance along my inner thigh, forcing the fabric high enough to reveal my cotton panties.

His pupils dilate at the sight of them. When I attempt to smooth down the material, he slaps my fingers away.

"Ow!" I'm more surprised than hurt.

"Leave it."

"But—"

"But what?" His gaze flicks to mine, almost daring me to argue.

"You're making me uncomfortable," I blurt.

"How?"

Nerves tremble in my belly.

Why do I need to explain this to him?

He shifts closer until our bodies can brush. "Are you sure about that? Because you seem to like the way I touch you. In fact, my guess is that I turn you on."

Blood surges to my face.

He's not wrong, damn him.

When I remain silent, unwilling to admit the truth, his gaze stays locked on mine as he reaches out and carefully strokes his finger along the seam of my pussy lips. A thin layer of cotton is all that separates my naked flesh from him.

The harsh intake of my breath gets trapped in my lungs. It takes a herculean effort to remain motionless when all I want to do is squirm beneath him. The blunt tips of his fingers hover over my clit before pressing insistently. His gaze sharpens as my teeth sink into my lower lip to stop the whimper from breaking free.

"You didn't answer the question."

Not once does he let up on the insistent pressure. The way he touches me is exquisite torture. Any moment I'll burst from the pleasure that is attempting to swallow me whole. The sensations he's carefully stoking to life are almost too much for the confines of my skin.

A quick search of my brain comes up empty. "Question?"

His lips quirk as a chuckle escapes from him. "Do I turn you on?"

Oh.

Right.

"I'd prefer not to answer that."

"Hmmm." His expression turns contemplative. "I'll take that as a yes."

"We should get back to work." The way his fingers hover over me, assaulting my senses, makes it impossible to think.

"Remove the panties and you can continue reading."

It takes a moment for his words to sink in.

"What?" My eyes widen as my voice rises with each syllable. "You can't be serious."

"I'm as serious as a heart attack."

My heartbeat thunders against my ribcage. "But—"

He shakes his head. "No buts. It's a simple request. Nothing will happen that you don't want."

That's exactly what I'm afraid of. As much as I'm trying to convince myself that I'm disgusted by his touch and him...nothing could be further from the truth.

When I continue to stare, willing him to back down, he asks, "Are you forgetting what information I have?"

"That's blackmail."

He shrugs. "Never said it wasn't. You can take them off yourself or I'll do it for you. Your choice."

That's not a choice and he damn well knows it.

My mouth feels like the Sahara. There's not a drop of refreshment to be found for miles.

His fingers drift from my center to the slim band encircling my hips. "Guess I'll do it—"

"Fine!" I huff out a frustrated breath and try to keep my nerves under control so they won't break loose before tossing the book to the side.

My fingers tremble as I grip the thin fabric. His attention stays pinned to mine. More than anything, I want to rip my gaze away, but I find myself unable to break the invisible connection that binds us.

I'm caught in the crosshairs of his eyes. All the different flecks of green dance, sucking me into their beauty like a vortex. A heady concoction of fear-laced excitement pumps wildly through my system, making it impossible to get a firm grip on my thoughts.

When he lifts a brow, I force myself to shove the cotton down my thighs until I'm able to kick it away. The thick wool material of my skirt falls over me, shielding my center from his hot gaze.

"Was that so difficult?"

I swallow past the thick lump that has wedged itself in the middle of my throat. The heaviness of his palm settles on the bare skin below the hem. His fingers flex before curving like talons into the supple flesh. I can't help but stare at the place we're now connected. There's such a contrast to our bodies. His skin is a dark, sun-kissed hue while I'm pale. Where I'm soft, he's calloused and hard. As much as my mind wants to reject the notion, there's something infinitely sexy about his large hand wrapped around my bare leg, holding me firmly in place.

"Time's ticking. Shouldn't you continue?"

I jerk back to awareness, gaze snapping to his. It would be impossible to miss the smirk that lifts his lips and the humor that flares in his eyes. He's loving this.

Loving that he's so easily able to knock me off balance.

"Yes." My hand quivers as I pick up the book and delve into chapter three.

After a few paragraphs, his fingers glide to my knee before drifting upward again. The tempo of my voice increases as his hand slips beneath the fabric, sliding over the curve of my hipbone. My breath comes out in a rush as it descends. Back and forth he strums, never moving toward the juncture between my thighs. As much as I attempt to concentrate on the words, it's impossible with the way he caresses my flesh.

His hand stills as he asks a question, seeking clarification.

My brows knit together and I scour my brain for the answer.

How can I be expected to pay attention to the story when he's touching me like this?

My face heats as I flip through a couple of pages. Honestly, I should already know it, but my brain appears to be malfunctioning.

When I resume reading, his fingers glide across my bare skin. Only this time, they drift along my inner thigh, edging dangerously close to my pussy. Even though I keep my attention focused on the page, the heat of his stare burns holes into me. Probing for answers to questions he has yet to pose.

When his hand ventures closer, grazing my bare lips, I shoot from the bed and the book falls to the floor. If that happened any other time, I'd immediately drop down and pick it up before dusting it off to make sure there wasn't any damage.

As I stare warily at him, the paperback is all but forgotten.

"You startle easily." There's a beat of silence as he rises to a seated position, scooting to the side of the bed closest to me. "Hasn't anyone ever touched your pussy before?"

Shaking my head, I retreat a few steps, needing more distance.

Only then do I acknowledge that we could have this entire house between us, and it wouldn't be nearly enough.

"I think we should change that."

"What?" My eyes bulge. "No."

Gaze fastened to him, I back up until my spine hits the far wall and I'm flattened against it.

He crooks a finger as his lips curve. "Come here, Delilah. I won't hurt you. Promise."

When I remain still, he says, "Don't you believe me?"

I chew my lower lip with indecision.

That's the crazy thing. As much as he's pushed me, he hasn't done anything to hurt me.

When he extends his arm in my direction and waits patiently, I find myself stepping forward until I'm close enough for his fingers to nab mine. Once he captures them in a tight grip, he tows me forward until I have no other choice but to step between his thighs.

Inclining his head, he holds my stare. "Wrap your arms around my neck."

Instead of questioning the directive, I do as he says, pressing myself against him. There's a teeny tiny part of me that wishes I were just as bare chested so I could feel the hard lines of his torso. As soon as that sly thought enters my brain, I shove it away.

My heart picks up its tempo when his large hands settle at the back of my thighs. There's a moment of stillness, as if he's allowing me a second or two to get used to the feel of them before they're sliding upward to cup my bare cheeks. His gaze stays fastened to mine as he palms the softness, testing the shape and weight.

A reluctant whimper rises in my throat.

He never stops squeezing.

Pulling and tugging at the flesh.

My eyelids feather shut so I can better focus on how good his hands feel.

"Do you like this?" His voice is several octaves lower than it was just a few minutes ago.

As loath as I am to reveal the truth, it bursts free before I can stop it. "Yes."

A chuckle escapes from him. "You don't have to sound so upset. If you like the way I make you feel, then enjoy it. There's no shame in that."

Easy for him to say.

A heavy silence settles over us as he continues to massage me. It's as if he understands exactly how I want to be touched, which doesn't make the least bit of sense, since not even I know that.

It's disconcerting.

But how can I focus on that when there is so much pleasure reverberating through every cell of my being?

My eyelids spring open when one hand slides to my knee before lifting my leg until it can wrap around his lean hip.

"Relax," he croons when my muscles turn rigid.

That's impossible.

Not when I'm spread open against him.

My arms tighten around his neck as he maneuvers the other leg into the same position on the opposite side. If I thought I was spread wide before, it's nothing compared to now. My knees are bent as I sit astride him, the plaid skirt stretching against my splayed legs as the tips of my breasts brush against his naked chest. The warmth of his breath drifting across my parted lips is nothing short of intoxicating.

It's as if he's woven a spell around me. That's the only thought circling through my brain as my chest rises and falls in quick succession. It feels as if we're both hanging in suspension.

Me waiting for what he'll do next.

Him waiting to see if I'll allow it.

Once I'm settled, both palms return to my backside before dragging me so close that I'm able to feel the thickness of his erection pressing insistently against my core.

His eyelids have fallen to half-mast as he flexes his hips.

A moan escapes as I fight to remain still when everything inside me is in chaos, only wanting to writhe against his rock-hard length. He massages my ass until my muscles gradually lose their rigidity.

In the back of my brain, I realize he's attempting to lull me into a false sense of security. And yet, I can't stop my body from turning pliant under his tender ministrations.

That's the one thing Jasper never was.

Gentle.

He was more like a battering ram I was constantly attempting to escape from.

This encounter couldn't be more different.

He squeezes the rounded curves one last time before stroking upward to my hips and then around to my thighs. The firm pressure of his hands feels so amazing that I barely notice that he's inched my skirt upward until I feel the cool air of the room drift over my bare flesh. My eyelids jerk open, and I find myself staring down at his dark head as his attention remains fastened on my exposed center.

His fingers lock around my thighs as if to hold me firmly in place so I can't escape his gaze. Even though I can't see it, I feel the intensity of it burning into my flesh. Air gets jammed in my chest until I become lightheaded.

"Mmm, you're bare."

He flicks his gaze to mine long enough for me to glimpse the heat that explodes in his eyes before lowering it again. His fingers tighten, biting into the soft flesh as he stretches my lips further apart.

"You're so fucking pretty. So pink and delicate."

My mind empties, unable to believe we're actually having this conversation.

That he's staring at me like...

Like...

He wants to devour me.

One hand loosens from around my thigh as he reaches out and strokes the tip of one blunt finger along my slit. The shock of his touch feels like a lightning strike.

"So damn soft. Just like silk."

He continues to caress me from the bottom to the top, circling my clit before retracing his path. He repeats the maneuver over and over until I want to scream in frustration. My belly dips as desire crashes over me, threatening to drag me to the very bottom of the ocean.

So.

Much.

Pleasure.

It feels like I could easily drown in this chaotic mix of sensations.

Happily so.

Just when I don't think I can take another second of this onslaught, one blunt tip dips inside my heat. A whimper escapes from me as he buries himself deep inside my body. Even though it's only one finger, there's a slight stretch.

"Fuck," he mutters.

As my inner muscles contract around him, his thumb settles over my clit, rubbing soft circles that make my eyes roll back in my head. I'm on the verge of splintering apart when he drags his finger from me and the ache growing within becomes even more ferocious. When my inner muscles clench at nothingness, he drives back inside, and a scream builds in my throat.

It's not a conscious decision to roll my hips, more like an instinct. A need to meet him head on. It doesn't take long for us to fall into a steady rhythm. My core tightens. I'm desperate to see through this orgasm that's building and cresting within. I've touched myself late at night when I couldn't fall asleep, but it never felt anything remotely like this. That pleasure was paper-thin in comparison.

"That's it, sweet girl," he murmurs, voice deep and low. "Come for me."

Just as my head lolls back and my mouth opens, a loud buzzing noise shatters the silence of the room and has me jerking to attention. My eyes pop open as the shrill sound fills the air.

The orgasm that had been within reach dissipates into nothingness as a deep ache fills both my lower belly and core. It's so sharp and painful that it becomes necessary to blink away the tears of frustration that prick my eyes.

When the phone buzzes again, I slip my hand into my wool blazer and wrap my fingers around the slim device before yanking it free and glancing at the screen.

One word flashes across it.

Mom.

Shit.

Shit.

That's when I realize the time. I'm twenty minutes late picking her up from school. It doesn't feel like I've been here for more than a half an hour. Instead, almost ninety minutes have sped past.

Austin slips his finger from my body as I scramble off his lap. My chest heaves as my eyes latch onto his. I expect a full-fledged smirk to be lifting the corners of his lips. Instead, his mouth is set in a grim line. Almost as if he's as irritated with my mother's poor timing as I am.

He reaffirms my suspicions when he growls, "Let her know that she cheated both of us out of your orgasm."

Laughter wells inside my throat.

I can't imagine saying something like that to my mom.

She'd keel over.

Before I can tell him that I will most definitely *not* be apprising her of what I've been up to, Austin lifts the same finger that had just been buried inside my body to his lips before sucking it inside. His eyelids sink as a hum of pleasure vibrates in his broad chest.

My mouth tumbles open as a fresh wave of shock crashes over me. I'm almost ashamed to admit that a burst of arousal detonates deep inside my core before leaking onto my thighs. Pressing them together does nothing to stymie the sharp shaft of need rushing through me.

"Just like I suspected—delicious."

Oh god.

"Now that I've had a taste, I'm going to need more."

When he rises to his feet, my gaze drops to his shorts. It would be impossible not to notice the massive boner that tents the athletic material. My mind tumbles back to yesterday and the way he strutted around naked. Not that I have anything to compare the length of his cock to, but it had seemed longer and thicker than what I imagined.

There'd been a few times when Jasper grabbed my hand and forced me to touch him through his jeans. He didn't feel anywhere near as big as Austin.

I'm jarred from those thoughts when the phone rings again. This time, I don't bother glancing at the screen.

"I have to go."

Afraid he'll find a way to detain me, I fly into the hallway and down the staircase before grabbing the handle and practically ripping the door off its hinges. Once the cool autumn breeze slaps at my over-heated cheeks, I gulp in a big breath and pray it clears my head so I can once again think straight.

It doesn't.

Not even close.

As I start the engine and shift into gear, my gaze is drawn to the front porch. My eyes widen when I find Austin leaning casually against the doorframe with my panties dangling from one finger.

The very same finger that had been buried deep inside the warmth of my body.

This time, the smirk curving his lips is unmistakable.

DELILAH

Dread pools at the bottom of my belly as Mom turns onto the campus of Hawthorne Prep. While I've never felt as if I fit in, I never felt unsafe. Like my wellbeing was threatened by the other students who attend this school.

That's no longer the case.

I glance at my mother, wishing it were possible to confide in her. So much has changed in such a short period of time. And none of it is good. Other than breaking up with my boyfriend, she has no idea what else is going on.

Yesterday after third hour, I turned the corner in the hallway and caught Mom talking with Jasper. His head had been bent as if he was in need of consoling, and even from the distance that separated us, I could see the sympathy filling her blue eyes before she pulled him in for a quick hug.

Why is she so blinded by him?

After a couple months of us being together, I discovered that Jasper had a Jekyll and Hyde personality. He acts one way in front of adults and another with his peers. And if he doesn't like you…

Watch out.

He's a formidable and dangerous foe.

It's doubtful Jasper will ever change.

Why should he?

The guy gets everything he wants.

Well…he's not going to get me.

He can go fuck himself, for all I care.

Instead of stomping past, I'd spun on my heel and stalked off in the opposite direction.

So, no…I don't feel like I can share any of this with her. She wouldn't believe me. Plus, our relationship still feels fractured from my convo with Pembroke. I heard her whispering on the phone last night, pleading with him not to break off their affair. The thought of her begging him for anything makes me sick to my stomach.

Doesn't she realize that she can do better than a married man?

I snap out of those thoughts when the car door slams shut, and she stares at me with a raised brow from the other side of the glass.

With my backpack in hand, I scramble out of the vehicle before reluctantly trailing after her to the sprawling stone building. The closer it looms, the more my belly spasms with nerves. As soon as I step inside the bustling corridor, my muscles tense, and my shoulders hunch as if it's possible to make myself smaller.

Less noticeable.

My steps quicken as I beeline for my locker. The plan is to grab the books I need for my morning classes and then hightail it to my first period. I don't care if I'm the only student in there and have to wait around for twenty minutes. If that verifies my status as a friendless loser, so be it.

As soon as my locker comes into view, I realize that I've made it through the hallway without a barrage of nasty comments hurtled at me.

Is it possible the worst of it has blown over?

Hope tentatively rises that life will soon return to normal.

My happiness is short lived when I catch sight of Sloane and Jasper. She's wrapped around him like a python as he lounges near a locker situated across from mine. Instead of paying attention to the pretty blonde, his gaze is centered on me. A shiver of dread slithers down my spine as I force my feet into movement. The sooner I get my books, the quicker I can hustle to class.

Even though it goes against every instinct, I turn my back to him. My fingers shake as I spin the dial on my locker. It takes three attempts and a curse muttered beneath my breath before I finally hit the numbers correctly. Just as I jerk the metal handle, Sloane sidles up beside me. I give her a sidelong glance as I root around for my books.

"Hey," she says in a syrupy voice. "How's everything going?"

"It's fine," I mutter, wishing she would stop pretending we're friends.

"That's good. I just wanted to check in and make sure you were okay. There's so much gossip flying around the halls. It's all anyone can talk about. You're so brave to be here. If this were happening to me, I'd refuse to show my face."

"There's not much choice in the matter," I say flatly.

"I guess not. Your scholarship probably hinges on attendance or something like that."

"Actually, my classes and grades are important to me. *That's* the reason I'm here."

Her attention flickers to the boy across the hall. I can practically feel his gaze burning holes into the back of my skull.

She steps closer and whispers, "You must miss Jasper."

I almost snort.

Not really.

"If he dumped my ass, I'd be devastated," she adds when I remain silent.

It's so tempting to tell her that I'm the one who broke up with him, but he's already spread around the story that I cheated to save face and make me look bad.

Well, mission accomplished. I've quickly become public enemy number one. Exactly what he wanted.

"I really appreciate your concern, but I'm fine."

"Come on, Delilah, admit it. Wouldn't life be easier if you were together again?"

I shake my head. "Nope. We're better off apart."

At least, I am.

She studies me for a handful of seconds. When the silence begins to stretch, I can't help but shift beneath her penetrating stare as some of her faux friendliness falls away.

"You do realize how lucky you were that Jasper Morgan ever gave you the time of day, right?"

Lucky.

Sure.

A sharp edge enters her voice. "He's hoping you can work through your differences. If I were you, I'd beg his forgiveness." She pauses. "Is there really anything worse than not having a boyfriend senior year?"

Ummm…yeah. There is. And that's being sexually assaulted.

"Strange. You don't have a boyfriend," I point out.

Her smile turns brittle. "Oh, don't worry about me. I have my eye on someone."

Whoever the unlucky guy is should run for his life. Maybe consider changing his name and relocating across the country. When she's through with him, he'll be nothing more than an empty husk of a human being.

When I remain silent, she snaps, "What should I tell him?"

I can't help but throw a glance over my shoulder to where my ex lingers. As soon as our gazes collide, he flicks his tongue between his lips and makes a lewd gesture.

My belly clenches as disgust rushes through me and I abruptly cut off eye contact. "That I'm not interested."

She leans closer before whispering, "Girl to girl, I think you're making a huge mistake."

The mistake was dating him in the first place.

"Then you should go out with him," I say with false brightness. "You two would be perfect for each other."

Her eyes narrow as her expression twists. "Just remember that you could have made this all stop."

Unwilling to engage in this pointless conversation, I grab my books and slam my locker shut before striding away, needing to put as much distance as possible between myself and Jasper. By the time I walk into first hour, my heart is jackhammering a painful tempo. Any second, it'll lurch out of my chest.

Unfortunately, the day only goes downhill from there. At the end of each hour, I linger, asking the teacher a slew of questions until there's less than a minute left before the start of the next class. Then I say a quick goodbye and race through the halls, sliding into my seat with seconds to spare.

When the bell rings for lunch, I head to Ms. Pettijohn's room and ask if there's anything that needs to be graded. If she's surprised by my unexpected presence, she doesn't let on. It's a welcome relief when she sets a thick stack of papers in front of me.

"I'll be in the teacher's lounge if you need anything."

I nod as she strides from the room, leaving the door ajar.

Only now, when I'm alone, does the tension leak from my muscles. I'm almost done with the freshman assignments when movement from the hallway catches the corner of my eye. I automatically glance in that direction and my belly crashes to my toes. Jasper and two teammates loiter outside the classroom door. Once my attention has been secured, his lips lift into a sly grin.

That's all it takes for his silent message to be conveyed.

No matter where I hide, he'll find me.

In this moment, I feel like a hunted animal. Panic floods through me as I jerk out of my chair and back away from the door. Only now do I realize how much he restrained himself when we were together. He'd push and prod, but it never went far enough for him to take what he wanted with brute force.

There's no longer a reason for him to hold back.

"Mr. Morgan, Mr. Wendt, Mr. Andrews, is there something I can help you with?"

Ms. Pettijohn.

Everything inside me wilts. My mind reluctantly tumbles back to yesterday and what almost happened in the library. It's only a matter of time before he finds me alone again.

And when he does, he'll make me pay.

Jasper flashes an easy smile. "Nope, I just needed to stop and grab something from my locker."

"Then you should probably get to it before lunch is over."

His gaze flickers to mine again. "See you around, Delilah."

A sick feeling churns in my belly as he disappears down the hallway with his friends.

The older teacher watches them before her gaze slices to me. I'm almost afraid she'll bring up the situation. It wouldn't surprise me if she's heard all the rumors flying around school. Most of my teachers have been giving me inquisitive glances.

She clears her throat and asks instead, "Were you able to get through all the assignments?"

For the second time in a matter of minutes, relief rushes through me. "Yes, I did."

"Excellent. Like I said before, you've been invaluable this year."

"Thank you."

On wobbly legs, I return to the desk and pick up my books before heading out. In the corridor, I pass Summer. We make brief eye contact before she shifts her attention away. It's so tempting to pull her aside for a conversation, but I have no idea what to say or if she'd even believe the truth.

Her own brother thinks I'm a liar.

As soon as I escape school grounds at two o'clock, the worst of my anxiety drains away. Within minutes of pulling into Austin's circular drive, I find myself on the front porch and ringing the bell. This time, the door immediately swings open. He doesn't leave me waiting.

Of course his chest is bare. At this point, I wouldn't expect anything less from him. The guy apparently has some kind of aversion to wearing clothes.

Not that I'm complaining. He's like a Greek god carved from marble. I'd like nothing more than to pull up a chair and study every hard line.

"Let me guess, you haven't showered yet?"

His lips lift into a slow grin. Even though I steel myself against it, the heated look that flashes in his eyes does funny things to my insides. It's like there's a swarm of angry butterflies attempting to fight their way free by any means necessary.

When he heads to the staircase, I don't bother trying to talk him out of it. We both know it won't do any good. This time, I follow closely behind, my gaze licking over his exposed skin with an unapologetic intensity.

The closer we get to his bedroom, the more excitement rises inside me. Once I cross over the threshold, he saunters to the bathroom as if taking a shower in my presence is a normal, everyday occurrence.

And strangely enough, that's exactly the way it's beginning to feel.

A week ago, I couldn't have imagined any of this playing out.

Much like the previous two days, he doesn't bother closing the door. The difference is that this time, I don't bother looking away. Instead, I perch on the edge of the bed and watch as he strips off the shorts and boxers until he's naked before reaching into the shower stall and turning on the water.

My mouth becomes bone dry as I stare, fascinated by the ripple of muscles and the tightly harnessed power lying beneath his skin. Once he steps inside the glass enclosure, the spell is broken and I force myself to look around the room, trying to find something to occupy my mind.

It doesn't work.

I can't stop thinking about him and shooting curious glances inside the fogged-up space. By the time the water stops running and Austin steps onto the bathmat, I'm a jittery, impatient mess. He grabs a towel from the silver rack before bringing the plush material to his face and drying it.

"I can feel your eyes licking over me," he says, words slightly muffled by the material.

My heart skips a beat at being called out. It's tempting to deny the accusation, but what would be the point?

He knows.

We both do.

When he lowers the towel, his gaze skewers mine. Instead of looking away, I force myself to hold his stare.

One brow lifts as his voice drops, becoming deeper. "Feeling bold, are we?"

I swallow past the thick lump that has lodged itself in the middle of my throat. Honestly, I don't know what's gotten into me this afternoon.

This isn't me.

It's never been me.

I'm a lot meeker.

I'm a look-before-you-leap type of girl. I've had to be. I can't afford to make mistakes the way other people can.

But I don't know...

There's something about Austin and the way he watches me. It's almost as if he wants to eat me up in one tasty gulp.

Then there's the fact that my life has imploded and is careening out of control.

Maybe I'm tired of always playing it safe.

Being overly cautious.

Especially when he makes me feel things I never have before.

He holds out the towel. "Mind helping?"

I stare as the question circles through my brain.

I hear what he's not saying.

It's not a demand. He's giving me a choice.

I could tell him to go to hell, but...

I don't want to.

That's all the encouragement I need to rise to my feet and close the distance between us before taking the plush material from his outstretched hand. A fresh wave of nerves skitters across my skin as he turns, giving me the broad expanse of his back. Without his gaze burning into mine, I can once again breathe.

I swipe the soft cotton across his shoulder blades. It seems like the safest place to start. Transfixed, I watch the beads of moisture disappear from his skin. Austin stands perfectly still as I lose myself in the task. Even through the towel, I feel the heat radiating from him in heavy waves.

Once his shoulders and arms have been thoroughly dried, my movements drift along his spine, swiping over him one vertebra at a time before skimming across the sculpted muscles of his back.

Everything about him is hard and sinewy.

There's nothing soft about the guy.

When the large swath of skin has been finished, I run the towel over his waist as my gaze dips to the taut muscles of his backside. Air gets wedged in my lungs as I sweep the cotton over one cheek and then the other.

God, he's beautiful.

I never thought I'd say that about a guy's ass, but it's one hundred percent the truth. I'm struck with the strange urge to sink my teeth into the muscular flesh.

A groan rumbles up from within his chest. It's like he knows exactly what I'm thinking as I continue to stroke the cotton over him before sinking to my haunches to dry his thighs. A smattering of dark hair covers his legs as I reach his calves and work my way upward.

Before I can rise, he turns in a semi-circle, and it becomes necessary to crane my neck in order to meet his hot gaze. The arousal filling his eyes is almost enough to knock me on my ass.

After a breathless moment, my attention settles on his erection. I'd be lying if I didn't admit that I'm ridiculously curious about the thick length that stands to attention. My face isn't more than a handful of inches away. It wouldn't take much for me to close the space that separates us and swipe my tongue over the bulbous tip. My belly hollows out at the thought.

It takes effort to stop my fingers from shaking as I reach out and run the cloth over his rigid length. His cock grows even longer and thicker beneath my touch. A guttural sound escapes from him. My teeth sink into my lip as I force my gaze away from his boner and glance upward. The tortured expression marring his face is a surprise.

"Am I hurting you?" The question is barely a whisper.

"No, it feels good." His hands are clenched at his sides. *Too good.*

Air escapes from my lungs like a slow leak as I carefully use the cottony material to stroke his balls. I was wrong when I said there wasn't anything soft about him.

Everything about Austin is hard and muscular.

Physically imposing.

I wouldn't have expected to find any vulnerabilities.

My curiosity gets the better of me and I reach out and run my fingers over his sac.

I'm right.

They're soft and pliable.

His breathing picks up tempo as I continue playing with him. Arousal curls in the pit of my belly like a whisp of smoke, intensifying the ache in my core.

I didn't realize it was possible to feel so needy.

There's something about this newly gleaned knowledge that's exhilarating.

And a little bit scary.

Maybe more than a little.

Unable to resist, I trace a path from his sac up the curved length of his cock. Once I reach the crown, I stare at the clear moisture that gathers at the tip. If I didn't know better, I'd think it was water. We're so close that the masculine fragrance of his shower gel along with the musky scent of his arousal teases my senses. It's intoxicating and makes me lose my head.

What other explanation is there for closing the distance and flicking my tongue across the small slit where the wetness has beaded?

A hint of saltiness explodes in my mouth.

He groans when I do it for a second time.

"Delilah…" he growls, voice sounding almost feral.

His fingers stroke along my jaw as I lick him like he's an ice cream cone before deciding to suck the mushroom-shaped crown between my lips.

"*Fuck*," he mutters.

Just when I contemplate drawing him farther inside my mouth, he gently pushes me away. Before I realize what's happening, he hunkers down and scoops me up, crushing me to his naked chest. And then he's stalking into the bedroom and depositing me in the middle of the queen-sized bed. I bounce twice as my gaze stays fastened onto his. There's a ferocious look brewing in his eyes.

I can't tell if he's pissed off or...

Something else entirely.

Or maybe a potent combination of both.

Instead of being frightened by the naked male staring down at me, desire floods my body before settling in my core.

No words are spoken as he looms over me, covering my body with his heavy weight. I'm pinned to the mattress in the most delicious way possible. His hard length is nestled against the apex of my thighs, pressing insistently. It wouldn't take much for him to shove a hand under my skirt and yank my panties to the side. I can't believe I'm even thinking this, but I wouldn't stop him. The sensations rushing through my veins feel much too amazing.

I want more.

His lips hover over mine, ghosting back and forth until I want to scream with the pent-up desire gathering inside me like an impending storm. The second I open my mouth to say his name, his tongue plunges inside, tangling with my own. Sparks of bright color explode inside my brain as our teeth scrape and lips brush. It feels as if I'm being consumed one needy breath at a time.

And yet, I'm still an active participant. He's not being overly rough. There's no need for me to fight him off. For each thrust, I parry. There's a give and take I wasn't expecting from him. It's as if he wants me to explore him in the same way he's acquainting himself with me.

I lose track of how long our lips stay fused before he nibbles at the corners of my mouth, sweeping his velvety softness over mine with achingly deep strokes that make my head spin.

Just when I don't think I'll be able to withstand another second of this sweet torture, his teeth rake over my chin before sinking lower to the column of my throat. I can't help but tilt my head, allowing him greater access to my flesh.

My fingers graze over lips that now feel swollen. I've kissed Jasper many times and it's always been more of an assult. One I had to fight off, afraid it would escalate before careening out of control.

Austin slides lower, his mouth hovering over one taut peak. When the warmth of his breath penetrates the material of my shirt and bra, my back arches as the need to get closer thrums through me.

"Greedy, aren't you?"

Apparently so.

A pleased note weaves its way through his voice as if the realization makes him happy.

When I remain silent, he bites down on one stiff bud. A gasp explodes from my lips as pain bursts inside me. It's quickly chased away by sparks of pleasure.

Unable to lie still, I shift restlessly as he drifts further down my body before reaching the waistband of my skirt. With his gaze locked on mine, he untucks the snowy white material and presses his lips to the trembling flesh. His fingers slip beneath the band as he drags the material down, exposing more of my skin. Sharp teeth scrape against my belly as his hand snakes under the hem of my wool skirt, shoving it upward and baring my panties to his sight.

Today, I'm wearing pale pink ones. They're cotton and certainly nothing fancy but they're the nicest ones I own. He groans at the sight before scooting further down my length until his mouth can hover over the thin fabric. My breath hitches as air gets caught in my lungs.

For just a moment, time stutters to a stop and hangs in suspension.

An inch or two separates us before he closes it, stroking my already sensitive clit with the tip of his nose. Newfound awareness explodes inside me as the room goes still until all I hear is the harsh intake of his breath.

"You smell so damn good."

My belly plunges at least ten stories as the feeling of being in free fall consumes me.

As he slides the tip of his nose across my slit, more sensation ignites within, rocking me to the very core of my being.

Oh.

My.

God.

"Your panties are fucking soaked."

He's right. They're drenched. I'm so turned on it's painful.

I'm a throbby mess.

My teeth sink into my lip to stifle the moan rising in my throat.

With a tug of the elastic band, he yanks it down until the top of my pussy is exposed. A growl escapes from him as he stares intently, eating me up with his eyes. I shift as need spirals through me. If I'm not careful, it'll consume my soul until there's nothing left.

When he presses his lips against my naked flesh, another round of explosions detonates inside me.

"You know what we're going to do now?"

I shake my head as excitement surges throughout me. I'm almost dizzy with anticipation.

"Get to work."

Yes!

Wait…what?

I blink as he shoves away and rises to his feet.

Work?

Now?

Laughter vibrates in his chest as he swings away, sauntering to the dresser before yanking open the first drawer and grabbing a pair of underwear.

I force my gaze to the ceiling and attempt to settle everything that riots beneath the surface of my skin. It's not easy. Blood roars through my veins as a dull ache settles uncomfortably in my core, throbbing a harsh beat.

It's only when he looms over me that I realize he's thrown on black athletic shorts while I'm still sprawled on the mattress, heart thudding painfully in my chest.

"We should probably get to it." He glances at the black sports watch wrapped around his wrist. "Otherwise, we'll run out of time." His gaze spears mine. "Wouldn't want that to happen, would we?"

By the smirk dancing across his lips, he's reveling in my confusion.

Asshole.

How am I supposed to focus on reading when I'm this aroused?

"You know what?" he says, interrupting the chaotic whirl of my thoughts. "Let's make things a little more interesting. Take off the panties."

DELILAH

By the time the alarm buzzes on my phone, I'm a scattered mess of hormones barely able to concentrate. It's disheartening. If I'd thought I was turned on earlier, it's nothing compared to the sensations currently rushing through my body.

I just want to come.

Scratch that.

I want Austin to make me come.

I never imagined a time when I'd beg for sex, but that's the point I've reached. While reading *The Kite Runner*, Austin's hand was shoved up my skirt, playing with me. He'd stroke my lips, slipping his fingers inside my heat before falling into a steady rhythm, only to slide them out and caress my clit. Every time I moaned, my words fading away, he'd give the top of my pussy a little slap and tell me to keep reading.

It was torture.

Exquisite torture, but torture nonetheless.

Each time I felt like I was on the verge of tumbling over the edge into oblivion, he'd yank me back from the precipice. The orgasm would slowly melt away, leaving a profound ache in its place. And then he'd begin all over again, carefully stoking the flames of my desire until I wanted to scream.

Only now do I realize that I was wrong about Austin.

He's just as savage as Jasper.

Instead of inflicting pain, his punishments leave me aching and desperate for more.

If his goal is to bring me to my knees, it's only a matter of time before he accomplishes it.

He pops a brow when I set the book on the bed.

"Time's up already?" he asks. "That went fast."

Too fast.

Barely does it feel like we've begun. Although, I was more focused on what he was doing than the story I was telling.

"Can't your mother find a different way home? Maybe Pembroke? They could probably sneak in a quickie if they really wanted to."

And here I didn't think it was possible for anything to dampen my arousal.

Turns out I was wrong.

I shoot him a scowl before sliding off the side of the bed and rising to my feet. The sooner I get away from him, the easier it'll be to clear my head.

And kick myself for allowing everything to spin so far out of control.

"What? It's true," he says with a chuckle.

"I don't want to talk about it," I grumble.

Thankfully, Austin will be back in school tomorrow and there won't be a need for afternoon tutoring sessions at his house. I wait for a wave of relief to crash over me.

It doesn't happen. If I'm being honest, there's a fair amount of disappointment lurking within.

It's a troublesome realization. I need to get out of here before I totally lose my mind.

With my backpack in hand, I head for the door. "I'll see you at school tomorrow."

"Actually, you'll see me before then. I'm picking you up in the morning."

My feet grind to a halt as I turn and stare, thrown off by the comment. "What?"

With his hands folded behind his head, he lays stretched out on the mattress as if he doesn't have a care in the world.

"I'm pretty sure you heard me the first time."

I shake my head. "No, I'll grab a ride with—"

"It's not up for discussion," he says. "I want to see Jasper's face when we arrive together."

My heart sinks like a heavy stone. It's not like I deluded myself into believing there was anything real between us, but…

I guess for a moment or two, I forgot that this is nothing more than a game of revenge. He wants to make Jasper pay.

And maybe he wants to make me pay, too.

I hate myself for the disappointment that wells inside me.

The words escape before I can stop them. "Is what happened really worth going to war over? Wouldn't it be better to drop the entire thing and move on?"

One second, he's lounging on the bed, the next he's on his feet and stalking toward me with anger blazing from his eyes. Gone is all the softness that had been filling them when I'd been reading to him.

"No. That guy has fucked with me for the last time. I don't give a shit if I get kicked out of Hawthorne Prep. As long as I take him down with me, that's all that matters."

My tongue darts out to dampen my lips. "Don't you see that it's not worth it? Jasper Morgan isn't worth it. You're giving him way too much power."

When he prowls closer, I retreat, wanting to keep as much distance between us as possible. It's almost a surprise when my spine hits the far wall. He eats up the space until he can cage me in with his muscular body, looming so close that it becomes impossible to see anything but him. It's as if my world shrinks down until it can only encompass Austin. Even when he steps away, I'm afraid that won't change.

"It's worth it to me."

The way his warm breath wafts across my parted lips shouldn't be so intoxicating. And it certainly shouldn't weaken my knees or have me wanting to lean forward in search of more.

"I'm going to rub you in his face every chance I get," he growls.

The sensations rampaging through me shatter into a million broken pieces.

Revenge.

Austin doesn't want me. He wants vengeance. I'm just the instrument he'll use to achieve it.

I flatten against the wall, fighting for breathing room. "I'm not interested in being your pawn."

He steals the space between us as his lips brush over mine. "Everything that once belonged to Jasper will be mine. First, I'll take his girl, and then his position on the team. You know what the best thing about it is?" He searches my eyes. "There's not a damn thing he can do about it."

Some battles are worth fighting.

But Jasper isn't one of them.

"Please, don't do this. Just let it go."

The chuckle that escapes from him is deep and dark and swirls around me before he nips my lower lip with sharp teeth and tugs the plump flesh. Pain flares before a burst of arousal races after it. Need arrows straight to my core and explodes.

As tempting as it is to shove him away, a bigger part of me wants to drag him closer until I can feel his lips coasting over mine.

I don't understand what he's doing to me.

How can I want him so much when this is nothing more than a game?

DELILAH

$\mathcal{M}$om frowns as she peeks out the front window. "Why is that Hawthorne boy picking you up for school? I thought we agreed that you would stay away from him."

The curtain slips back into place as she swivels around to face me. Her hands settle at her hips as she glares. I was really hoping to sneak out the door before she figured out who I was catching a ride with.

I should have known better.

When I try to slink past, she steps in front of me, blocking my escape.

It's almost impossible to believe that this is what our relationship has deteriorated to. There was a time when she trusted me to make good decisions.

Those days are now long gone.

When I finally meet her gaze, it's filled with suspicion. As if I'm the one who has been lying and sneaking around.

Doesn't she see that her affair has created this wedge between us?

One I have no idea how to repair.

When I remain silent, her voice grows sharp. "I'd like an answer. Why is that boy picking you up for school?"

"Because I'm tutoring him."

She purses her lips and continues to glower. "I thought that ended yesterday."

"It was supposed to." The lie escapes before I can think better of it. "But since it worked out so well, Ms. Pettijohn asked if I would continue working with him."

Her brow furrows as she folds her arms against her chest. "Why didn't you tell her no?"

I clear my throat and glance away. "I thought the tutoring would look good on my scholarship applications."

Her lips grow even thinner as she grudgingly admits, "I suppose that's true."

When she doesn't say anything more, I hasten my pace toward the door.

I make it two steps before she blurts, "I just don't want you getting tangled up with the wrong people. Not when you're so close to making your dreams come true."

Tangled up with the wrong people?

I almost snort.

"I ran into Jasper yesterday," she continues.

When I swing around, she inches closer before reaching out to comb her fingers through my hair in a way that's reminiscent of my childhood.

"He's so hurt by your breakup. He just wants the chance to talk with you, maybe work everything out."

Unable to stop myself, I roll my eyes.

Hard.

"He's lying to you."

Her mouth falls open. "Why would you say something like that? You should have seen him. He was practically in tears."

Tears my ass.

"Because it's the truth. You've never been able to see past the façade Jasper projects. A handsome, rich, popular football player whose father is mayor of this town. He's not nice, Mom. And he's certainly not a good person. You need to trust me on that."

Her eyes are so wide, they're in imminent danger of falling out of her head. "I really don't know what's gotten into you lately. You're not the same sweet girl you once were and it's disheartening."

My face scrunches, contorting with shock. "Are you being serious?"

"I certainly am. You've been so different lately. And I think it has everything to do with that boy. He's been a problem since he arrived. If you think I'm going to sit idly by and allow you to get involved with that low life, you're mistaken. You might be eighteen years old, but you still live under my roof, young lady. And you'll follow my rules. You're done with Austin Hawthorne."

It's so tempting to fire back with her affair, but I keep my lips clamped shut so I won't say something hurtful we'll both end up regretting. It's only when I swing around and head to the door that I realize that I'm shaking from head to toe.

"Delilah! We're not done discussing this."

She's wrong about that.

It takes every ounce of self-restraint not to slam the door. Anger and resentment churn through me, building like a storm, as I stalk to the G-Wagon idling in the drive and drop onto the seat.

Austin throws a questioning glance in my direction as I stare straight ahead. My teeth are clenched so tightly that it feels like they'll shatter into a million pieces.

"Rough morning?"

"Yup." I pop the P at the end but refuse to say anything more. I'm trapped between warring factions, unable to do anything about it.

He pulls out of the drive. "Sorry to hear that."

"Are you?" A snort escapes before I flick my gaze in his direction. "Because you're part of the problem."

"How so?"

Seriously?

"For one, the only reason we're together is because you're using me to get back at my ex. And two, Jasper has been filling my mother's head with a bunch of bullshit and now she's pissed off and concerned about me spending time with you."

"Bad influence, huh?" he says with a smirk as if he's proud of the designation.

It's tempting to smack him.

"She's afraid you'll corrupt me."

"Can't blame her for that. I've certainly been doing my best."

I shoot him a sour look.

A smile trembles around the corners of his lips as his palm drops onto my upper thigh. Even though his grip isn't tight, it feels like my bare skin is being singed alive. It wouldn't surprise me to find a permanent tattoo of his handprint I'll sport for the rest of my life. My anger isn't enough to douse the ember of desire that flares to life in my core with that one innocuous touch.

It's ridiculous.

If there were a way to stomp it out, I'd do it in a heartbeat. I don't want to feel this way about Austin. Not when this isn't anything more than a game.

"Maybe I should introduce myself so she can see that I'm not as bad as she thinks."

My pulse trips and it takes a moment to find my voice. "Why would you even bother? You don't actually give a shit what happens to me."

His gaze stays pinned to the ribbon of country road as we speed toward school. When his jaw locks, the muscle in his cheek tics a mad rhythm. My heartbeat pounds as I wait for him to deny the accusation.

Oh god, why would I want that?

Am I a total glutton for punishment?

Even though alternative rock plays from the stereo and filters through the cabin, the silence that blankets us is deafening.

His fingers tighten, biting into the soft flesh, marking me in a way that can never be undone.

"Is that what you want, Delilah?" he asks softly. "For me to care?"

The question circles viciously in my brain.

I don't know, and that's part of the problem. Without everything that sits between us, the answer would be much clearer.

When I remain silent, he growls, "Don't forget that this is a game you started."

How are we back to this again?

"It's not," I explode. This argument is a constant circle, and I don't know why I bother. He will never believe me. "I had nothing to do with it."

"He just oh-so-conveniently found out after I shared that with you in private, huh?" He glares, skewering me straight through the heart with that one angry look. "What else did you tell him?"

I shake my head. "Nothing. I never said a word about our conversation. Why would I?"

"How should I know? Maybe you get off on humiliating people the same way he does."

My mouth dries. "You know that's not true."

"Do I?" There's a pause. "How would I know that?"

My tongue darts out to moisten dry lips. "Because we weren't together. I broke up with him the day after you picked me up along the side of the road."

His lips lift into a snarl. "Stop lying. You were together the week after that."

My shoulders slump under the heavy weight of his accusation.

Jasper was so careful to plan it all out.

More like diabolical.

Only in hindsight do I understand that. He asked me to keep our breakup a secret so it would look like I was a willing participant in his plans. And now there's nothing I can do or say to prove my innocence.

All I have is my word, and that's nowhere near good enough.

"I don't know how he found out about the dyslexia, but it wasn't from me." My hand settles on my chest. "I would never do something like that."

Barely am I aware of passing through the iron gates and onto the carefully manicured property. Trees dot the landscape along with rolling hills, but none of it registers. My gaze stays pinned to Austin's profile as the winding road opens up to the parking lot. He pulls into a space near the back.

It's only when he shifts the SUV into park that he swivels, giving me his full attention. The anger simmering in his expression leaves me wincing as my spine presses into the door handle.

"How the hell would I know what you'd do?"

Air leaks painfully from my lungs. "I'm not like these people." I gulp. "You have to realize that."

With a cock of his head, he continues to stare. There's not an ounce of softness to be found. "That's funny, because I really didn't think so either." He reaches out, stroking a finger along the curve of my jaw. His voice becomes as wintry as his eyes. "Turns out I was wrong."

I jerk away from his touch as if scalded before wrapping my shaking fingers around the door handle and yanking it open. Autumn air wafts over my cheeks, but it does nothing to cool them. With my backpack clutched at my chest, I stalk through the parking lot. It only takes Austin a handful of steps to reach my side. He plucks the bag from my hands before slinging one brawny arm around my shoulders and hauling me close.

His warm breath drifts over the outer shell of my ear. "Don't be angry. You can't blame me for not trusting you. For all I know, you're still involved with him and this is all a game to humiliate me."

When I stutter to a halt, he does the same.

"I'm not with Jasper," I whisper. "I don't want anything to do with him."

For a long, painful heartbeat, he studies me as if he's able to discern the truth for himself.

"Only time will tell, won't it?"

Tears prick the backs of my eyes. I've never felt more helpless. "I suppose so."

It's only seven thirty in the morning and I'm already exhausted. What I should have realized sooner is that Austin will never believe me. Or fully trust me. Doubts will always linger in the back of his mind.

If he insists on moving forward with this charade, I need to protect myself against him, because even now, I can feel myself falling.

As these thoughts circle viciously through my head, movement from the corner of my eye catches my attention and I turn to see Summer and Kingsley exiting his Mustang.

The moment her gaze lands on me, her brows snap together. The lighthearted smile dancing around her lips dissolves, only to be replaced with a scowl.

"Austin!"

I wince as her snapped-out voice travels across the parking lot and people turn to stare.

He glances in her direction before lifting a hand in acknowledgment.

"Does your sister know what you're up to?"

From her surprised reaction, my guess is that she doesn't.

"Nope. And I'd like to keep it that way. Summer's been through enough already. She doesn't need to spend any more time worrying about me."

I nibble at my lower lip as my belly twists into a painful knot.

Great.

More lies and deception.

How has this become my life?

"Wait up!" she calls out again, voice growing closer.

Even though we stop near the sidewalk, I can tell by the way Austin's muscles have tightened that he's reluctant to engage in conversation. It doesn't take Summer long to catch up. Kingsley isn't far behind. What I've noticed is that he's never far from her. Almost as if he can't bear the thought of her out of his sight for long.

It's a far cry from how their relationship started out the first day of school. And that's with his fingers wrapped around her neck as he shoved her against the lockers in the hallway.

It put the two boys instantly at odds.

She shoots me a glare before turning her attention to her brother. "Can I talk to you for a sec?"

"Sure."

When he doesn't budge, her lips thin, wilting at the corners. "In private."

Austin shakes his head and glances toward the school. "Can we do this another time? I need to head inside and speak with a couple of teachers."

"I guess so," she mutters, shooting me another frown.

"I'll catch you later, okay?"

In that moment of silent connection, something passes between them, and her expression turns to one of concern as she nibbles her lower lip before glancing at her boyfriend. He shrugs and wraps an arm around her shoulders as we all head inside the stone building.

Just as my heels strike the marble of the corridor, Austin whispers, "Showtime."

That one word sends my belly plunging.

All I wanted to do is make it through this day unscathed.

No longer am I sure that's possible.

Within seconds of us entering the congested hallway, heads swivel in our direction before doing a double take. I've never felt more on display. By the time we reach my locker, I can practically feel everyone's eyes crawling over me as the whispers and comments drone around us.

I stifle the urge to run and hide.

When the hair at the nape of my neck prickles with unease, I glance around and find Jasper glaring at us. The hostility filling his expression is enough to make my pulse trip.

Before I realize what's happening, my spine is pressed against the lockers and Austin's lips have crashed onto mine. When I don't immediately open, he nips my lower lip. Surprised, a gasp escapes from me and his tongue delves inside my mouth to tangle with my own.

My palms slip between us, settling on the hard planes of his chest. Even through the fabric of his button-down shirt, I can feel the chiseled lines and the heat that emanates from him. In the beginning, my intention had been to push him away, but the longer his mouth slants across mine, the more everything fades to the background, and I forget this is nothing more than a meaningless display solely meant for Jasper's benefit.

Just as my fingers curl into the starched material and I lose myself in the kiss, he's ripped away. My eyes widen when I find the two boys standing toe to toe. Tension vibrates in the air as people stop, craning their necks, not wanting to miss the fight that is seconds away from breaking out.

"What the fuck do you think you're doing?" my ex growls before shoving Austin in the chest and knocking him back a step. "Keep your grubby hands off what's mine."

I wince, afraid Austin will retaliate and find himself in even hotter water with Pembroke. And this time, there won't be anything I can do to save him. I take a step forward, ready to intervene if necessary. As mixed as my feelings are about Austin, I don't want to see him get expelled.

He doesn't deserve it.

He doesn't deserve any of this.

His eyes sharpen, the smirk never faltering from his face. "She isn't yours, Morgan. She belongs to me now." He flicks a hard stare my way, almost daring me to argue. I know exactly what will happen if I do. The silent promise is there, lurking in his eyes. "Isn't that right, Delilah?"

A growl vibrates from Jasper's chest as he glares. Hatred and jealousy swirl through his stormy gray depths. The intensity is almost enough to have me shrinking away. Instead of giving into the urge, I straighten my shoulders and hitch my chin. "Yes."

"Tell him who owns you," Austin says softly.

I swallow down my growing nausea, hating him for making me say it in front of everyone. "You do."

"Louder for the people in the back."

Heat floods my face. "I belong to you."

"I always knew you were nothing more than a fucking whore!" Jasper bares his teeth before swiveling toward me and leaping forward.

A scream rises in my throat as Austin slides in front of me, blocking the other boy.

After pushing him back a step, he wags a finger. "Ah, ah, ah. No touching my property, Morgan. Unlike you, I don't like to share my toys."

And here I thought it couldn't possibly get worse.

Hot licks of humiliation sting my cheeks.

I glance at the people pressing in on us, hanging on every word. By the end of first hour, it'll spread like wildfire, and the entire student population will have heard some twisted version of what happened this morning.

"You think this is over?" Jasper snarls. "Not by a long shot. You're messing with the wrong fucking guy."

"Nah. It's over. I won. She's mine." He leans in before whispering something that I can't quite make out.

Fury flashes in Jasper's eyes as he grips Austin by his shirtfront and hauls him close. Instead of fighting back, the dark-haired boy grins.

"Go ahead, hit me."

Jasper smashes his lips together as he vibrates with impotent rage.

"Let him go, Morgan," Kingsley snaps, shoving his way through the press of bodies.

Jasper's gaze never deviates from Austin. His face has turned a mottled red hue as his chest rises and falls in quick succession. I've witnessed my ex lose his temper lots of times but have never seen him pushed this close to the edge.

"*Now.*"

A murderous haze fills Jasper's eyes as he shoves Austin away.

"Do yourself a favor and leave." Kingsley stares him down, daring him to argue.

My ex remains still, hands clenching at his sides as if he's unsure what to do.

My breath stalls, wondering if he'll lose the internal battle and throw a punch.

Summer lays a hand on her brother's shoulder before talking to him in a low voice. Austin's gaze stays riveted to the other boy.

"You think you can fuck with me, Hawthorne?" He shakes his head. "When I'm done with you, you'll wish you never set foot in this town."

"Too late for that. Got anything else?"

Jasper's hard-edged gaze slices to me. "I'll be seeing you around, Delilah."

A shiver slithers down my spine as he stalks away. Even though he didn't threaten me, that's exactly how his growled-out words come across.

As a promise of retribution.

Now that Jasper has disappeared down the hallway, the tension vibrating in the air dissipates and the crowd gradually disperses.

I release a shaky breath, relieved they didn't come to blows.

Since Summer is still talking with Austin, now would be a perfect time to grab my books from my locker and scurry to class. I take one step before her cool gaze skewers me in place. Dread pools in my belly as she eats up the distance between us and gets in my face.

"I don't know what kind of game you're playing, but it needs to stop," she growls. "Haven't you caused enough damage already? Are you actually trying to get him expelled from school?"

My eyes widen.

Is that what she really thinks?

Thick emotion gathers in my throat.

"Summer," Austin says, voice softening, "it's not—"

With a scowl, she wheels toward him. "Yeah, it is. What are you even doing with her? After the shit she pulled with Jasper, how can you stand the sight of this girl?"

I shake my head. "That's not…"

My voice dies as her expression turns ferocious.

From the moment the twins arrived at Hawthorne Prep, it was obvious they shared a close relationship, and that Summer was protective of him. I've witnessed her go after other people on his behalf.

What I never expected was her wrath to be turned on me.

Before she can say anything else, Kingsley drops down and wraps his arms around her thighs before hoisting her off the floor and over his shoulder. With a shriek, she dangles upside down. Her fists pound against his back as he carts her through the hall. My eyes widen when he gives her ass a good smack. I can't imagine anyone other than Kingsley manhandling her and living to tell the tale.

Now that the crowd has thinned, I stalk to my locker before spinning the dial and pulling out my books. Everything that just happened replays through my brain and a fresh wave of mortification crashes over me.

Slamming the door shut, I spin around, ready to take off when I smash into a hard chest. Austin's fingers wrap around my biceps to hold me in place as I glare.

"Was it really necessary to embarrass me in front of everyone?"

Instead of releasing me, I'm hauled closer. "What's wrong? Don't like it when the tables are turned? Sucks to be humiliated in front of the school, doesn't it? Consider yourself lucky that it was a small group and not a couple hundred people."

The heavy weight of his recriminations has my shoulders collapsing. If I honestly thought apologizing again would do any good, I'd drop to my knees and beg his forgiveness.

But we both know it won't.

A gasp escapes from my lips when he drags me to a small alcove tucked between two classrooms before pressing my back against the wall. He's close enough for me to feel the thickness of his erection digging into my lower abdomen.

"What's the matter, Delilah? Nothing to say?"

I tilt my neck until our gazes can fasten and find stormy green depths staring back at me. Was it only a few weeks ago when he'd watch me with lust filling his eyes?

Now, there's nothing but distrust and hate.

Maybe the lust is still there, but it's buried beneath all the other emotions jockeying for position.

"No."

"Good. It's just like I told Jasper—you belong to me, and I'll do whatever I want with you."

His words slice through my beating heart with the precision of a scalpel. It's almost unbelievable how much pain they're capable of inflicting.

"Everyone—*especially your ex*—needs to understand who owns you."

"It will never be you," I whisper.

A cruel smile flashes across his handsome face as he presses into me. Just when I think he'll brush his lips across mine, he angles his head until his mouth can hover at my ear. "Know what I think? That you want to be owned. But only by me. Are you really going to tell me that you don't enjoy my hands on you?" There's a pause. "Come on, sweet girl, tell me the truth. Because you were falling to pieces less than twenty-four hours ago. Every time I slid my finger from your body, your pussy clenched, trying to draw me back inside all that wet warmth."

Even though I don't want his seductive words to set me on fire, that's exactly what they do. I clench my thighs in a feeble attempt to stifle my growing arousal.

It doesn't do a damn bit of good.

As much as I hate admitting the truth, Austin's right. I want to belong to him. The way he touches my body makes me forget all the reasons why it's a disastrous idea.

When his warm breath drifts across my ear and neck, shivers explode across my flesh.

"Are you going to admit it?"

What would be the point?

Deep down, we both know the truth.

I try one last time to reason with him before it's too late and the situation careens any further out of control. "You need to let this go before you get kicked out of school."

"How can I do that when we've only just begun?"

Even though his response doesn't surprise me, my heart sinks.

Before anything else can be said, the bell signaling the start of first hour rings throughout the halls. Even though I can't see around him, I hear people's rushed footsteps scurrying past us.

His grip never relents.

"Austin…" My voice trails off when his lips settle over my pulse.

"If you're not with Jasper, then it shouldn't matter what happens to him…right?"

I freeze.

When I remain silent, one hand snakes between us before settling over my breast.

"Give me your words. I want an answer."

He squeezes the soft flesh before flexing his palm. A sigh is on the verge of escaping from me when his fingers wrap around the hardened tip of my nipple, giving it a pinch.

"We're not together," I gasp.

His eyes continue to study mine, picking through all the bits and pieces of information. "Are you sure about that?"

He tweaks the little bud.

"Yes!"

Releasing the tip, his hand drifts down my ribcage before sliding beneath my skirt. His fingers strum my bare thigh, moving dangerously close to the edge of my panties.

My breath catches as my eyes widen. Before I can protest, one finger strokes across the seam of my lips.

His eyes darken as he smirks. "Already nice and wet, huh? That didn't take long. I'm beginning to think your ex didn't understand you at all. What he needed to do was stroke your petals softly and you'd open like a flower. The problem with Jasper is that he thinks everything needs to be taken with force. Between you and me, I'm pretty sure he enjoys it."

The gentle pressure never lets up. I can't stop my eyelids from falling to half-mast as arousal explodes in my core. It doesn't matter if we're standing in the middle of an empty hallway and anyone could stumble upon us.

All that matters is—

"What the hell are you doing, Hawthorne?"

Irritation flashes in Austin's eyes as his hands fall away and he swings around.

"Nothing that concerns you. So, feel free to move it along."

Duke steps to the side until he's able to meet my gaze. His tone softens. "Delilah? Are you all right?"

I comb my fingers through my hair before slipping past the other boy. "I'm fine."

Eyes narrowed, Duke gives me a quick once over as if checking for bodily injury before glaring at Austin. "Come on, I'll walk you to class."

A shudder gallops down my spine. I can practically feel Austin's gaze burning holes into my back. It takes every ounce of self-restraint not to throw a glance over my shoulder.

"Thank you."

When I reach Duke's side, he wraps a muscular arm around my shoulder and propels me forward, leaving the other boy to stand alone in the alcove.

A shaky burst of air escapes from my lips.

The day can only go up from here, right?

DELILAH

As I round the corner of the hallway after fourth hour, my pace slows when I catch sight of Austin leaning casually against my locker, staring down at his phone. It's enough to make my belly hollow out. I don't understand what it is about him that affects me this way.

What I do know is that I felt this attraction from the first moment I saw him in the office and showed him around school. His gaze never deviated from mine as he stood too close, crowding into my personal space. After that, I did my best to avoid him since I had a boyfriend, but it was never enough to evict him from my mind.

I have no idea if anything can do that.

Even though I should hate him for what he's doing, I don't.

I understand his anger and why it's directed full force at me.

For a handful of seconds, I allow my gaze to rove over him while he's unaware of my presence. Even though his posture is relaxed, the tightly harnessed power is there, simmering beneath the surface, ready to break loose. And that notion turns me on and sets my blood on fire.

A tiny voice in the back of my head prods me to close the distance.

The pull is magnetic, and I'm powerless to resist the lure of him. Even when I understand that it's bad for me.

After a handful of seconds, he straightens, turning as if he's able to feel the penetrating intensity of my stare the same way I'm aware of his. It's just another strange connection we have when there should be nothing. Our gazes collide and electricity sizzles through my veins as my pulse kicks up a notch, thumping an insistent beat.

Instead of giving into the attraction thrumming through my veins, I stay rooted in place, needing to prove to him as well as myself that he doesn't have total control over me. When I don't budge, one side of his mouth hitches as if he knows exactly what thoughts are circling through my head before he eats up the distance between us with long-legged strides.

The closer he gets, the harder it becomes to breathe. His gaze stays fixated on mine, and I find myself trapped within his green depths.

Drowning helplessly in them.

Is there a more frightening feeling than being rendered completely incapable of saving yourself from certain death?

That's exactly the way it is with Austin.

Every time we're together.

"Ready for lunch?"

The haze clouding my brain gradually clears. "In the caf?"

It's the last place I want to go.

All those people…

They're still buzzing about what happened this morning. Austin and Jasper together in the same space will only add to it.

"Where else would we go?" There's a pause before his voice dips. "How else can I rub you in Jasper's face if we're not sitting across from him?"

The deep scrape of his words is enough to turn my blood cold. Nerves burst to life inside me. "Can't we go somewhere else?"

I'm tired of pretending that I don't hear the whispered comments or see the sly glances aimed in our direction. It's exhausting. All I want to do is hide and regroup.

When he remains silent, unmoved, I force myself to whisper, "Please."

Austin is so intent on pushing Jasper over the edge. After the confrontation this morning, it wouldn't take much. I'm afraid his plan will backfire, and Austin will be the one to bear the brunt of the punishment.

Which will mean expulsion.

I know how it works around here. The cards are neatly stacked against him. They have been from the very beginning. Contrary to what Jasper and his father proclaimed at the fundraising event, we are not one big happy family.

These people want the Hawthornes gone. And they'll seize upon the smallest infractions and flimsiest of excuses to accomplish their agenda.

His eyes darken as he reaches out and drags a finger across my lower lip. Back and forth he strums. "You know how much I love that word when it falls from your lips."

Arousal curls like a whisp of smoke in the pit of my belly.

"Can you offer something even more tempting than parading you around in front of your ex? If so, I'm all ears."

Nerves detonate in my core as my mouth turns cottony. "What is it that you want?"

The smile that lifts his lips moves at a glacial pace. "Oh, I think you can guess."

The ravenous look in his eyes is all the answer I need. Even if it weren't written across his expression so clearly, I'd still know. He's been nothing but upfront about what he wants and why.

It's what pricks at me the most.

It's also a stark reminder that this is nothing more than revenge.

A way to make me pay.

It doesn't mean anything.

More importantly, *I* don't mean anything.

When he steps closer, I lift my chin to hold his penetrating gaze.

"Just know that I'm hungry and need to eat. It can be you or lunch. The choice is yours."

My breath catches at his blunt words and my mind tumbles back to yesterday and what it felt like to have him between my thighs. That's all it takes for liquid heat to flood my panties.

He strokes a finger over my lip again. "What's your decision?"

It takes effort to shake off the thick fog as it slyly wraps around me. This is exactly what Austin's dominating presence does. It wouldn't take much to forget my own name.

One look, one touch and I'm putty in his large hands.

"Ms. Pettijohn's room? It'll be empty at this time of the day. She always eats in the teacher's lounge."

He lifts a brow. "You sure about that? I don't want to be interrupted when I'm dining on you."

My belly plummets as that mental image flashes unwantedly through my brain.

"Yes," I squeak.

His eyes glint as a smile simmers across his lips. "Then by all means, lead the way."

It only takes a few minutes to weave through the hallway and find her classroom. My fingers tighten around the knob before turning it. When the door opens easily, I peek my head inside and find the room empty.

I jolt when his hands slide around me and he growls near my ear, "Better hurry up, sweet girl. I'm famished." He cups my breasts through the fabric, palming the softness.

Even though it's tempting to close my eyes and enjoy his touch, I slip from his embrace before backing into the sun-filled space. He follows me in, closing the door quietly behind him.

My eyes widen when he clicks the lock. "What if she returns before the end of lunch?"

"If we leave it open, my guess is that she'll catch quite the eyeful." He jerks a thumb toward the narrow window that allows people in the hallway to glimpse inside the room. "We'll need to sit in the corner where she—or anyone else walking by—can't see us. How embarrassing would it be to get caught having your pussy eaten?"

I gulp.

Embarrassing doesn't begin to describe what it would be.

When he stalks closer, I retreat, trying to keep the same amount of distance between us.

He smirks. "Do you want me to chase you, Delilah? Because I'd be more than happy to oblige. I like the hunt. There's something immensely satisfying about capturing your prey."

Oh god.

My muscles tighten and a fine tremble racks my body. I force myself to stand still as he saunters closer. Whether it's from fear or excitement, I have no idea.

All right, that's a lie.

I know *exactly* what the cause is.

Excitement thrums wildly through my blood, turning my insides into a giddy mess.

When no more than a foot separates us, he reaches out and strokes a finger along the curve of my jaw. The touch is light and airy. Everything Austin is not. He caresses my lower lip before pressing the blunt tip inside my mouth.

It's not much.

Just an inch or so.

Enough to taste the slight saltiness of his skin.

When my tongue strokes over it, his eyes darken, turning into liquid pools of green.

"I can't stop thinking about the way you sucked my cock yesterday."

When he presses further inside my mouth, I draw him in deeper. It's not something I consciously think about, more a reflex.

"Fuck," he growls. "Was that your first time?"

I give my head a slight nod.

"I can't believe you never did anything with Jasper."

When he finally pulls his finger free, a strange sense of loss fills me.

"I wanted to wait, and in the beginning, he was fine with that. He made a big deal about my virginity and how he would be the first one to have me. It's like he both loved and hated the idea that I'd never had sex before."

His hands wrap around my hips before lifting me onto the closest desk and sliding on the chair. He turns my body until I'm able to stare down at him. His gaze stays locked on mine as he forces my legs apart. Only then does he stroke his fingertips along my calves. The drift of his hands lulls me into a contented place, and I stop worrying about how easily it would be to get caught.

"How long were you together?"

The way he caresses my skin drives me to distraction and I'm barely able to concentrate on the words coming out of his mouth.

What did he ask?

Oh, right.

"Ummm…six months."

"Why'd you date him in the first place?" Each pass brings him closer to the apex of my thighs. Barely has he touched me and I'm already a puddle of need.

"I…" My voice trails off as arousal ignites in my core. "I thought he was different."

His movements still. "Let me get this straight. He didn't strike you as an asshole right off the bat? Shocker."

My lips quirk at the corners. "I didn't really know him back then. I'd only seen him around. He was a popular football player, and I thought he was nice looking. I'd crushed hard on him freshman and sophomore year. So, when he finally noticed me, it seemed like a dream come true. My mom was ecstatic about it." I bite my lip before admitting, "It hasn't been easy for her since Dad died. I've always tried to do what was expected. I knew how badly she wanted me to fit in with the students at HP, and dating Jasper solidified that."

He listens intently before leaning forward and pressing his lips to my calf.

"And that's what you wanted?" he asks softly. "To fit in with all these self-absorbed pricks?"

Eyes never faltering from mine, his lips wander farther up my leg before he nips at the delicate flesh behind my knee. Air gets wedged at the back of my throat, making it impossible to breathe. I don't think I could look away even if I tried. There's something about the intensity of his stare that draws me in and holds me captive.

My tongue darts out to lick my lips. "Of course I wanted to fit in. Who doesn't?"

"Is that the way you still feel?"

I shake my head. "No. My eyes have been opened and I see the way most of these people are."

Especially after this last week. Not only has it been a brutal lesson, but it's made me realize that I don't have many friends here.

"What about Carmichael?" Even though his voice remains quiet, there's a sharp edge to it.

My brows pinch as I try to grasp the direction this conversation has veered in. The way his fingers continue to drag along my skin make it a challenge. "What about him?"

"Is he a friend?"

"I've known Duke since elementary school."

"That doesn't answer the question." He presses a kiss against the flesh behind my knee.

"Yes, he's my friend."

"How good of one?"

I blink. "What?"

He pauses as his eyes narrow. "Has he ever touched you, Delilah? That's what I'm asking."

"Touched me?" I echo. For some reason, the question doesn't penetrate. "What do you mean?"

I'm transfixed by how the green flecks in his eyes darken. "Has he ever stroked his hands over you? Or kissed you?"

"No, I told you—we're just friends."

He continues to stare as if trying to work out a puzzle in his head. "Maybe he feels differently. Can't say I know him well, but he doesn't seem like the kind of guy to involve himself in a situation if he doesn't have a dog in the fight."

Well...that's probably true. Most of the time, Duke is an island unto himself. There aren't many people he trusts at Hawthorne Prep.

My attention is drawn back to him when he shoves the material of my skirt up and brushes another kiss along my inner thigh. Not once does his gaze stray from mine as his lips inch upward.

"He was pretty quick to steal you away this morning. I didn't like it. And I sure as shit didn't like his hands on you either. No one touches you but me."

When I remain silent, Austin's teeth sink into the supple flesh of my inner thigh and a whimper escapes from me. I'm walking a fine line between pleasure and pain without any idea as to what side I'll crash onto.

"Do you understand what I'm saying?"

"Yes."

"Good girl. For the moment, you belong to me."

For the moment.

His hands slide around my hips before dragging my ass to the edge of the desk. My fingers grip the linoleum top, curling around the thick surface as he presses my thighs farther apart.

My gaze darts to the door as anxiety threads its way through my voice. "Austin, we shouldn't. Not here."

With a smirk, his attention settles on my panty-covered core. My face heats, knowing that he can probably see the growing wetness on the cotton. There's no way to hide it.

"Fuck, I can smell you from here."

When I attempt to close my legs, he forces them wider until my knees practically touch the desk.

His hot gaze fastens on mine again. "I told you that I'd be eating lunch one way or another, and that's exactly what I plan to do."

A ragged breath escapes from me. The most damning part—the part I'm loath to admit to even myself— is that it's not just embarrassment eating me up alive.

It's arousal as well.

So much that it feels like I could drown in it.

He has me splayed open on a desk in the middle of the afternoon at school. Ms. Pettijohn could return any second and find Austin's dark head between my thighs. If I were thinking clearly, I'd shove him away and escape from the room.

But that's not even a thought in my mind.

Not with the way he's running his hands over me and pressing his soft lips against my naked flesh. The heady pleasure that follows in their wake is intoxicating.

Until this week, I had no idea it existed.

Now that the curtain has been ripped away, I want to experience more.

I want to experience everything.

His fingers dance over the thin fabric stretched across my core.

"So damn wet," he mutters more to himself than to me.

My head spins as he strokes the material with careful fingers. A whimper builds in my chest before attempting to fight its way free. For a few seconds, I keep it trapped deep inside where it can't see the light of day.

Where he can't feast upon it.

That becomes impossible when he hooks a finger into the side and stretches it across my opening so that I'm bared to his sight.

"So fucking pretty," he growls. The words vibrate in his chest, echoing throughout my head and the empty room. "I haven't been able to stop thinking about your bare pussy after getting a glimpse of it. Made my fucking mouth water."

Those dirty words send a thick shaft of need straight to my core. When it bursts into flames, I spread my thighs wider.

With a tortured groan, he leans forward and his warm breath drifts across my aching flesh. As delicious as it feels, it's nothing compared to the first lap of his tongue. The world goes dark as arousal explodes like a brightly colored firework inside my lower belly.

"Mmmm. You taste so damn good. Sweet. Like honey. I'm not sure if it's possible to get enough of you."

My muscles loosen as I sink into the sensation.

"You like that, baby? Does it feel good?"

"So good," I groan.

There's nothing I wouldn't do to feel more of this.

Beg.

Plead.

Grovel.

I don't care.

"You realize that I'm the only one who will ever be able to give you this, right?"

I truly hope that's not the case. After experiencing something so amazing, how can I possibly consider going a lifetime without enjoying it again?

Unwilling to dwell on that disturbing thought, I push it aside and focus on the pleasure unfurling inside me as he licks from the bottom of my slit to the very top before circling the tip of his tongue around my clit. The sensations wreak havoc inside me, shattering everything I thought I knew. Any moment, I'm going to come undone, splintering apart into a million jagged pieces that will never be put back together again.

"No one else, Delilah. Only me."

I'm so afraid he's speaking the truth.

"Please..."

The velvety softness of his tongue strokes over my center. "Please what, sweet girl? What is it that you need?"

My mind cartwheels until forming words isn't possible. Worse than that, I'm not even sure what I want. How can I ask for something I've never experienced before?

"More," I finally whisper.

"More of this?" He thrusts his tongue deep inside my pussy. The way he strokes my insides makes me want to spread myself wider. There is so much pleasure roiling inside me that self-combustion seems imminent. It's almost too much for the confines of my flesh.

It doesn't take long before he falls into a steady rhythm.

My head lolls back, hanging between my shoulder blades as I arch, attempting to get closer. The muscles in my lower belly coil tight. I'm going to—

The door handle rattles.

With a gasp, I shove Austin away before nearly tumbling off the desk and onto the floor. My wide eyes slice to his smirking ones.

Oh my god!

We've been caught.

Any moment, the door will swing open, and Ms. Pettijohn will stride into the classroom. She'll take one look at the two of us locked away in here and know *exactly* what was going on. I don't need a mirror to tell me that my face is flushed and clothing askew.

Austin rises to his feet as if there's no rush and we're not seconds away from being caught. His demeanor doesn't change as he grabs my hand and pulls me to Ms. Pettijohn's office. Just as we step inside the dark space, the classroom door opens with a creak and footsteps follow.

He flattens against the wall before dragging me to him until my backside is perfectly aligned with his front. One strong arm snakes around my waist, pressing me close enough to feel the thickness of his erection digging into me. His other hand settles against my collarbone. Even though the touch is light, my pulse flutters erratically beneath it. There's something about the way he holds me, the dominance of our positions and the pressure he exerts. Even though I'm scared, it's not enough to quash the hot licks of arousal from flaring to life.

I don't understand how I can enjoy this.

When a whimper escapes from my lips, he whispers, "Shhhh. We wouldn't want Pettijohn to discover us in her office, now would we?"

I give my head a little shake.

"Good girl." He nips at my earlobe, and it takes every ounce of self-control not to moan. "That's the second time you've been cheated out of an orgasm. And you were so damn close."

My eyes widen as the arm wrapped around my waist loosens before his hand slips beneath the band of my skirt and delves into drenched panties. When I shift, attempting to deter him, his other hand tightens around my throat.

It's not much, just enough to subdue my movements.

"I would have preferred you come on my tongue so I could watch your expression, but this will have to do."

No.

No.

No.

I shake my head as his fingers settle over my clit, rubbing soft circles. I'm already so turned on and swollen from the way he licked me. I don't think I can take more of this sweet torture before falling apart.

My ears stay pricked, listening for the slightest sound as the older woman moves around the classroom. There's the shuffling of papers and the opening of a desk drawer before the soft strains of music from a radio fill the air. Every noise feels like an explosion.

The slightest movement of our bodies has me fearing that she'll step inside the office to investigate. We'll both get expelled, and then I can kiss my one-way ticket out of this town goodbye.

"How are you even more soaked than when I was eating you out?" He chuckles softly in my ear. "I think someone enjoys the risk of getting caught. Maybe you're not the good girl you've always pretended to be."

When I shake my head, he accuses, "Liar."

As much as I want to deny his words, I can't. What he's saying is true.

"You know what I think? That you like it dirty."

As frightening as the thought is, he might be right.

His breath grows harsher, echoing in my ears, as his fingers keep up a steady rhythm. I can't help but writhe against him, so close to coming. It takes every ounce of strength to stop the wave from crashing over me. With each caress, my willpower falters. I'm terrified that I won't be able to keep all this pleasure trapped inside. The grip around my throat intensifies when I struggle against him.

"Just let it happen," he commands.

I squeeze my eyes tightly closed as his fingers glide across my damp flesh and a moan escapes from me.

Ms. Pettijohn's chair scrapes across the floor, and then there's the sound of footsteps. My eyes fly open in horror as air gets trapped in my lungs.

The strikes of her low heels against the tile grow closer.

Louder.

She's headed this way.

She must have heard us.

Me.

She heard me.

The office is only a six-by-six square foot room. There's nowhere to hide. No way she won't discover us.

Austin's fingers still over my clit. Even though he doesn't move, the firm pressure drives me insane. It's almost more agonizing than when he was rubbing me. Even when her willowy shadow falls across the crack between the wall and the door, I squirm in his arms, attempting to find relief.

Just as she's about to step inside the office, a familiar voice calls from the hallway, "Clarissa, do you have a moment?"

Not even the risk of discovery is enough to dampen the pleasure threatening to overtake me. It's only a matter of seconds before I lose all control.

And he knows it.

By the sound of his heavy breathing, he's all but glorying in it. He wants me to come undone with our teacher a few steps away. When his grip tightens around my throat, I lift my chin, tipping my head so the back of my skull rests against the solid strength of his chest. He strokes the long column of my neck as his other hand begins circling.

"Mmm, I could get used to this. One hand wrapped around your delicate throat and the other stroking your pretty little clit."

I whimper as my body throbs an insistent beat.

"You know what you're going to do now?"

I can only imagine.

When I remain silent, he whispers, "Come all over my fingers."

Oh god.

There's no way for me to keep these explosive feelings contained any longer. They're too much for the confines of my skin.

"Of course," Ms. Pettijohn says before swinging away, footsteps fading into the hallway.

Relief weakens my knees as he presses against my clit. That's all it takes for my world to splinter apart. When I slump, his fingers once again wrap around my throat as if to keep me firmly in place.

"Shhhh," he murmurs in my ear. "You need to be quiet."

My teeth sink into my lip in order to keep everything trapped within.

But it's hard.

So hard.

Especially when all I want to do is scream out my pleasure.

At the moment, I don't care who hears.

Or sees.

I've never felt more out of control.

But I've never felt so free, either.

DELILAH

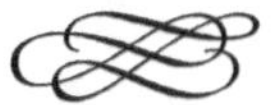

"*I* could always catch a ride home with my mom," I tell Austin outside the football stadium, cautious hope weaving its way through my voice. The more time I spend with him, the more I...

No.

I don't even want to think along those lines.

He shakes his head. "You're staying. I want your ass in the bleachers."

"Because you want me to watch you, or you want Jasper to see me watching you?"

As soon as the words escape, I wince.

Why did I even bother to ask?

Deep down, I know the answer.

I'm a fool for hoping that something will shift or change our relationship. Especially after our conversation this morning. It doesn't matter if he enjoys touching me.

He doesn't trust me. In his mind, I'm no better than Jasper. He entrusted me with secrets that were then used against him.

Austin flashes a grin before stroking his fingers over the curve of my jaw. It's something he does often. For just a second or two, I find myself leaning into his touch before realizing what I'm doing and drawing back.

"It'll totally fuck with Jasper's head."

Exactly.

My shoulders wilt under the unexpected weight of my disappointment. Needing to break the physical connection, I take a hasty step in retreat until we're no longer touching. It's all too easy to lose myself when I'm in his arms.

"Guess I'll see you after practice," I mutter, irritated for allowing myself to fall deeper when he feels nothing.

Before he can say anything else, I swing around and stalk to the student section in the stands where we sit for home games. Even though I ignore him, I feel his gaze tracking my movements. Not that it's a hardship to sit and watch Austin practice—his body is a thing of beauty and athletic grace—but I don't want to be used to incite more bad blood between these two. I'd rather head home.

Plus, a little breathing room would probably help me get my head on straight.

Pockets of students dot the bleachers as I make my way over to them. Most of the spectators are girls. Each group I pass stares openly before putting their heads together and whispering behind their hands. The tips of my ears burn as I keep my expression neutral.

The fact that I was dating Jasper last week and now I'm with Austin only seems to solidify my status as a whore. What's laughable is that these people should know better. I've spent my time at HP trying to fly under the radar, never doing anything to garner unwanted attention. Most would call me boring. Apparently, my past track record is nothing when compared to the rumor mill that is constantly churning at Hawthorne Prep.

When I'm far enough away from everyone and unable to hear their chatter, I drop my backpack onto the long stretch of metal bench. If I'm going to be stuck here for two hours, I might as well get a head start on my homework. If there's time later tonight, I can look over some of the photos I took the other day and start putting together a portfolio of possibilities for the art show.

I pull out my pre-calc book and get to work. Fifteen minutes later, my attention is drawn to the team as they walk onto the turf for practice. The head coach blows his whistle and the guys huddle around him, listening intently to what's being said.

Even though I don't consciously search for Austin, it only takes seconds for my gaze to zero in on him. There's something about his presence that commands my attention. I glance at the small groups of girls hanging around and realize I'm not the only one affected.

If there were a way to fight this growing attraction, I'd do it in a heartbeat, but there's not.

I've tried everything.

I'm like a rabbit caught in a snare, unable to free itself. The more I struggle, the more entrapped I become.

After several failed attempts to refocus on my work, I shove my book and notebook to the side before pulling out my camera. I remove a shorter lens in favor of a longer one and lift the Nikon to my face. Once Austin is in view, I adjust the lens and the image sharpens. My finger hits the shutter button, and the camera clicks in rapid succession.

My mouth dries as I continue snapping shots.

The way his white practice pants hug his lean hips and thighs has a reluctant burst of arousal exploding in my core. His waist is narrow and tapered. There's not an ounce of fat on him, and the pads make his shoulders seem even broader than they already are. With the gold helmet in place, I can't see his face clearly, but I feel the zip of electricity sizzle through my veins and know he's watching me.

Eye contact is abruptly severed when Jasper plows into him. Austin stumbles a few paces before straightening to his full height and swinging around. A couple guys flank my ex, ready to jump in if needed. Jasper's hands remain clenched at his sides.

Air gets clogged in my lungs as I wait for Austin's reaction. My gaze bounces between the two as the tension on the field turns suffocating. It's almost as if Jasper is waiting for Austin to lose his shit and make the first move.

Realization dawns.

That's exactly what he's doing.

Coach Baker and several of his assistants stare at the boys.

All the other players do as well.

The field becomes still. Everyone seems to be waiting for an explosion to rock the stadium.

Heart pounding, I worry my lower lip, hoping that Austin won't take the bait.

Because that's exactly what this is—*a trap*.

A slow grin spreads across Austin's face. Even from here, I see the flash of white teeth in the sunlight. He dusts off the front of his jersey with both hands before taking a step in retreat.

As he does, Jasper lurches forward. Even though I can't see his face, his tense stance screams that he's all but itching to tackle his teammate to the ground. Barely contained rage bristles from him. His friends grab his jersey, pulling him back, as the coach's whistle rents the air.

My shoulders collapse as relief floods through me. Maybe I shouldn't care what happens to Austin, but I do. Life at HP would probably be easier if he were expelled. But I don't want to see that happen.

I don't want Jasper to win.

It's obvious from the taunting smile on Austin's face that he was prepared for a fight.

It's all part of the plan.

That's all I am to him.

A plan.

Jasper swings around and glares at me. I can't help but recoil from the fury filling his expression. That's when I slip the camera back into the case and refocus on pre-calculus. My insides are a jangled mess, and I need something to calm them.

"Hey."

My head snaps up as Summer and Everly settle on the bench beside me. "Hi."

Distrust glints in the dark-haired girl's eyes, and I get the feeling she's trying to figure me out.

Her attention deviates to the field for a moment or two before returning to me. "What are you doing here?"

I should have expected Summer to seek me out. "Watching practice."

Her gaze sharpens as she tilts her head. "Who are you here to watch? Austin or Jasper? Maybe both?"

That last question is like a punch to the gut. Is that really what she thinks? "I'm here for Austin."

Her gaze crawls over me, silently probing for answers. There's something strange about staring into eyes that are the exact same vibrant shade as Austin's.

I'm used to seeing them all heated up.

Even when they're full of distrust.

Hers are colder.

"I don't understand what's going on between you two. And he won't say a word. Care to explain?"

Unable to hold her probing stare, mine slides to the field and fastens on Austin. That's when I realize he's watching us. I blow out a steady stream of air as his words from this morning echo throughout my head. He doesn't want his sister knowing what he's up to. Probably because she'd put the kibosh on it. Much like his twin, Austin is a force to be reckoned with.

I rack my brain, trying to pull a story out of my ass.

Something she'll believe.

Even if it's reluctantly.

But what?

"The rumors flying around school are true," I blurt. "We're seeing each other."

Her brows skyrocket across her forehead as her expression turns ferocious. "Why would he want anything to do with you after the shit you pulled at the fundraiser?"

It takes effort to keep my voice from trembling. "That didn't have anything to do with me. It was all Jasper. I would never purposefully hurt Austin."

"That's not what your ex has been telling anyone who'll listen."

"He's a liar."

A humorless laugh falls from her lips. "Funny you would say that when you two were dating for half a year and you seemed to be in on the setup."

"I know," I admit. The optics are terrible. "I've wanted to break up with Jasper for a while. I just had to work up the courage to do it. I knew he'd make my life hell and that's exactly what he's done."

Summer's brow furrows as she studies my face. "Honestly, I'm not sure what to believe." A few seconds of silence slowly tick by before she says, "When we first got here, you were one of the few people who were nice to us." Her gaze gets drawn to the field. Even though her boyfriend is there, I know she's watching her brother. "The rest of them were ruthless assholes."

"I know. I'm sorry I couldn't do more," I murmur.

When it comes down to it, I'm nothing like Summer. She's so much stronger. Maybe that's because I've spent years trying to be invisible. Breaking out of my shell doesn't come easy.

When Austin's sister clears her throat, my attention snaps back to her. "If you hurt him, I'll kick your ass. Do I make myself clear?"

"Perfectly."

I don't bother telling her that I suspect it'll be Austin who inflicts the pain. For him, there aren't feelings involved. For me...

That's no longer the case.

I can lie all I want to him, but I refuse to hide the truth from myself.

Now that she's issued a warning, I expect Summer and Everly to take off. It's a surprise when they remain seated. It takes a while for the thick tension to dissipate and for Summer's expression to soften as she becomes absorbed in the practice.

What's obvious is that she only has eyes for Kingsley. They share several heated glances that make me feel as if I'm a voyeur intruding on a private moment. Everly catches my eyes before rolling hers with exaggeration. My lips twitch in response. It feels good to loosen up. It only makes me realize how much I miss having girlfriends. I haven't had true ones since middle school. Sloane and her minions were never my friends.

What's that old saying?

Keep your friends close and your enemies closer?

That's exactly what I was doing.

I'm happy that Summer has found someone who loves her so completely. Kingsley is strong and so is she. They're a perfect match.

If there's a kernel of envy blooming at the bottom of my belly, I ignore it. I've never been prone to jealousy. If I were, Hawthorne Prep would be an even more miserable place since everyone here is loaded.

But to have a real relationship with someone who gets me, someone I could share my hopes and dreams with, someone who had my back, a partner, that would be nice. For a short period of time, I thought I'd found that with Jasper.

I couldn't have been more wrong.

So, am I a little bit jealous for the first time in my life of what someone else has?

Maybe I am.

I shift my gaze and realize that Everly is wearing a wistful expression as well. It makes me wonder why she isn't dating anyone. When she first arrived, she stirred quite a bit of interest. Strangely enough, it seems like all the guys who were flirting with her in the beginning have backed off.

Almost as if someone deliberately scared them away.

Once practice wraps up, the three of us rise to our feet and grab our backpacks before making our way to the track that circles the field. I'm thankful that most of the tension has dissolved. I can only hope that the tentative peace we've managed to find lasts.

As I wait for Austin to finish up in the locker room, I feel the stares from the other girls directed my way. Now that I'm with Summer and Everly, I don't feel quite so alone. That's always been the hardest part about being at Hawthorne Prep—the loneliness.

The feeling of not fitting in or belonging.

"Did you want to grab something to eat after this?" Everly asks.

"I'm starving and Dad probably won't be making an appearance anytime soon, so I'll be on my own for dinner as usual."

Summer glances at her phone. "Wish I could, but I've got too much homework."

A smirk curves her lips. "Yeah, sure. I think there's something else you want to study."

Summer's cheeks pinken before she uses her elbow to jab her friend in the side.

Everly laughs before the happy sound dies on her lips as Duke joins us.

Her blue-green eyes turn guarded as she folds her arms tightly across her chest. It would be impossible not to notice the way the atmosphere shifts with his imposing presence.

"Hey," I say in a friendly tone, wanting to defuse the strange tension that vibrates in the air.

He gives me a chin lift in greeting before doing the same to Summer. Then his gaze narrows on Everly, and his eyes harden. The edges of his lips curl into a snarl as the two stay locked in a silent battle of wills. My gaze bounces between them, only now realizing there's a problem.

That's when an uncomfortable silence descends, blanketing the four of us.

Just as it grows stifling, I clear my throat. "Did you need something?"

He rips his attention away from Everly long enough to say, "I thought you might want a ride home."

We don't live far from each other, and sometimes he drops me off when I've needed a ride. I've always appreciated the way he looks out for me.

Before I can respond, a thickly muscled arm snakes around my body, hauling me close as I'm inundated with a fresh masculine scent.

"That's not necessary, Carmichael. I've got her."

Duke glares at Austin for a long, uncomfortable moment before refocusing on me. His voice softens. "Is that the case?"

"You heard me say that it was," Austin snaps.

Duke takes a menacing step toward us. The blond lacrosse player is just as tall and broad as Austin. Honestly, he might be a bit bigger. Other than that, they're evenly matched. "Is it a problem if I want to hear it from Delilah?"

Before they can come to blows, I blurt, "Thanks for asking, but Austin will take me home."

He searches my eyes carefully. Like everyone else, I can see him trying to figure out what's going on between us. "You sure about that?"

"I am," I say, forcing a bright smile.

Duke presses his lips into a tight line before jerking his shoulders into a shrug. "All right. Guess I'll catch you tomorrow."

I nod as he stalks away. It would be impossible not to notice how people scurry from his path. No one wants to have a run-in with him. It's only when he's disappeared around the corner of the stadium that Everly releases a pent-up breath.

"I really hate that guy," she mutters.

My gaze swings to her in surprise. "Really?"

Duke has never been anything but kind to me. I know he can be brisk and is rough around the edges, but I've always felt that deep down, he has a heart of gold.

All right...maybe not gold.

But he's a good guy. Certainly better than a lot of people around here.

Everly's teeth rake across her lower lip as she glares at the place he was last seen before disappearing. "Sometimes, I think he goes out of his way to be an asshole. Especially to me, and I have no idea why. I barely know him."

My brows pinch together as I mentally comb through their past interactions. "I think it just takes time for him to warm up to people."

She snorts. "I think you're way off base and he's a jerk. I wish he'd just leave me alone. I'm tired of putting up with his crap."

What I don't mention is that it sucks to be a scholarship kid at Hawthorne Prep. Even if it's not openly talked about, everyone knows that the only reason we're here is because the board pays our tuition.

There are always little offhanded remarks or jokes made at our expense.

And we're both more guarded because of it.

Ironically, Duke is more accepted than I am. He's a gifted student and talented athlete. The problem is that he has a huge chip on his shoulder. He goes out of his way to remove himself from social situations and people. Honestly, when I think about it, he was that way when he was younger and we attended public school.

Kingsley joins us, wrapping an arm around Summer before hauling her close and brushing his lips across hers.

"For fuck's sake," Austin grumbles. "The last thing I want to see is you maul my sister."

Not bothered by the comment, Kingsley flashes a grin. "Then you should turn away, because it's about to get rated R real quick around here."

Summer slaps at his chest but doesn't stop him from taking her mouth in a possessive kiss that sizzles in the air surrounding them.

Austin rolls his eyes before propelling me forward, away from the trio.

"We're out. I'll catch you later," he tosses over his shoulder.

That's all it takes for nerves to explode across my skin as we head to the parking lot.

DELILAH

I fiddle with the hem of my skirt before smoothing my palms over the fabric, attempting to stretch it farther down my thighs. Every time I shift against the leather seat, it slides upward.

As we leave the rolling grounds of Hawthorne Prep behind, a breath of relief escapes from me. This place has become more of a prison. One I'm happy to escape from.

Admittedly, the day was easier to get through with Austin at school. I didn't have to worry about being openly hunted by Jasper. My mind wasn't consumed by thoughts of where he would turn up next and what he would do if he found me alone.

To be honest, I'd been so preoccupied with the dark-haired boy and whether he was going to lay hands on me that I barely gave my ex a passing thought. It's demoralizing to realize just how quickly I can be reduced to a quivering mass of hormones.

When I continue to fidget, he reaches out and wraps his hand around my thigh. He hits the turn signal, swinging onto the long stretch of country road that leads to town. The way his palm sears my bare flesh is almost enough to make me forget about everything churning through my brain. In that moment, my world shrinks down until it encompasses just the two of us.

"You all right?" he asks.

I glance from his fingers draped possessively around my leg to his face. He flicks his gaze to me, searching my eyes before his stare returns to the road.

"I'm fine."

Well…as fine as I can be, considering the circumstances. It's not something I allow myself to dwell on, since there's nothing I can do to change the situation. I just need to get through it. And that includes Austin. I need to find a way to survive him without falling any harder.

"Did you have any convos with Jasper today?"

I shake my head, thankful there weren't any unexpected run-ins. "No."

When I peek at him, I find his lips compressed into a tight line.

"You don't believe me. You think we're still together."

In that moment, I realize just how far apart we are. It's as if he's standing on one side of the ocean and I'm on the other.

The night we spent talking in the car tumbles through my head, and I can't help but wish it were possible to go back to a place where our relationship was less complicated.

"I'm not sure what to believe," he says carefully, somber gaze latching onto mine. "Part of me wants to trust you're being honest and had nothing to do with what happened. But there's another part that's afraid you two are playing me." He shrugs. "That's where I'm at."

"Tell me what I have to do to prove that I'm not lying." Desperation fills my voice.

His jaw locks and he takes his foot off the accelerator, dropping his speed as we cruise through the sleepy little town.

When he remains silent, I swivel toward him. "Austin?"

His profile looks as if it's etched in stone.

Just as I open my mouth to plead, he gives his head a brisk shake.

Frustration wafts off him in heavy waves. "I'm not sure there's anything you can do that will make me believe you. Too much has happened."

My shoulders collapse as everything inside me wilts. Unsure what to say, I turn away and stare sightlessly out the passenger side window. The remainder of the ride is made in painstaking silence. By the time we pull up in front of my house, I just want to escape his presence.

I'm done playing games.

There's no doubt in my mind that when this is over, someone will be hurt. And more than likely, it'll be me. I don't mean anything to Austin. He's made that perfectly clear. And Jasper is incapable of caring about anyone other than himself. None of this would be transpiring if I'd realized that sooner and never gotten involved with him in the first place.

Unfortunately, what they say is true—hindsight is twenty-twenty.

When my fingers tighten around the handle, he reaches out and lays a hand over mine to stop me from leaving.

"We're not done here."

Angry with the way this conversation has played out, I snap. "I think we are."

Everything happens so fast. One minute, I'm trying to shake him off and the next, I'm hoisted onto his lap with no other choice but to straddle his thighs.

My palms land on his chest before curling into the soft T-shirt. "What are you doing?"

"Finishing our conversation." His hands wrap around my waist as if anchoring me to his lap.

My brows rise at his audacity. "And I don't get a say in the matter?"

"Nope."

Air gets sucked from my lungs as he shifts me until I'm nestled against his hard length. The same heat that flares to life inside me at the contact is echoed tenfold within his eyes.

"Are you really interested in proving your innocence?"

One flex of his hips and my eyes are rolling back in my head. He might have given me one orgasm this afternoon, but it's not nearly enough. I'm greedy for more. In a matter of seconds, my skin comes alive, arousal exploding in my core.

The way he turns me on...it's like a light switch being flipped inside my body. One moment, I'm pissed off and the next, all I crave is his hands on me, making me forget everything that sits between us.

There's nothing normal about the way he makes me feel.

Somewhere in the back of my head, I know I should put a stop to this, but it's so hard to think straight when his thick erection is pressing insistently against my clit. Another thrust has those thoughts scattering. My jaw slackens and my head tilts, exposing the long column of my neck as my hair tumbles down the back of my wool blazer.

"Yes," I groan.

"Then give me yours."

At first, his words don't register, and I'm unable to make sense of them. His hands are still locked around my hips as he grinds against my pussy. My brain grows fuzzy from the contact. If he keeps this up, there's no way I won't come. I can already feel it building like a storm within.

"I want your virginity," he growls when I remain silent.

He gathers up the thick length of my hair before slowly winding it around his fist. Without causing pain, he holds the strands taut so I'm able to feel the tug against my scalp. A moan escapes from me as I roll my hips against him, desperate for more.

Why him?

Why does he affect me like this?

"Did you hear me?" he says in a voice strung tight. "I want to be the first man to have you."

The first...

Not the last.

Not the only.

The *first*.

All he cares about is denying Jasper the opportunity to claim me. It'll just be another thing to rub in my ex's face.

I didn't think it was possible for all the pleasure rushing through my veins to dissolve, but that's exactly what happens. In its place is a hollow emptiness. His grip on my hair tightens as I lift my head to meet his gaze.

"What happens after I let you in my body? Will that somehow exonerate me? And you'll finally believe I had nothing to do with the shit Jasper pulled?" There's a pause before I drop the final question. "Or will you continue to think it's all a game?"

Confusion flickers across his expression. "I don't know."

"Then there isn't much point in talking about it, is there?"

He narrows his eyes and tilts his head. "And if I said that it would prove your innocence without a shadow of a doubt, you'd do it?"

I allow the question to bounce around in my brain for a handful of moments before jerking my head into a nod. "Yes."

A growl rumbles up from deep within his chest.

His grip intensifies and there's a flash of pain along my scalp before I allow my head to tip further back, easing the sensation and baring the slender column of my throat. My back arches and my breasts thrust forward. My breathing picks up its tempo as his fingers stroke along the exposed length before dipping into my cleavage and retracing their path upward, settling under my jawbone.

"Your pulse feels like the wings of a bird beating frantically against a cage." He presses ever so gently, and the tempo quickens. It's a steady thud against the pads of his fingers. Any second, my heart will explode from my chest.

No one else will ever be able to incite these kinds of feelings within me.

Only him.

"What we do together can't have anything to do with Jasper," I whisper.

His hips rise slowly until the thickness of his erection can stroke against my core and a shudder of pleasure explodes inside me.

"I don't know if that's possible," he murmurs. "I'm not sure if I can separate the two of you in my head."

The softly spoken admission isn't enough to kill the desire rushing through my veins. At this point, I'm not sure anything can.

His gaze drops to the apex of my thighs as he shoves the material up so that he can see my panties. "All I'd have to do is unzip my fly and I could slide right inside your heat. Already I know it would be a tight fit. Your virgin cunt is so tiny. I'd have to take it nice and slow. Lick you first to get you ready to take me."

Oh god.

His dirty words dampen my panties with even more arousal as he thrusts. One hand is splayed against my throat while the other stays wrapped in my hair to keep me locked in place. Maybe I wanted to flee the vehicle ten minutes ago, but it's no longer a thought in my head. It feels like there's a fire burning through my body as he slides his thick length against me. The sweet friction makes me want to scream with pent-up frustration.

There's a desperate part of me that wants him to lower his fly and pull out his cock. He's probably right about me having to stretch around him, but it would feel so damn good.

The burn of it.

Knowing that he's shaping me to fit him.

I'm so far past the point of caring if the neighbors or people passing by catch a glimpse of us parked in his SUV. I'm burning up inside, and he's the only one capable of dousing the flames.

My eyelids flutter closed as he rocks against me.

"Fuck, you've soaked the front of my pants."

If I were in my right mind, a comment like that would embarrass the hell out of me.

"Do you have any idea how much I want to make you orgasm again?"

"It can't be more than I want it," I groan.

I crack open my eyes just enough to see him smirk before a tortured chuckle escapes from him. "I haven't come in my pants since I was fifteen years old. But that's exactly what's gonna happen."

"Is that what I do to you?" I ask, turned on by the idea of him losing all control because of me.

His fingers press against my throat as he continues to fist my hair. I couldn't imagine anyone else touching me like this.

His expression turns fierce as he thrusts again. "You know it is. From fucking day one."

"I felt it, too," I whisper, wanting him to know the truth.

Emotion flickers in his eyes. "Do you have any idea how much I want to believe you?"

"Austin..."

Another upstroke has his cock dragging across my clit. That's all it takes for me to fall apart. The hold on my hair intensifies, the sting only adding to the pleasure ricocheting throughout my body. His fingers slide upward until the thumb and forefinger are pressing into the bones of my lower jaw, holding me in place. That too, somehow, only enhances the sensations unfurling inside me. A scream builds in my throat and tears from my lips. There's no way to stop it from pouring out.

He doesn't attempt to muffle my screams. They echo throughout the cabin and ring in my ears. It wouldn't matter if there were a crowd of onlookers gathered around the vehicle, I wouldn't be able to stop it from happening.

Austin groans as his cock continues to stroke my panty-covered pussy. My inner muscles clench and contract, searching for something to lock around. As amazing as this feels, I know it would be so much better if he were inside me, filling me to the brim. My hips buck as I writhe against him.

It's only when the last tendrils of orgasm dissipate that I return to my senses.

"You're so fucking beautiful when you come undone."

I huff out a breath as a massive wave of exhaustion crashes over me, threatening to suck me under. The emotional upheaval and toll this week has taken is finally catching up with me. All I want to do is curl up against his chest and fall asleep. Maybe when I wake again, the worst part of it will have passed.

Austin releases his hold on my hair before stroking his fingers along my jaw. A shiver slides through me as he trails them down the column of my throat to my collarbone.

Not in a million years would I have expected either of those things to be a turn-on.

Having experienced it now, there's no denying that it is. There's something about the possessiveness of his touch and the feel of being at his mercy. It only heightens the sensations wreaking havoc throughout my body.

His gaze stays pinned to mine, searching it as I sit astride his lap. I have no idea what he sees within my eyes.

The truth?

My tongue peeks out to dampen my lips as I rack my brain for something to say.

He beats me to the punch.

"You should probably go."

There's a gruffness to his voice that wasn't there before. Whatever openness had been in his expression has vanished. For a second or two, I consider pleading my case but decide against it.

What would be the point?

It's the same conversation we've had half a dozen times. He doesn't believe me. And nothing will change that.

For Austin, this is a game of revenge.

That's all it'll ever be.

That's all *I'll* ever be.

DELILAH

As I step inside the house, Austin's Mercedes peels away from the curb with a roar of the engine that echoes in my ears before fading into the distance. With a huff, I lean against the door and squeeze my eyes tightly closed.

I'm overwhelmed by the rush of emotions. I've never felt so conflicted in my life. As much as I want to hold myself back so these feelings won't continue to flourish, that's no longer an option. The moment he looks at me, all my good intentions are thrown out the window. He makes me want things that aren't possible. Things he can't give me.

Or maybe I should say—won't give me.

"Where've you been for the past two hours?"

Startled, my eyelids fly open, and I find Mom sitting in the armchair facing the door. Her face is drawn and there are lines of tension bracketing her mouth.

I clear my throat. "I stayed at school to watch practice."

She jerks a brow as her voice drops. "Football practice?"

"Yes."

"Since when are you interested in that? You certainly weren't when you were with Jasper."

The lie shoots out of my mouth before I can stop it. "Everly asked me to hang out with her."

I can almost see the wheels in Mom's brain turning. "Everly Donahue?"

When I jerk my head into a nod, her eyes narrow. "The new girl who's friends with Summer Hawthorne?"

I wince, not expecting her to know who Everly is, much less who she hangs out with. "Yes."

"Is she the one who drove you home afterward?"

Shit.

I consider lying again but quickly discard the idea. Mom has already proven that she's paying more attention than previously.

"No. Austin drove me home."

The edges of her lips wilt. "I thought I made myself perfectly clear this morning when I said I didn't want you hanging around or getting involved with that boy. Whether you want to see it or not, he's trouble. He'll only bring you down."

For the second time in a matter of minutes, I squeeze my eyes closed before releasing a steady breath and forcing them open again. "I promise you that he's not trouble. I wish you could take my word for it and trust me."

"Unfortunately, that's no longer possible. You've proven over the last week that you're not capable of making good decisions." Her voice turns quiet. "I don't think I've ever been more disappointed in you."

My eyes widen as my mouth drops open.

I...can't believe she just said that.

"What?"

"You heard me. I'll be damned if I let some punk waltz in here and turn your head, undoing all our carefully laid plans."

"That's not going to happen."

"Oh really? Then why have you been lying to me?"

I blink, thrown off by the question. "I don't know what you're talking about."

"Just this morning, you told me that Ms. Pettijohn asked you to continue tutoring that Hawthorne kid."

My mouth turns cottony. Too late, I realize where this conversation is heading. It feels like a train crash is taking place in front of my eyes and there's nothing I can do to stop it.

"I spoke with Clarissa after school. Imagine my surprise when she told me she never asked any such thing of you."

"Mom—"

"You were also kissing that Hawthorne boy in the hallway this morning. Everyone was talking about it."

Oh god.

When I remain silent, she continues, voice escalating with each snapped-out word. "And that, he and Jasper almost got into another fight. It's unfortunate that didn't happen. Then he'd be tossed out on his ear." She glares. "I look at you and it's like I don't even know you anymore."

"That's not true," I whisper. "I haven't changed. I'm still the same as I've always been."

"Maybe you don't want to see it, but you have. And it all started with Austin Hawthorne. He's the problem. Both Jasper and Edmond think—"

"I don't care what they think," I growl, losing my patience.

"Delilah!" Her eyes widen in shock.

"Why are you listening to either one of them? Jasper's a liar. How do you not see that?"

"And yet, you're the one who has been caught in several lies. And he's always been perfectly nice. Even when I see him around school, he's always happy to chat."

"He's a phony, Mom. He never showed you his true colors."

No, he reserved all that for me.

She waves a hand. "Just stop. I can't believe you're trying to throw him under the bus when he's been so good to you." She leans forward. "You know, he told me the real reason you broke up with him."

That's highly doubtful.

"You were seeing that other boy behind his back." She squints and shakes her head. "Like I said, I don't even know you anymore."

"That's not what happened."

"You know what? I don't want to hear any more of your lies. We've reached the point where I can't trust anything that comes out of your mouth."

Hot licks of pain slice through me. I can't believe she's saying this. I've always been a good kid and never caused her a single moment of worry. Instead of listening to what I have to say, she's accusing me of lying.

Maybe part of that is my fault. I've hidden things, especially when it had to do with Austin.

"I don't want you spending any more time with him, do you understand?"

I press my lips together before muttering, "Yes."

Her eyes narrow as if she doesn't believe me.

I almost laugh.

Of course she doesn't.

She believes Jasper.

And apparently, Edmond.

"I'm being serious, Delilah. He's bad news and I don't want you within ten feet of him."

"I got it."

Needing to shut down this conversation before I say something I'll regret, I stalk to my bedroom and slam the door. Tears prick the backs of my eyes as I collapse onto the bed. At every turn, my life becomes more twisted, and I have no idea how to untangle it.

The irony is that it's her affair with Pembroke that put me in this precarious situation in the first place.

DELILAH

I'm ripped from the shadowy depths of slumber when a heavy weight drops on top of me. A bloodcurdling scream gathers in my throat as a large hand covers my mouth and my nostrils, making it impossible to draw in breath. My hands rise, latching onto a muscular forearm and clawing at it to free myself.

The person doesn't budge.

Fear slices through me, unable to believe that something like this could happen. Sure, we don't live in the best neighborhood, but this is Hawthorne. It's always been a quiet community.

"Shhh. It's just me."

Everything within stills as the deep voice echoes in my brain.

Austin?

What the hell?

As silvery moonlight slants in through the open window, my eyes gradually adjust to the darkness and the boy straddling my waist. As swiftly as fear bloomed to life inside me, it drains, leaving a million questions to circle in its place.

"I'm going to remove my hand. You need to be quiet," he warns. "I doubt you want your mother to find me here."

When I raise my brows, his palm disappears, and I can once again suck in a full breath. His gaze stays pinned to mine, waiting for what I'll do next. But he's right, if Mom discovers him in my room at this time of the night, she'll lose it.

And probably lock me in a convent where I'll never see the light of day.

"Why are you here?" I hiss, glancing at the clock on the nightstand. It's well after midnight. We didn't exactly part on the best of terms this afternoon. Honestly, I wasn't sure where we stood.

His brows slide together as he searches my face. It's as if I can feel the heat of his gaze warming my skin. One look is all it takes for my brain to click off and my body to come alive.

It's maddening to feel this way.

Just when I think he won't respond, he shakes his head. "Truthfully? I don't have a clue."

The disappointment that rises within me is instantaneous and all consuming.

Why am I surprised?

Better question—why does it even matter?

I'm much too afraid to inspect my thoughts and feelings for an answer.

"I just knew I couldn't stay away. Not after today." Another heavy silence falls over us as our gazes cling. My hands drift to his chest and his eyes search mine in the darkness as if it's possible to sift through all my innermost thoughts and dig down to the truth.

If only it were that easy.

Everything inside me cautiously lifts. I'm almost afraid to ask. "Do you believe me?"

"I want to." His voice turns solemn.

"That's not good enough," I whisper.

A sharp shaft of grief slices through me. It feels as if my heart is breaking into a thousand tiny pieces, and I can't imagine it being put back together again.

"I know, but I want to believe you. What I feel..." His words trail off into nothingness.

"Tell me."

His fingers lock around my wrists, removing them from his chest before leaning forward and pressing them into the mattress above my head. His face hovers inches above mine.

"Things I don't want to. Things I wish I didn't."

My heart skips a painful beat before pounding into overdrive at the reluctant admittance.

"Is that really so bad?"

"I don't know." He shakes his head as if genuinely confused. "There've been girls before, but none have ever made me feel the way you do. And I'm afraid you're just toying with me."

"I'm not." Now it's my turn to examine his eyes. "I had no idea what Jasper was planning to do. The day after you picked me up on the side of the road and took me home, I told him we were through. I no longer cared if he made my life hell. I just needed to be free of him." My mind tumbles back to that conversation. "He lost it and then stomped out of the house. I thought it was over between us. But then he picked me up for school Monday morning and was acting as if he were genuinely sorry. He asked if I would keep our breakup a secret because of the fundraiser. He was being so nice, and I thought if giving in made it easier afterward, then it would be worth it. He set both of us up. Not just you." I gulp and force out the rest. "He knew I had feelings for you, and he found a way to ruin it."

"Jasper didn't ruin anything," he murmurs. "Because I'm here. As much as I've tried to hold you at a distance, I can't do it."

"What I'm telling you is the truth," I whisper, needing him to believe me.

Leaning forward, his lips brush over mine. Back and forth they sweep until I'm dizzy with the sensation. I draw his warm, minty breath into my lungs as his tongue licks at my mouth.

A whimper escapes from me as I shift beneath him, restless for more. When I lift my arms, attempting to tangle them around his neck, his fingers tighten, pressing them back to the mattress.

"I want to touch you," I whisper.

His lips curve as he shakes his head. "I don't think I could stand that right now. I refuse to come in my pants for a second time today."

Even thinking about what happened in both Ms. Pettijohn's office and in his vehicle this afternoon is enough to have my core throbbing with need. He kisses the corners of my lips before settling over the fullness as his tongue brushes across the seam. When I open, he steals inside.

Austin is all sharp edges, but there's a softness to him as if he's trying to hold back and take this slow. The self-control he exerts only makes me want him more. It also makes me wonder what it would be like to see him when he's not holding back, being gentle because he knows that's what I need.

Powerful.

Dominating.

Forceful.

Those are the adjectives that spring to mind when I think about Austin Hawthorne.

Barely harnessed energy on the verge of breaking free.

The way he touches me is enough to set my body to flames.

Now that I've sampled a taste, I can't imagine not having more. There's no way any other man will ever measure up. When his mouth fuses to mine, the velvety softness of his tongue wreaking havoc inside me, it feels like I'll lose a piece of myself. In that moment, I realize I'll never be the same again.

This boy will ruin me for all others.

And yet, that innate knowledge isn't enough to stop this moment from unfolding.

Whatever happens, I refuse to regret it.

He pulls away just enough to mutter, "So damn sweet. Do you have any idea what you do to me?"

Maybe. But only because he does the exact same thing to me. He turns my world upside down and inside out. I have no idea how I'll ever fight my way free of him.

When his mouth resettles on mine, I open, only wanting him to delve back in so I can forget everything that rages outside this bedroom. The caress is fleeting before he's sitting back, creating distance between us.

Too much distance.

My body aches as I shift restlessly. His fingers loosen from around my wrists before stroking down my bare arms until they can reach my ribcage. His gaze tracks the steady movement as his palms settle on my breasts, squeezing the softness. Unlike when he touched me in the hallway before school, the way he handles me now is gentle.

Just as my eyelids flutter shut and I arch into his palms, the warmth disappears. He grips the hem of my tank and drags it upward until he can peel it away, tossing it to the carpeted floor alongside the bed.

His gaze fastens onto my breasts. "How are you this beautiful?"

No one has ever stared at me so openly. It's almost as if he's trying to soak up every single detail and commit it to memory. Heat flushes my cheeks and chest as my arms rise to shield my nudity.

"Don't do that." His voice drops, becoming rougher. "Don't ever hide yourself from me." His arms rise, shackling my wrists once more before dragging them above my head to the pillow. "Leave them there."

It's a struggle to do as he says and not move them. When he sits back, eating me up with his eyes, I can't help but shift beneath his penetrating stare.

"You have nothing to be embarrassed about."

"I'm not," I lie.

"Good. I've been fantasizing about what you looked like beneath your uniform since we met. Now, I finally get to see every damn inch. I can take my time and spread you out. I can stare at you for hours if that's what I want."

The low hum of his voice and the meaning of his words strums something deep inside I didn't know existed. The thought of him doing exactly that is such a turn-on.

His thumbs and forefingers settle around each turgid peak before giving them a small pinch. A sizzle of pain zips through me before it's chased away by a flash of pleasure.

"Such stiff little nipples."

A whimper escapes from me and my back bows. Need spirals

through me as the buds become impossibly hard. When he tweaks them for a second time, a fresh burst of arousal explodes in my core before throbbing insistently to life. He stays focused on my chest, playing with me, twisting and pulling until it feels like I'll self-combust.

Darkness fills his eyes as they flicker to mine. "You like that, don't you?"

There's no point in denying it. More than that, I don't want to. "Yes."

His hands are so big and yet he knows exactly how much pressure to apply to give the most pleasure. Before I'm ready, his fingers disappear. I cry out in protest before he leans down, drawing one aching peak between his lips and sucking it greedily into his mouth.

I twist beneath him. So badly do I want to tunnel my fingers through his hair, but I'm afraid to move. Afraid to disobey him. Just when I can't bear another moment of this exquisite torture, he releases me with a soft pop. His warm breath feathers over the other aching tip and a shiver slides through me as he draws me farther inside his mouth.

With every tug, pleasure ricochets throughout my being.

Even though he's barely touched me, it won't be long until I'm falling to pieces.

"Austin," I moan.

He nips the hard point and another round of explosions detonates at the bottom of my belly. Just like this afternoon, my panties are now completely soaked. I have the feeling he'd ruin every single pair if given half the chance.

"What, sweet girl? What do you want?"

His hands drift along my sides until they can cup my breasts before pressing the rounded curves together. His tongue circles one stiff bud before doing the same to the other side.

"Tell me," he growls as he continues licking my nipples. "Tell me what you want."

"You," I gasp. "I want you."

"Good. Because I want you, too."

He drifts down my ribcage, peppering kisses as he goes. His tongue licks over me, leaving a trail of desire in its wake. The cool air of the room wafts over my newly dampened flesh. My breasts throb, aching for more of his attention. It's tempting to cup them with my hands and squeeze their softness, to pluck my own nipples as he kisses a path to my panties.

I'm not sure how much more of this erotic torture I can stand. My head is clouded with so much pleasure that it feels as if I'm drowning in it. A yelp escapes from me when his teeth sink into my pubic bone.

Again, the pain is chased away by need. A flood of it rushes through my body before settling in my core. He buries his nose in the cotton at the top of my slit before circling it around my clit.

"These should probably go, don't you think?"

God, yes.

But wrapping my lips around those three little letters feels impossible. I'm a puddle of need, writhing beneath him as delicious sensation reverberates through every cell of my being.

"Is that what you want me to do?" He lifts his face, and the warmth of his breath disappears.

"Please." Pleading tones fill every syllable.

It's a relief when he doesn't make me beg and the cotton is ripped away in an instant. They're down my hips and thighs before being carelessly discarded.

And then I'm bared to his sight.

He's touched my breasts and yanked my underwear to the side, but this is the first time he's seen me completely naked. Moonlight streams in through the window, bathing me in a silvery glow as Austin sits back to silently look his fill. He resettles between my legs, shifting them to make room. My thighs are spread wide, and my arms are still stretched out overhead. There's no way to hide from his piercing stare. I can almost feel the heat of his gaze licking over every inch. Admiring every dip and curve. His palms settle on my inner thighs before pushing them wider to expose my center. He's stared, but never like this.

Never so intently.

His gaze lifts to mine. "Don't move a single muscle."

His body rises, stretching over me before clicking the small lamp beside the bed. The room fills with light. Even though it's not overly harsh, I squint and try to adjust to the illumination.

"Why—"

"I need to see you."

Embarrassment gathers in my cheeks and spreads to my chest as he resumes his position between my legs.

"Austin," I whisper. "Please turn it off."

"No. I want to see every inch of you." His green eyes flicker to mine, and the heat radiating from them nearly singes me alive. "I want to see what now belongs to me."

The possessiveness of his words arrows to the very heart of me before exploding on impact.

His voice deepens, turning into more of a feral growl. "You belong to me, don't you, Delilah?"

"Yes." It's not a question I have to think about. I've never wanted to belong to anyone the way I do to him.

He rises to press a kiss against my mouth. When his tongue licks the seam of my lips, I open, and he delves inside. There's a tangle of softness before he pulls away, dropping a kiss against each breast before hovering over my center. His hands press my thighs impossibly wide until it feels as if every single inch of me is on display.

"So fucking pretty," he groans before his mouth settles over my pussy.

That one soft touch is enough to leave me whimpering. Especially when he spears his tongue deep inside my opening before licking me from top to bottom and then back again. When he sucks my clit gently into his mouth, every muscle tightens as sharp tendrils of need curl in my core. A whimper slips free as I arch off the mattress. Unable to help myself, I widen my legs, needing to feel the firm pressure of his lips roving over every fragile inch.

"How will I ever get enough of you?"

I silently echo the sentiment. Not in a million years would I have suspected that physical intimacy could feel this amazing. He nibbles at my clit before licking along the length of my opening and spearing his tongue deep inside my heat.

"Such a sweet little pussy," he groans before attacking my flesh.

Intensity gathers inside me like a storm as his dirty words push me over the edge. My body becomes whipcord tight as my inner muscles convulse and I find myself falling into an abyss of riotous sensation.

A scream wells in my throat and I slap a palm across my mouth to keep the sound trapped inside. My body writhes beneath him as his hands lock around my thighs to keep me firmly in place. It's only when the aftershocks fade that he lifts his head and recaptures my gaze.

His tongue darts out to lick the shininess that coats his lips. "Fucking delicious."

Even though the last remnants of orgasm have barely faded, his words bring a sharp ache of desire to my core.

His gaze stays locked on mine as he presses a kiss against my swollen pussy before rolling off the bed and rising to his feet. Before I can ask what he's doing, his fingers grip the edge of his T-shirt and drag it up his sculpted chest. He discards the material before flicking open the button of his jeans and tugging the zipper. The denim is shoved down lean hips and thick thighs before he kicks it away.

That's when I realize he isn't wearing boxers.

Why that's sexy as hell, I have no idea.

Even though it's been less than thirty-six hours since I've seen him naked, I'm starving for the sight of him. With his sinewy muscles on display, he stills, allowing me to look my fill.

I can't imagine any other man being this magnificent.

He's gorgeous.

Utter perfection.

He keeps telling me how beautiful I am, but he's the stunning one.

My gaze falls to his cock. It's ridiculously long and hard. Standing to attention. The head is engorged, making it look even bigger and more intimidating. My mouth waters, remembering what it felt like to draw him inside me.

There were so many times when Jasper tried cajoling me into

giving him a BJ and I always refused. The thought secretly disgusted me. I didn't want him anywhere near my face. When his sweet words didn't work, he'd get angry and become forceful. It's a miracle I came out of that relationship with my virginity intact. I'm so glad that I did, because I couldn't imagine this moment unfolding any other way than with Austin.

My tongue darts out to lick my lips as he steps closer. Unwilling to be a passive participant in this experience any longer, I move to the edge of the bed. When he's no more than an inch away, I glance up until our gazes can fasten as my tongue flicks over the tip of his erection. A groan slides from him as his eyelids fall.

Inching forward, I draw his crown into my mouth. He hisses out a breath as his fingers tangle in my hair, holding me firmly in place. With a flex of lean hips, he slides deeper inside me. It doesn't take long for his breathing to turn harsh as we fall into a steady rhythm.

Five more pumps and he pulls away.

When a sound of displeasure hums through me, he smirks and leans down, hands sliding over my cheeks. "The next time I come, sweet girl, it'll be in your pussy." He presses a kiss against my lips before nipping at them. "After that, we'll explore your sucking abilities in more depth." His eyes grow dark. "Watching my dick disappear between those pouty pink lips is hot as fuck."

"Promise?"

A groan rumbles up from his chest as he presses another kiss against my mouth. "Damn right I do."

And then he's setting me free and rising to his feet before kneeling on the mattress between my legs. His hands slip behind my knees as he pulls them up and forces them further apart. It only takes one arch of his hips until the head of his erection can slide through the wetness of my lips.

Sensation ricochets throughout my body as I shift, wanting to feel the slide of him deep inside my heat instead of merely teasing me with the tip. He stares at my core as he strokes his length against my sensitive flesh.

"Austin," I whimper. "Please."

His eyes lift, pinning me in place. There's so much heat and arousal brimming within them that it feels like they could scorch me alive.

"Don't rush me. This first time needs to be gentle in order to make it good for you. After that," he growls, voice deepening, "I won't make any promises. The next time I have you, I'm going to fuck you hard. I'll turn you over and mount you from behind. So let me take this nice and slow. You deserve that."

I nod, wanting his tenderness as much as I want his forcefulness. That's when I realize that with him, I can have both. He's opened up a whole new world I had no idea existed, and I want to take my time and explore it all.

He continues to tease, stroking his thick erection against my core until I'm writhing beneath him.

"Your pussy is so nice and wet. Ready for more?"

I nod.

"Good. Because I need to bury myself inside that sweet little cunt." His gaze falls to my core. "As much as I fucking hate thinking about the two of you together, I can understand why Jasper wanted to keep you a virgin."

His gaze slices to mine.

"Your pussy is so fucking perfect. If I didn't want you so bad, I'd hold off, but there's no way I can do that. I need to make you mine."

Even the thought of him pulling away and denying me is enough to have icy cold tendrils of panic wrapping around my heart. "Please don't. I need you inside me."

A groan escapes from him as he flexes his hips. "Don't worry. I'm going to fill you all the way up. You'll get all the cock you need."

My muscles loosen as relief crashes over me. "Thank you."

"You can thank me afterward."

It's tempting to laugh, but I'm racked with too much tension to summon the sound.

Another long stroke and the head of his cock is pressed against my opening. Air gets trapped at the back of my throat as everything inside me stills.

A growl rumbles from deep within his chest. "Fuck. Are you on the pill or should I grab a condom?'

"I'm on the pill."

He squeezes his eyes tightly shut. "Good, because I really don't want to wear a rubber. I want to feel your tight heat surrounding me." He swallows thickly, the corded muscles of his throat working. "I'm clean. I haven't been with anyone since we moved here."

"Okay."

He cracks open his eyes and holds my stare. "Are you sure? Once I take you uncovered, I won't wear anything again. I'll want that pussy bare every single time."

"I understand. I've been on it for a while."

He jerks his head before pressing farther inside me. It's not much. Just an inch or so. There's a pinch as my body adjusts to his girth. Austin is both long and thick. I can't imagine what it'll feel like to have him buried deep inside my body.

The thought is as thrilling as it is scary.

With a flex of his hips, he works his way in another inch before stopping.

"You're so damn wet," he mutters, teeth tightly clenched, a bead of perspiration breaking out across his brow.

I wriggle against him, needing him deeper inside me.

"Don't be greedy. You'll get what I give you."

He swats my clit with the tips of his fingers and a thousand little fireworks explode within me. I whine and writhe against him, unable to help myself. It's as if my body has a mind of its own and I'm no longer in control. There's something wonderfully liberating about the sensation. When he slides free, I cry out in frustration before he glides back inside. There's another pinch of pain and I wince.

"Are you all right?" A muscle tics in his jaw.

I nod as my teeth scrape across my lower lip.

"Should I stop? Because I will, if that's what you want."

God, no.

"Please don't."

In response, he pushes a little farther inside until he's buried halfway. My gaze drops to the place where we're now intimately connected, and a wave of heat rolls over me.

How is he only halfway inside my body?

"I don't think you're going to fit," I whisper.

The edges of his lips quirk. "I promise, it will. You were made for my cock. Do you know that?"

I feel the same, but still…

There's so much of him. Pain radiates from my center as I stretch around his size. When he pulls out, a strange emptiness settles in my core, and it leaves me feeling hollow and bereft.

"Look at my dick. Do you see how wet you are for me?"

We both take a moment to stare at his thick erection. The tip is swollen and purplish in hue, as if it'll explode any second. He's right about it glistening with my arousal. That's all it takes for more desire to flood me.

As he slides back inside my heat, his fingertips settle over my clit, rubbing soft circles. The way he caresses my delicate flesh while splayed completely open as his dick pins me to the mattress is enough to have the thin whisps of another orgasm curling through my lower belly.

His hips rock, sliding deeper inside with each movement. As the intensity continues to build, I arch, needing more.

"I can't go any further without causing you pain," he grounds as if loathe to do that.

"I know. I want you to make me yours. I want to belong to you in this way."

He groans. "Only me. You'll belong to only me."

His teeth drag across the fullness of his lower lip as if he's having a difficult time holding himself in check. His fingers disappear from my clit as he lowers himself until his chest is pressed against my breasts and my legs can wrap around his lean waist.

His mouth hovers over mine. "I'm sorry, sweet girl. This is going to hurt."

Just as I open my mouth to tell him it's okay, he jerks in one swift movement, impaling me with his cock. My eyes widen as shock reverberates throughout my being. His lips crash onto mine to swallow down my cries as his tongue thrusts inside my mouth. Once he's buried deep inside my abraded body, he goes completely still.

With our gazes locked, he whispers, "Breathe."

A burst of air escapes from my lungs as he gives me time to adjust to the intrusion.

"I'm going to move, all right?"

I gulp down my growing nerves. All those delicious sensations spiraling through me have disappeared, leaving only searing pain in their place.

A tear escapes from the corner of my eye.

"I'm sorry." He braces on his elbows and thumbs away the wetness. "Don't cry. Give it a few minutes and it'll get better. I promise."

I nod and attempt to put on a brave face. This hurts more than I anticipated. But still…I like the heavy weight of his body pressing into mine. And there's a closeness between us that wasn't there before. When he broke through the thin barrier of my virginity, he destroyed the ones standing in our way.

When he drags his cock from my body, a breath of relief escapes from me. The sound hasn't even left my lips when he presses back inside. Even though I try to keep the whimper trapped in my lungs, it proves to be an impossible task.

His gaze stays locked on mine as he remains still, allowing me to adjust before carefully withdrawing and repeating the movement. The pain fades so gradually that I don't realize it's happened until arousal once again stirs in my core.

My eyes widen as I cautiously raise my hips to meet his. The tension filling his face lessens as he rocks against me. It's almost a shock when pleasure once again blooms in the pit of my belly, feeling very much like it did before he forced his way inside my body.

His jaw locks, the muscle in his cheek ticking a mad rhythm. "I won't last much longer."

My own tempo increases as I meet each thrust.

"Fuck," he grunts before tensing. His cock swells, becoming even larger, before jerking. He squeezes his eyes shut and throws his head back, the thickly corded muscles of his throat on display.

I can only stare in awe as his tightly held control falls away. It's the most beautiful thing I've ever witnessed in my life.

He continues to grunt, his pelvis grinding against mine, as his release seems to go on forever. The warmth that floods my womb heats me up from the inside out. I don't think I've ever felt closer to another human being than I do in this moment.

I wish it could last forever.

After the final shudder racks his body, he collapses. His harsh breath fills my ears as I wrap my arms around him and hold on tight.

"I'm sorry," he whispers.

A chuckle bursts free. "For what?"

"I wanted you to come a second time."

"Are you forgetting that you gave me three orgasms today?"

He lifts his head and meets my gaze with a smirk marring his expression. "That's true." He presses a quick kiss to my mouth. "Next time, you'll come with me buried deep inside your pussy."

A shiver of anticipation dances down my spine at the thought of doing this again.

"Do you have any regrets?"

I shake my head. "Nope. I'm happy it was you."

"I'm happy it was me too."

He searches my eyes as his expression turns serious. "Now that you've given yourself to me, you're mine." There's a pause as his voice deepens. "You belong to me."

I nip his chin with sharp teeth. "I wouldn't want to belong to anyone else."

The tension leaks from his muscles. "Better not."

Needing to break the seriousness that has fallen over us, I ask, "So…how long do we need to wait until we can do that again?"

When a chuckle slips free from him, ricocheting off the walls, I know the question has done exactly what it was meant to.

DELILAH

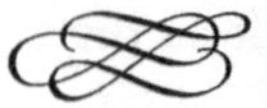

*A*ustin's fingers lock around mine as he tows me through the first floor of Kingsley's house. Even though I've been here several times, I can't help but stare at the opulence that surrounds me. Heavy crystal chandeliers hang from the double story ceiling and antique furnishings that are polished to a high shine fill every room. There's an ocean of gleaming hardwood throughout the first floor. The oversized paintings that take prominence on the walls look as if they belong in a museum rather than a home. It doesn't escape me that just one piece of artwork from the Rothchild collection could probably buy us a new house.

There was a game earlier this evening and the Hawks crushed their opponents. Jasper started out playing the first quarter, but after an intercepted pass and touchdown, he was pulled out and replaced by Austin.

By the end of the first quarter, the game had turned around. I couldn't help but notice how cool and collected Austin appeared on the field. It didn't take long for the fans filling the stands to cheer his name.

Since our arrival at the party, classmates have been slapping him on the back, telling him what a great game it was. A few stopped, wanting to discuss some of the plays. Instead of eating up their praise and attention, he gave them a chin lift in acknowledgment and a curt thank you. If this were Jasper, he'd be reveling in their admiration, soaking it in.

Austin is nothing like my ex. It's something I've known in the back of my head, but to catch more glimpses of it is reassuring. The last thing I want to do is make the same mistake twice.

My belly hollows out as my attention resettles on him. No matter what I'm doing or where I'm at, I can't keep my gaze off him for long.

He's so handsome.

Devastatingly so.

It seems almost surreal that we're here tonight as a couple.

A real couple.

He's not rubbing me in Jasper's face and using me to piss him off. After spending the night in his arms, a shift has occurred. It feels like we might actually have a real shot at a relationship.

"Do you want something to drink?" he asks over the pumping beat of music that echoes off the cavernous walls of the mansion.

"Just a water," I say, raising my voice to be heard.

Fighting through the mass of bodies, we make our way to the kitchen, where the booze is flowing freely. People are taking shots and playing drinking games. He grabs a bottle of water from the fridge and a red Solo cup of what's on tap for himself.

We both take a drink as his gaze coasts over the sea of students. "Let's go outside and sit by the firepit. It's too damn crowded in here."

The house is wall-to-wall people. Kingsley doesn't throw parties often, so when he does, no one wants to miss it. Classmates chatter excitedly about the victory on the field now that the team is closer to making it to state.

Although, let's face it, there's probably a good number of kids in attendance who don't give a crap about football. They want to get wasted and have a good time. I've never been one of those people. When Jasper would drag me to parties, I was always careful not to drink too much. I didn't quite trust him not to take advantage of me.

It was yet another red flag I turned a blind eye to.

I slant a look at Austin. Maybe he lashed out because of hurt feelings, but even then, he wasn't intent on inflicting damage. A chill slides through me, thinking about what Jasper would have done had the situation been reversed. There's no doubt in my mind that he would have burnt the school to the ground along with everyone in it.

That's exactly the kind of person he is.

Unwilling to dwell on those disturbing thoughts, I shove them away. We're here to have fun. I want this to be a fresh start. One where we can let go of the past and move forward.

I glance at the crowd pressing in on us. My hope is that we don't have to stay long. I'd much rather go somewhere quiet and continue getting to know one another.

As we push through the French doors onto the patio, the cool night breeze wafts over us. It makes me wish I'd worn a cozy sweatshirt instead of a thin sweater. Goose bumps ripple across my flesh as I lift my hands to rub my arms.

We dodge the pockets of people who are standing around and talking. A few notice Austin and attempt to wave him over. He doesn't give them the time of day. I certainly can't blame him for that. Most have been assholes. Unable to think for themselves, they've taken their lead from Jasper. It was even worse when Kingsley was against the twins.

"Looks like your fan club is trying to get your attention," I joke.

It's kind of amazing that they've done such a quick one eighty. It just goes to show you how fickle our classmates really are. They don't care about Austin. They care about winning football games and making it to the championship. They care about having another banner to hang in the hallway.

It's as if he can read my thoughts.

"They're not my friends," he says with a snort. "Come Monday, half of them will pretend I don't exist."

Sadly, there's not much I can say to that since it's the truth and we both know it. We're outcasts, but for different reasons. The funny thing is that Austin should fit in. He's stupid handsome, a gifted athlete, and his descendants founded both the town and school. He should be treated like royalty. But he didn't grow up here, and there's too much bad blood between his ancestors and this community.

I'm not sure if there's anything he can do to change it.

Once outside, Austin drops onto the plush couch and pulls me onto his lap. It feels like second nature to thread my arms around his neck. Two weeks ago, I couldn't have imagined doing something so intimate. I couldn't even picture being alone with him in the same room.

And now everything has changed.

It was rough in the beginning, but it's all worked out and I couldn't be happier. I have the boy I've secretly longed for since we first met. The very same one who only has to glance in my direction and my pulse kicks into overdrive, thumping a painful beat against my flesh.

His hands settle around my hips to lock me in place. I can feel the heat of them singeing me through my jeans. It's enough to make me wish that we'd skipped the party all together. But how could we do that when he's the reason the Hawks won in the first place? If there's going to be any movement with our classmates, it'll be made now. Plus, it's Kingsley's party and Summer is here. Even though Austin has set aside his issues with him, he's still protective of his sister.

For the time being, I'll happily snuggle against his broad chest as the bright orange flames twist in the firepit. The heat is just enough to warm my chilled skin as silvery moonlight pours over us. The music from inside is more muffled, but faint wisps along with the steady bass can still be heard as the fire's reflection dances in his eyes.

It's impossible to believe this boy now belongs to me.

Just like I belong to him.

It's almost too good to be true.

"Are you cold?" The concern that weaves its way through his voice strums something deep inside. It wouldn't take much to fall even harder for him.

Instead of admitting that I'm freezing, I shrug. "A little."

"Want to head back in the house?"

I shake my head. "No, I'd much rather stay on the patio where it's less crowded."

One hand slides into the thickness of my hair before he pulls me close enough for his lips to settle over mine. As they do, I open and the velvety softness of his tongue slips inside my mouth to tangle with my own. That's all it takes for the noise and people to fade to the background. I can't help but open more fully until he's able to devour me.

That's precisely what it feels like.

Being consumed in the best way possible.

"Get a room," someone shouts, breaking into the protective bubble that surrounds us.

"Or don't," another guy laughs. "I wouldn't mind watching that girl get fucked."

Austin strokes his tongue against mine before reluctantly pulling away. He glances around, spotting one of the loudmouths near the pool.

"Hey, Garrickson?" Austin calls out, voice raised over the noise of the party.

The redheaded kid glances at us with a stupid grin on his face.

"Shut the fuck up."

Austin's attention locks on his friend. "You, too."

Their smiles dim in wattage as they glance at each other before swinging away.

"So fucking childish," he grumbles.

"Welcome to high school," I say lightheartedly, not wanting them to ruin our night.

His expression eases and his lips hitch. "Yeah, I guess so."

A burst of wind whips over us and a shiver scampers across my skin. When I press closer to his warmth, he grabs the hem of his sweatshirt before yanking it up his body. As soon as it's removed, he drags it over my head. I shove my arms through the sleeves as the material settles around me. It's so warm and smells exactly like Austin. It takes every ounce of my willpower to resist bringing the thick cotton to my nose and inhaling a lungful of his masculine scent.

"Better?"

"Much," I say with a contented smile. "Thank you."

For the second time, I burrow against his brawny chest before tilting my head and slanting a look up at him. "Aren't you cold?"

"Nope. I've got you to warm me up."

His hands slip beneath the hem of the sweatshirt before drifting along my ribcage and settling under the gentle swell of my breasts. All he has to do is inch his thumb upward a bit and he would be touching me. The sweatshirt is so oversized that no one would be the wiser. Our gazes cling as he strokes my bare flesh. I lose all sense of time as people come and go, no one daring to intrude on the moment we're having.

When the hair at the base of my neck prickles, I'm struck with the feeling of eyes crawling over me. It's different than the curious stares that have been aimed in our direction for most of the evening.

Unable to shake the disturbing sensation of being watched, I lift my head and scan the area. It doesn't take long for my gaze to collide with Jasper's. Instead of looking away, his attention stays locked on mine as he lifts the Solo cup to his lips and downs the contents. He doesn't pay attention to Sloane and one of her minions as they hang on him. His broody stare stays locked on me.

A jolt of unease slides through my body before settling at the bottom of my belly like a heavy stone. No matter what I do, it's impossible to dislodge. I'm knocked from the strange paralysis when Austin nips at my lower lip.

My gaze slices to him.

He searches my eyes. "What's wrong?"

I force a smile, unwilling to bring up my ex. "Nothing."

Steeliness grows in his eyes as his jaw locks. "Don't lie to me."

Heat suffuses my cheeks as his gaze shifts, settling on someone over my shoulder. "Looks like we have an audience."

The sinking sensation in my gut grows. I wish Jasper would move on and leave us alone. It's over. He did his damnedest to keep us apart and it didn't work. I'm sure he's furious. The guy is used to getting his way and has no idea how to handle rejection or walk away from a fight.

"Unfortunately."

The corners of his lips tilt as his hand slips from beneath the sweatshirt and slides around the back of my skull before propelling me forward.

"Let him watch. You belong to me now."

"Austin…"

The last thing I want to do is provoke Jasper's temper. It's like poking at a wild animal. You never know how he'll react, and I'm not looking to get mauled. Barely have I managed to escape from him unscathed. I'd like to keep it that way.

Before I can deter him, the firm pressure of Austin's lips settles over mine. Even when his tongue slips inside my mouth, there's no losing myself in the caress. I'm much too aware of the narrowed gaze drilling into the back of my skull.

Uncomfortable with the PDA, my palms settle against his chest before pushing him away. As we break apart, he sends me a curious look.

Before he can ask any questions, I blurt, "I need to use the bathroom."

His eyes narrow as the intensity of his stare grows. "Are you sure that's all it is?"

Thrown off by the question, I stare. "Of course. What else would it be?"

He shifts, muscles tensing as his gaze flickers over my shoulder. When they resettle on mine again, suspicion mars his expression. After the other night and everything we shared, it feels like a slap in my face.

"I'm not sure…maybe you don't want Jasper to see us together."

Air stalls in my lungs before I admit in a calm voice, "You're right, I don't. But not for the reasons you assume."

The mistrust that brews in his eyes slices through my heart with the precision of a scalpel. I'd really hoped we could put this mess with Jasper behind us. Maybe it was delusional on my part to think we could move on so easily.

I clear my throat and untangle myself from him before rising to my feet. "I'll be back in a sec."

His gaze probes mine as if searching for answers to questions he has yet to ask. After a long moment that only intensifies the tension vibrating in the air, he murmurs, "I'll be here waiting."

I force a smile. "Okay."

With that, I weave through the thick crowd, making my way to the set of French doors that lead to the kitchen. A little time to clear my head is exactly what we both need. I refuse to be a pawn in a game of revenge. If Austin wants to be with me, he needs to stop thinking about my ex.

As I open the door and slip inside the house, I wince. The decibel level of the music is like an assault and the vibrations of it echo in my bones. One glance tells me that people are even drunker and rowdier than thirty short minutes ago. As I consider turning around and retreating outside, I get shoved from behind. The force sends me stumbling farther into the space.

"Sorry," a girl from my AP psych class mumbles, tipping the red cup to her lips and draining it.

It's definitely time to get out of here before this party spirals any further out of control. I'll use the bathroom and then tell Austin I'm ready to go. This kind of thing has never been my scene, and it's nice that it isn't his either. It doesn't take long to find one of the first-floor bathrooms. The line, on the other hand, is at least ten deep. By the time I take care of business, it feels like twenty minutes have slipped by. As I retrace my steps to the kitchen, a couple girls stare when they realize whose sweatshirt I'm wearing. I hunch my shoulders and force my way through the thick press of bodies. It's just another reminder that I don't fit in with these people. They will never be my friends. And nothing will change that.

I pass by the massive stainless-steel refrigerator that looks more like it belongs in a fancy restaurant and realize just how thirsty I am before beelining for the appliance. I'll grab a water and then find Austin. One peek inside shows that all the non-alcoholic beverages have disappeared. If I want to quench my thirst with a beer, there are plenty.

Looks like I'm out of luck.

As I maneuver my way to the door, I bump into Aubrey. When I hung around Sloane's group, we were never close but always friendly. After all the issues with Jasper, I've gone out of my way to steer clear of her.

So it's a surprise when she flashes a smile. "How's it going?"

It's tempting to glance over my shoulder and make sure she's talking to me.

She usually takes all her social cues from her bestie. There's a hierarchy to the group. Only Sloane is allowed to think for herself. She's the brains of the operation. If she snubs someone, her girl gang doesn't need a reason to fall in line and follow suit.

"Umm, good. How about you?"

Maybe she's drunker than I realized.

The wattage of her smile increases. "Amazing. This party is so much fun. I love when Kingsley invites people over." There's a pause before she adds, "I gotta tell you—we're all *so* proud of Austin."

I blink, thrown for another loop.

Have I somehow entered a parallel universe where nothing makes sense?

Because that's exactly how this conversation feels.

"Really?" Shock weaves its way into my tone.

One hand smooths over the short skirt of her cheerleading uniform as she nods. "Who knew that he would turn out to be such a superstar?" She glances around before leaning closer. I can't help but mimic the movement. I have no idea what's about to tumble out of her mouth, but I would be lying if I didn't admit that I'm curious. "Don't tell Jasper I said that. He'd be so pissed."

That's an understatement.

The thought of his rage is enough to turn my mouth cottony. I can't help but remember the way he'd been staring outside and a shiver slithers down my spine. Any hope I'd had that we could peacefully co-exist has disintegrated.

"I won't say a word." I take a quick step in retreat, only wanting to find Austin and get out of here. I'm about to lift a hand and say goodbye when I spot the bottle of water hanging from her fingers. "Where did you get that?"

"Sorry, girl. I just grabbed the last one." She leans toward me again before dropping her voice to a conspiratorial whisper. "I'm trying not to drink so much this year. I need to get my grades up, otherwise I won't get accepted to college."

I've had several classes with Aubrey and grades have never seemed important. Apparently, now that we're in the final stretch of high school, she's decided to buckle down.

Better late than never, I guess.

"Bummer about the water, but good for you."

Just as I'm about to swing away, she says, "Wait!"

I stop and cock a brow as she thrusts the bottle in my direction.

"You can take this one."

My gaze drops to her outstretched hand before I wave her away. "It's all right. No worries."

She jiggles the container. "Go ahead, I just opened it. Never even took a sip. It's all yours."

When I hesitate, she rolls her eyes and cocks a hip. "Seriously, Delilah. Just take it. I wasn't that thirsty anyway."

Indecision swirls through me. "Are you sure?"

"Of course." She flashes that same bright smile. "I wouldn't have offered if I didn't want you to have it."

Even though I'm reluctant to take anything from her, I relent. She's being so nice. "Okay, thanks. I appreciate it."

She presses the plastic bottle into my hand. "No problem. Enjoy."

Feeling parched, I twist off the cap and tilt the opening to my lips before guzzling down a third of the cool liquid.

Ahhh...that feels so much better.

"Thanks, Aubrey. I'll catch you later."

Her voice rises above the music as I turn away, "Are you looking for Austin?"

I pause and glance over my shoulder. It's been about twenty minutes and I'm impatient to find him again. "Yeah."

"I think he's playing pool in the game room with Kingsley and a couple of the other guys from the team."

That comment surprises me almost as much as her beaming a smile and being so friendly. "Really?"

I figured we'd take off, but maybe him doing well on the football field has helped break through the icy social barrier that has been erected since the twins' arrival. If that's the case, I don't want to deny him the opportunity to make friends. Not everyone at Hawthorne Prep is bad. It just takes time to weed through them and find the good ones.

She nods. "Yup, pretty sure I saw him in there."

"Can you point me in the direction of the game room?"

Kingsley's house is easily ten thousand square feet. It's not difficult to get lost or turned around in the maze of rooms.

She glances toward the hallway. "Okay, you're going to head in that direction and then, after the first door, take a right." Her brow furrows. "Or maybe a left. I'm pretty sure it's a couple of rooms down from there."

I should probably call him.

Before I can reach into my pocket and pull out my cell, she locks her fingers around my hand. "It'll just be easier if I show you where it is. I've played strip poker in there a ton of times."

That's not a surprise.

From what I've heard, she's done way more than just play card games.

We only get a handful of steps before passing a group of her friends. When Aubrey stops to chat, a couple of them glance at me as if they can't figure out what I'm doing with the popular cheerleader. I'm silently asking myself the same question. At the moment, I feel very much like an unwanted third wheel. Unsure what to do, I shift before twisting off the bottle cap and taking another deep drink.

After a handful of minutes, I decide to find Austin on my own. Standing around with this particular group of girls is beyond awkward.

I stifle a yawn, covering my mouth with my hand, as a wave of fatigue crashes over me. It's a battle to keep my eyes open. I don't know what time it is, but it can't be that late.

Where did this exhaustion come from?

Then again, maybe I shouldn't be so surprised. This week has been stressful. I could probably crash for a solid twenty-four hours, and it wouldn't be nearly enough.

I need to find Austin so we can take off. I'm over this party.

"Aubrey," I say, tugging on her hand. "Thanks for your help, but I'm going to find him on my own."

With a glance, she holds up one finger. "Give me just a sec." She turns back to her friends. "I'll catch you guys in a bit. There's something I need to take care of."

Ugh. Why can't I shake this girl loose?

It's not like we're besties.

I should have snuck away without saying a word. "It's fine. I'll find him on my own."

Instead of responding, her grip tightens around my hand before she tows me through the kitchen and down the dark corridor toward the front of the house. At least, I think that's where we're going. I'm a little turned around. We pass by a couple groups talking and laughing. A few people say hello to Aubrey, but this time, she doesn't stop to chat.

She's a woman on a mission.

"Here we are," she singsongs in a high-pitched voice before grinding to a halt in front of a closed door. "Ready to find your man?"

God, yes.

Her words circle through my head.

Is that what Austin is now?

My man?

The idea makes my belly flutter with happiness.

Her gaze drops to the drink in my hand. "Looks like you're almost done with that water. Finish it up and I'll throw the bottle away."

My eyelids feel like they weigh a thousand pounds as I glance at the plastic container. Strangely enough, the near-empty bottle feels equally as heavy. Her words circle through my brain but don't penetrate. It's like I can't make sense of them.

"Huh?"

"Drink up," she encourages with another smile.

When I remain still, she huffs out a breath and nips the bottle from my fingers before removing the cap and lifting it to my lips, not giving me a choice in the matter. Even though Aubrey has been weirdly nice, I want to find Austin. A splash of cool liquid rushes down my throat and dribbles from the corners of my lips.

Sputtering, I swipe the back of my hand across my face.

"I think you're all set."

She gives me the once over before throwing open the door and shoving me across the threshold.

When I stumble into the large space, she laughs. "Are you all right?"

"Fine. Just a little tired." My words come out sounding strangely incoherent.

And my tongue...why does it feel so thick?

Like a piece of rubber sitting in my mouth. My brain feels so fuzzy. Kind of like when I was in the hospital and had my appendix removed. The pain meds they gave me made me feel like this.

How weird is that?

Aubrey giggles. "I think someone drank too much."

What?

No.

I shake my head. I'm not much of a drinker. I've always been too focused on my grades, graduating from high school, and getting the hell out of this godforsaken town.

But I'm sleepy, garbling my words, and I can barely keep my eyes open. It's like I've been run over by a Mack truck. Right now, nothing makes sense.

I glance around the room, but it's dark and shadowy. There's a small lamp on an antique side table near a curved sofa along with a pool table and another for cards at the far end of the room.

Wait a minute...aren't there supposed to be people in here?

Where's Austin?

I lift my hand to my face. Everything feels so confusing.

"You said he was here."

The slurring is getting worse.

"Hmmm. I thought he was." She saunters toward me before pressing down on my shoulder. The weight of it sends me crashing onto the couch. "Sit down and I'll find him. He couldn't have gone far. In fact, he's probably looking for you."

Is that what happened?

My body feels so heavy. Unable to hold myself up, I topple onto the cushions like a freshly cut tree.

"Timber," I whisper before a giggle escapes.

"Jesus. You're really bad. Hold tight, I'll be back in a sec."

"'Kay." My eyelids feather closed, and for one blissful moment, it feels like I'm dozing.

The next thing I know, strong hands are sliding under my arms and lifting me up. My hair gets swept away from my face as my name is called. It sounds like the voice is coming through a long tunnel, barely able to reach me.

It's annoying.

My eyelids flutter, but it's a struggle to open them. It's like they're cemented shut.

I'm so tired. I just want to go to bed.

Right here.

Right now.

I don't care anymore.

Just as I slip back into sleep, pain explodes in my cheek, and I squeak.

"Open your damn eyes," a deep voice demands.

It's one I recognize.

Where do I know it from?

When I don't respond, my face is slapped again.

Only harder this time.

"Stop," I force myself to say but don't think it comes out sounding as it should.

"You need to wake up," the voice says sternly.

"I'm awake." It takes effort to get the words out.

Whether they're actually coherent is debatable.

"We're going to take some pictures. You like pictures."

Do I?

Oh, right. Photography. Although, I prefer to be behind the camera rather than in front of it.

"Can you do that for me?"

I nod. "I want to go home."

"Be a good girl and I'll take you there."

Good girl...

Didn't Austin say that to me?

Yeah, he did.

And I liked it.

Liked the deep growl of his voice when it slid from his lips.

I'm repositioned like a ragdoll so that our faces are close. My eyelids flutter just before his lips crush mine. When he forces his tongue inside my mouth, I can't help but think that something is off. There's something different about his kiss, but I'm unable to put my finger on it.

Then again, I don't feel like myself.

From somewhere nearby, a flash goes off and the burst of light hurts my eyes.

He smacks my cheeks again. "We're not done yet."

"Ow!" I bat my hand but my limbs, like my tongue, feel thick and heavy. Almost like they don't belong to me.

It's an odd sensation.

"You look hot. Let's take off the sweatshirt."

A jumbled sound leaves my lips as I'm manhandled.

"She's barely awake," another voice says.

Only this voice is different.

Higher.

That's the last coherent thought that flits through my brain before I'm sucked back into the darkness and swallowed up.

Delilah and Austin's story continues in Princess of Hawthorne Prep

Pre-order Princess of Hawthorne Prep here -)
https://books2read.com/princessofhawthorneprep

See where it all began in King of Hawthorne Prep with Summer and
Kingsley.

KING OF HAWTHORNE PREP

My gaze wanders over the water as white-capped waves roll rhythmically toward the sandy shore. When the wind picks up, a warm breeze rustles through my hair, and I tip my face toward the sun before stretching.

Could life get any better than this?

Doubtful.

A family friend was kind enough to let us borrow their beach house in Door County for the week. Mom and Dad surprised us with the impromptu vacation a few days before we were supposed to leave.

The house we're staying at isn't like one of the newly renovated million-dollar monstrosities that flank us with their gargantuan square footage, swanky pools, and perfectly groomed lawns. But it's steps from the beach and has breathtaking views of Lake Michigan. At just fifteen hundred square feet, this house has three cramped bedrooms, an outdated kitchen, and a ton of seashell décor. Even so, there's something charming about it.

Sweat beads my forehead as I haul myself from the chair I'm sprawled on and saunter to the water's edge. It might look as inviting as the Caribbean cast in varying shades of cerulean and turquoise, but it doesn't feel like it. Especially when my skin has been crispifying for hours beneath the sweltering sun.

A breath hisses from my lips as the frigid liquid rushes past my ankles. The first couple of steps are the worst. As soon as numbness sets in, it gets better. Braving the water, I continue forward as the waves swirl around my calves. I do a little dance, bouncing up and down on my toes, trying to get used to the cold as it sinks into my bones.

I force myself to move deeper until the water reaches my hips.

It's now or never.

With that brief pep talk, I suck in a breath and dive beneath a wave as it peaks and curls. Water rushes around me, instantly chilling my overheated flesh. After a moment, I break through to the surface and expel the lungful of air from my body.

It's easier to submerge myself the second time as I dive to the bottom before trailing my fingers through the fine-grained sand in search of clamshells. When my lungs burn, I pop up again before floating on the surface so the sun can warm my skin. With my eyes closed, I stretch my hands and legs, allowing the waves to rock my body. My mind drifts as the rhythmic motion lulls me to a contented place. Every once in a while, I lift my head and search for our little blue one-story cottage to make sure I haven't drifted to far down the shore.

My plan is to make the most of our little beach vaca before returning to Chicago next weekend. There's so much that needs to be accomplished before senior year begins in the fall.

A couple of months ago, I registered for an introductory astronomy class at a local university about thirty minutes from the house. Next on the agenda are campus visits. I've scheduled tours for the University of Chicago, Northwestern, and the University of Michigan in Ann Arbor. My three dream schools have impressive astronomy programs. To round out the summer, I've snagged a volunteer position at the Adler Planetarium. I'm scheduled to start next Monday at nine o'clock sharp.

Long after my fingers turn pruney, I drag myself from the water.

As I trudge toward shore, a bleached clamshell glints in the sunlight from the bottom and catches my attention. Stilling my movements, I bend over to inspect it. A wave crashes over me, stirring up the sand and covering the shell. Once the debris settles, I turn, brushing my fingers across the bottom until they land on it again.

"Nice view."

I yelp and swing around, straightening to my full height only to come face-to-face with the most gorgeous boy I've ever seen. My breath gets lodged at the back of my throat as his mahogany-colored eyes pierce mine with unwavering intensity. Rooted in place, it's all I can do to take in the thick slashes of his eyebrows before my gaze slides to the slant of high cheekbones, and then on to a perfect cupid's bow of a mouth.

Damn.

He's seriously hot.

Like...*way out of my league* hot.

My heart riots painfully against my chest as I continue to stare. His brows rise as humor sparks to life in his eyes.

Is he waiting for a response?

Did he ask a question, and I wasn't paying attention? I hit the mental rewind button and quickly sift through our limited conversation.

Nice view.

Nice view?

Wasn't I bent over at the time with my ass in the air?

Heat slams into my cheeks with the force of a tsunami. That's *exactly* the pose I'd been striking. When he said *nice view*, he'd been commenting on my behind. The very same behind barely covered by a thin strip of fabric because the beach has been fairly empty since we arrived on Saturday. This guy is one of the few people I've seen.

"Ummm, thanks," I force myself to respond.

His lips slide into a smirk as if I've amused him.

I need to pull it together before I humiliate myself any further. Although, let's be honest, that ship has already set sail. Right now, I'm operating strictly in damage control mode.

Is it possible that he hasn't noticed my awkwardness?

Any chance of clinging to that unlikely prospect is blown out of the water when he tilts his head. "Did you just thank me for admiring your ass?"

All right, so he noticed.

The heat radiating from my face intensifies a few hundred degrees until self-combustion seems likely. Not to mention, welcome.

"Yeah," I mumble, attempting to rip my gaze from his, but that proves to be impossible. It's as if I've become ensnared by the dark depths assessing me in such a forthright manner. "Apparently I did."

The sound of his deep chuckle reverberates throughout my entire body before darting straight to my—

"I'm Kingsley." He steps forward, closing some of the distance between us. His proximity makes my heart pound faster. "And you are?"

Humiliated?

Embarrassed?

Mortified?

It's a dealer's choice.

"Summer," I mutter instead. When you daydream about talking with a really hot guy, this isn't exactly how you picture it playing out.

Relief rushes from my lungs when his gaze flicks from me to the house I'm standing in front of. There's something powerful about his stare, leaving me to feel as if he's able to pick through all my private thoughts, and it's a disconcerting sensation. I want to run and hide, but my feet refuse to move. I'm frozen in place.

He points at the house on the dunes. "Is that yours?"

"Yes." I clear my throat along with those disconcerting thoughts. "We're renting for the week."

He nods as his attention returns to me where it stays put. That same feeling of nervousness fills me. "Who knows, maybe I'll see you around, Summer."

A wave of heat wafts over me at the sound of my name sliding from his lips. I tamp down the response and shrug, trying to play it cool even though it's much too late for that.

"Yeah, maybe."

He flashes a wide grin as if not fooled by my nonchalance before taking off at a brisk pace down the beach.

Now that his attention is no longer focused on me, I'm free to look my fill as all those well-honed muscles shift and bunch as he jogs away. We're talking broad shoulders with a broad, muscular back that tapers into a trim waist. Loose black athletic shorts cover his trunk and thighs. My gaze drops, wanting to commit every detail to memory. Damn, even his calves are well-defined.

There's no way a guy built like that is in high school. He's definitely in college. I'd like to know what university he attends so I can submit an application. As his figure grows smaller in the distance, I realize I don't even care if they offer astronomy as a major.

I chuckle and shake my head at the thought of planning my future around a boy I spoke with for all of two minutes.

Never.

Going.

To.

Happen.

I have plans. Lots of them. And I would never derail a single one for a guy.

No matter how good-looking he is.

Once the boy fades from sight, I blink out of my thoughts and head back to the house. In all likelihood, I'll never see him again.

Want to read more of Summer & Kingsley's story?
Do it here -) https://books2read.com/u/4A7K8p

HEARTLESS

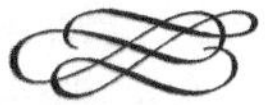

SKYE

"Yay! The bitches are back together again, and tonight we ride!" Lanie wraps her arms around me and squeezes tight. "It's been too long, girl! *Way too long!*"

A reluctant smile curves my lips. "I know. It's good to be back." The circumstances surrounding my return are less than ideal, but I'm happy to see Lanie again. She's been my best friend since middle school, and I've missed her. FaceTime and texting are nice, but it's not the same as talking in person. She links her arm through mine as we walk across the open field.

I glance at the cute cowboy boots that adorn her feet. When she told me that we were going to a field in the middle of nowhere, I didn't believe her.

That was my first mistake.

Second mistake?

Not going with sturdier footwear.

Instead, I'm wearing a pair of flimsy sandals. They're cute as hell, but that's not going to do me a whole lot of good across this terrain.

Lanie insisted we celebrate my return by dragging me to a bonfire in a farmer's field. Already, the place is crawling with drunk-off-their-asses, barely legal adults. Shouting and raucous laughter fill the balmy night air.

Even though I know it won't do me any good, my gaze coasts anxiously over the ever-swelling crowd. Nerves dance across my spine as I silently pray Hunter will be absent from the revelry. Or, if he is here, we'll somehow be able to avoid one another.

If I know Lanie—and I do—she'll be up my ass to cut loose and have fun. How can I do that when Hunter and I now attend the same college? At any given moment, I could turn a corner and smack right into him.

The thought of that happening makes me nauseous.

As much as I want to play it cool and act like my ex-boyfriend doesn't matter, the words slip from my mouth before I can stop them. "You don't think he'll be here, do you?" I shoot her a look that's rife with concern.

Lanie doesn't bother to ask who I'm referring to. She doesn't have to. She's all too aware of my past. She had a front row seat to our relationship and its demise.

"I don't know." She pauses and pops her shoulders into a careless shrug. "Maybe."

"*What?*" My feet grind to a halt as my mouth dries, turning cottony. I'm barely aware of the blades of straw poking my feet through the leather sandals. "But you said—"

Her expression hardens, transforming into one of impatience. "Even if he *is* here, the chances of you running into him are slim." She waves an arm toward the massive group of students who have gathered to mourn the end of summer by drinking themselves into a stupor. "Look around. Half the university is here. There's no way you're going to see him, Skye, so stop worrying about it and live a little."

My teeth sink into my lower lip before I suck the fullness into my mouth. No matter what Lanie says, I'm going to worry.

When I remain silent, my best friend plants her hands on her hips and glares. Here comes Lanie's version of tough love.

"Would you rather sit home by yourself on a Saturday night

because you're too chickenshit to show your face? Afraid that you *might* run into Hunter Price?"

I'm sorry, is that really a question?

From the annoyed expression that flickers across Lanie's face, I decide to keep those thoughts to myself.

"Skye Elizabeth Sinclair!"

I wince as my full name cracks through the air. It brings an unpleasant image of my mother to mind. This is what I get for living with someone who isn't afraid to call me out on my bullshit. Maybe I should have taken Dad up on the offer to live with him.

I decide to go with something close to the truth. "I was hoping to avoid him for a while," I mutter. "That's all."

And when I say a while, *what I really mean is forever.*

Is that really too much to ask?

Lanie sighs as her expression softens. Marginally. "I know, but you're going to run into him on campus or at a party eventually. It's inevitable. Accept it and move on."

I snort.

Easy for her to say. Lanie doesn't have any ghosts from her past that are ready to jump out and scare her.

I have a carefully constructed plan in place for the year. It involves lying low and flying under the radar, so Hunter doesn't even know I'm here. "Yeah, I guess..."

Unwilling to let me backslide, Lanie loops her arm through mine and pulls me toward the growing group of partiers. "It'll be fine. I promise."

Unfortunately, my bestie isn't in a position to guarantee me anything, and we both know it.

The closer we get to the party, the more my anxiety ratchets up. At least night has fallen. The only light emanates from the bonfire that flickers in the distance and the stars that twinkle across the dark velvety sky.

For the time being, I'll remain vigilant. There's really nothing more I can do.

I inhale a deep breath before carefully blowing it out.

Maybe Lanie's right, and I'm making a big deal out of nothing. It's been three years since we've seen each other, and a lot has happened since then. We've both moved on with our lives. I'm sure he's forgotten all about me. As those thoughts circle through my head, my shoulders loosen from around my ears, and my heart stops thumping a painful beat.

The moment we reach the outer ring of people, Lanie is swept off her booted feet and spun around in a tight circle like a rag doll. Her short floral dress flies around her thighs. Laughter rings throughout the air as her arms slip around her boyfriend's neck.

Jaxon Conway has a typical football player's physique. He's a mountain of a man—tall, broad in the shoulders, and muscular. He looks like he could easily bench press Lanie's VW Bug. I would be intimidated by him, but he's quick to laugh and has warm brown eyes. He's like a teddy bear—big and gruff on the outside but tender and mushy on the inside.

"Missed you, babe," he growls.

"It's only been a couple of hours since we saw each other!"

"Doesn't matter," Jax complains. "I still missed the hell out of you."

"Aww." Lanie's voice softens, becoming dreamy. "I love you so much."

"I love you more," he responds with enough heat to melt the panties off Lanie's body.

Ugh.

Make it stop.

These two are so sickeningly sweet that I get a toothache every time I'm around them. Although, if anyone deserves a good guy, it's Lanie. Like most girls in their early twenties, she's dated her fair share of assholes. Jaxon is almost too good to be true. Kind of like a mythical unicorn that sprang to life. He's an athlete who isn't interested in screwing as many girls as he can get his hands on.

Ever since I rolled into town a few days ago, Jaxon and Lanie have been glued together at the hip. I get the feeling he'll be our unofficial third roommate for the year.

Know what's been getting a lot of use?

My noise-canceling headphones.

Most nights, those two sound like they're auditioning for a porno. Let's hope it calms down soon.

Jaxon and Lanie coo at each other before their mouths fuse, and they start going at it like a pair of cats in heat. I clear my throat and glance everywhere but at them. If we were hanging out at the townhouse, this would be my cue to exit stage left. But we're not at home; we're in the middle of a field a few miles from town. There's nowhere for me to go, and no one for me to talk to.

Awkwardness descends as I flick a piece of straw from my shirt.

Maybe I should take this opportunity to grab a beer. There must be a keg around here somewhere. You can't have this many college kids congregating in one spot and not have alcohol. That would be considered sacrilegious, right?

With any luck, by the time I return, Jaxon and Lanie will have stopped mauling each other long enough for us to move on with our evening. It's not like he's being shipped off to war tomorrow and they'll never see each other again.

Sheesh.

My gaze meanders to them in hopes that they've gotten their fill of each other.

Nope. The face sucking has become even more intense. Any moment, clothing is going to spontaneously combust from their bodies.

I don't really want to be around when that happens.

So...a beer it is.

Not that either of them is paying me the least bit of attention, but I point toward the mass of bodies that have multiplied in the fifteen minutes since we've arrived. "I'm going to grab a drink." When my words are met with kissy noises, I say, "Try not to miss me too much while I'm gone."

Lanie waves a hand absently in my direction as they continue to get it on.

"Okay then," I mumble before reluctantly taking off on my own.

The number of people gathered here is a little overwhelming.

Lanie's right; half the university must have shown up. Everyone is talking, laughing, and drinking. In other words, they're having a great time.

Me, not so much.

It takes a good ten minutes to find the keg. Or maybe I should say *kegs* since there are six of them next to the back end of a midnight black pickup truck blasting music from massive speakers. I can barely hear myself think over the thumping bass. Then again, maybe that's for the best. It's a relief to get out of my head, even for a few minutes.

I locate the line for the beer and take my place at the end of it. I'm not much of a drinker, but I need something to smooth out all of the rough edges so I can relax and enjoy myself.

My flesh prickles with awareness, and I run my hands over my arms to banish the disconcerting sensation. I glance around, scouring the crowd for one face in particular but don't see him anywhere. That alone should alleviate my anxiety, but it doesn't.

My parting with Hunter wasn't what one would call amicable. I don't blame him for being hurt and angry. Whether Hunter understands it or not, I did what needed to be done. As painful as it was, I'd do it all over again. I loved Hunter more than life itself.

A part of me still does.

Probably always will.

If everything I've read online is true, then my sacrifices have been well worth it. Hunter will get snapped up in the NFL draft before graduating this spring. Ever since I can remember, that's been his goal. If one person deserves for all his dreams to come true, it's Hunter Price. Unwilling to dwell on my ex, I shove him from my mind and take in the scene before me.

People are gathered together in groups, greeting one another as if they're long-lost friends who haven't seen each other in decades. It's surreal to be surrounded by so many people yet feel so removed from it all. As if I'm more of an observer than a participant. Other than Lanie and Jaxon, I don't know anyone else. I'm sure people from high school attend CU, but I lost touch with most of them after I moved away.

By the time I make it to the front of the line, I'm antsy and ready to head back to my friends. Even if they're still going at it. Which is really saying something. I'd much rather stand around as a third wheel than be an island onto myself. I dig through my front pocket and hand over a couple of bucks in exchange for a blue plastic cup before it's filled to the rim with golden liquid.

The cute guy manning the keg flashes me an easy grin as his eyes drift over my body. When he's finished with his perusal, his gaze once again settles on my face. Kudos to this guy for not gawking at my boobs like he's never seen a pair of D cups before.

"Here you go, beautiful," he says, handing over the cup with a gallant flourish.

This little bit of silliness lightens my mood. "Thanks."

Our fingers brush as I take the Solo cup from him.

"Next time, cut to the front of the line." He gives me a flirty wink. "I got you covered."

I flash him a grateful smile. Maybe tonight won't be so bad after all.

With my drink in hand, I'm ready to make my way back to Jaxon and Lanie. Only now does it occur to me that they could have moved from the spot where I'd left them.

Who's to say I'll even be able to find my way back?

A knot of unease settles at the bottom of my belly. My fingers go to the purse slung across my chest. It's big enough to hold my phone, but that's about it. I could always shoot Lanie a text, but who knows if she'd hear it. And I have no idea how to navigate my way back to our apartment. The unsettled feeling that had taken up residence in my gut turns into full-on nausea.

Only now do I realize that walking away was a bad idea. I should have stuck to Lanie and Jax like glue. But standing around and watching them make out felt pervy.

And not in a good way.

With those thoughts swirling through my brain, I spin around and slam into a wall of impenetrable muscle. The impact knocks me off-balance, and I stumble back a step. Before I can fall, strong hands reach out and grab my shoulders, yanking me forward. My breath catches, and my heart pounds at the narrowly avoided tumble.

I shake my head to clear it as beer sloshes over the rim of my plastic cup and spills onto the ground at my feet. I'm lucky it didn't end up down the front of my top or the shirt of the unsuspecting person I plowed into.

How humiliating would that have been?

Ugh…I don't even want to think about it.

"I'm so—"

My voice falls off as I glance up, my gaze colliding with narrowed blue eyes. Hunter quickly sets me free as if his fingers have been burned. Neither of us breaks eye contact. All of the raucous noise of the bonfire dies away until it's just the two of us standing alone in the middle of a dark field.

This is the moment I've been dreading.

My eyes roam over his face, cataloging the myriad of changes that time has wrought. When I walked away, Hunter had still been a boy, his lean muscles beginning to thicken. Now the transformation has been complete, and he's a full-grown man. Hunter has always had size on his side, but somehow, he's managed to grow both taller and broader. He must be somewhere in the vicinity of six three or four. I have to crane my neck to hold his gaze. The graphic T-shirt he's wearing stretches tautly across the wide expanse of his chest and hugs the chiseled strength of his biceps. It's enough to make my mouth dry and my knees soft.

If I have one weakness, it's for thickly corded arms. All that tightly harnessed power waiting to break free…

A shiver of desire scampers down my spine before I stomp it out.

Unaware of the effect he's having on me, Hunter's deep voice cuts through my thoughts.

"What are you doing here, Skye?"

It's the harshness of his tone that has my gaze snapping back to his as heat floods my cheeks. I can't stop myself from staring. The little bit of cyberstalking I've done over the years has in no way prepared me for coming face-to-face with my ex-boyfriend. He's grown into his dark looks, becoming even more of a heartbreaker than he was in high school.

My tongue darts out to smudge my parched lips as nerves dance along my skin. I search Hunter's eyes, looking for any hint of softening, but there's none to be found. His gaze is as frigid and detached as I imagined it would be. The tiny kernel of hope that our time apart would be enough to heal our past wounds shrivels and dies inside me.

There is no forgiveness in his heart.

But then again, did I really expect there would be?

Maybe. It would have made coexisting on campus for the next year so much easier.

It's obvious from his terse behavior that Hunter would prefer to pretend I never existed in the first place. As much as I would love to give him that, I can't. Unforeseen circumstances have forced me home.

I straighten my shoulders and attempt to keep my voice level. I don't want him to hear the slight tremble that is working its way through my body. "I transferred to Claremont for my senior year."

His shadowed jaw ticks as he clenches his teeth. *"Why?"*

The way he bites out that one word leaves me wincing.

I take a quick step back and lift my chin, not wanting him to see how much power he still holds over me. Time has done nothing to diminish it. "That's none of your business."

Whether Hunter realizes it or not, he still owns a piece of my heart. It's better for both of us if he never suspects the depth of my feelings.

His hands tighten into fists as he closes the little bit of distance that I've managed to put between us. Instead of scrambling back the way every instinct is clamoring for me to do, I hold my ground until we're standing toe-to-toe. My heart pounds a painful staccato against my breast as his harsh breath feathers across my parted lips.

There was a time when I couldn't get close enough to Hunter.

Now I can't get far enough away.

Sorrow floods through every fiber of my body that it has to be this way between us. Next to Lanie, Hunter was my best friend. He was my first everything.

Date.

Kiss.

Love.

Heartbreak.

Everything we once shared has been blown to pieces, and we're nothing more than strangers. Actually, what we are is much worse. His animosity is palpable. It radiates from him in suffocating waves that threaten to choke the life out of me.

"You shouldn't have come back," he growls. "You don't belong here anymore."

That may be true, but there's nothing I can do about it. I'm here. And I'm not going anywhere.

I shift my weight and force myself to say, "Claremont is big enough for the two of us."

"No, it's not. Stay the fuck out of my way, Skye." His eyes flash with barely suppressed hostility. "You won't like the consequences if you don't."

Before I can summon up a retort, he stalks away. Rooted in place, I track his movements until he fades into the crowd. Not once does he turn around and acknowledge my presence. I've been dismissed. Relegated to the black hole that is our past.

Once he disappears from sight, my knees weaken as the pent-up breath rushes from my aching lungs.

I haven't been on campus for a full seventy-two hours, and in Hunter's eyes, I'm public enemy number one.

Want to read more of Hunter and Summer?

You can download the free prequel here -)

Get your FREE copy of Heartless Summer (bookfunnel.com)

You can check out the book here -)

https://books2read.com/u/m2Moq7

ABOUT THE AUTHOR

Jennifer is a USA Today bestselling author who has published twenty-five new adult novels. Her work has been translated into German, Dutch, and Italian. Jen has a bachelor's degree in history and a master's in educational psychology. She started out her career as a high school counselor before relocating with her family out of state and focusing on her passion for writing. When she's not tapping away at the keyboard and dreaming up swoonworthy heroes to fall in love with, you can find her bike riding or planning her next trip to the beach. She lives in Michigan with her husband and four kids.

If you would like to receive regular updates regarding new releases, please subscribe to her newsletter here-
Jennifer Sucevic Newsletter (subscribepage.com)

Or contact Jen through email, at her website, or on Facebook.
sucevicjennifer@gmail.com

Want to join her reader group? Do it here -)
J Sucevic's Book Boyfriends | Facebook

Social media links-
https://www.tiktok.com/@jennifersucevicauthor
www.jennifersucevic.com
https://www.instagram.com/jennifersucevicauthor
https://www.facebook.com/jennifer.sucevic

Amazon.com: Jennifer Sucevic: Books, Biography, Blog, Audiobooks, Kindle

Jennifer Sucevic Books - BookBub